PENG
MIDI

Author's and translator's bi

Bhisham Sahni was born in 1915 into a devout Arya Samaj family in
Rawalpindi (now in Pakistan). He earned a master's degree in English
literature from Government College, Lahore. Upon his return to
Rawalpindi he joined his father's import business and also began
teaching, staging plays, writing stories and becoming involved in the
activities of the Indian National Congress. He later earned a Ph.D.
from Punjab University.

After Partition, he and his family settled in Delhi, where he was a
lecturer at a Delhi University college and took to writing more
earnestly. His first collection of short stories, *Bhagya Rekha* (*Line of Fate*)
was published in 1953. In 1957, Sahni moved to Moscow, during which
time he translated several Russian books into Hindi, notably some
works of Leo Tolstoy. He returned to Delhi in 1963 to resume teaching.
He edited the literary journal *Nai Kahaniyan* from 1965 to 1967.

Sahni was recipient of the Sahitya Akademi Award for his novel
Tamas in 1976. He has also received the Distinguished Writer Award
of the Punjab Government, the Lotus Award from the Afro-Asian
Writers' Association and the Sovietland Nehru Award. His writings
include seven novels, nine collections of short stories, six plays and a
biography of his late brother, the actor and writer Balraj Sahni. Many
of his books have been translated into numerous foreign and most
major Indian languages. In 1998 he was conferred an honorary
doctorate by the Institute of English and Foreign Languages,
Hyderabad and the Padma Bhushan by the President of India. In
1999 he received the Shlaka Award, the highest literary award from
the Delhi government.

*****

Gillian Wright is a journalist and author living in New Delhi. She
studied both Hindi and Urdu at London University and has translated
two modern classics of Hindi literature, Shrilal Shukla's *Raag Darbari*
and Rahi Masoom Reza's *Adha Gaon*, published in English under the
title *The Feuding Families of Village Gangauli*. Her other books include
An Introduction to the Hill Stations of India, *Sri Lanka* and *Birds of the
Indian Subcontinent*. She has collaborated with Mark Tully on all his
books, including *No Full Stops in India* and *Heart of India*.

MIDDLE INDIA
Selected Short Stories

Bhisham Sahni

translated by
Gillian Wright

PENGUIN BOOKS

Penguin Books India (P) Ltd., 11 Community Centre, Panchsheel Park,
New Delhi 110017, India
Penguin Books Ltd., 80 Strand, London WC2R ORL, UK
Penguin Putnam Inc., 375 Hudson Street, New York, NY 10014, USA
Penguin Books Australia Ltd. Ringwood, Victoria, Australia
Penguin Books Canada Ltd., 10 Alcorn Avenue, Suite 300, Toronto, Ontario,
M4V 3B2, Canada
Penguin Books (NZ) Ltd., Cnr Rosedale & Airborne Roads, Albany,
Auckland, New Zealand

First published in India by Penguin Books India 2001

10 9 8 7 6 5 4 3 2 1

Typeset in Palatino by S.R. Enterprises, New Delhi
Printed at Chaman Offset Printers, New Delhi

To Martand
with all my love

CONTENTS

Introduction	x
Dinner for the Boss	1
Nandlal's Leela	12
Mother or Stepmother	33
Salma Aapa	39
Aham Brahmasmi	52
Paali	63
Genesis	89
Toys	97
The Witch	109
Seminar	133
The Sparrow	149
Before Dying	158
Straying	171
Wang Chu	183
Radha-Anuradha	207
The Wondrous Bone	225
Veero	231

INTRODUCTION

It has been a privilege for me to work with Bhisham Sahni, one of Hindi literature's most outstanding figures, whose many years as a teacher have made him a patient and supportive guide during this translation. The choice of stories in this collection is entirely his. I had thought that he would choose his personal favourites, but he preferred those which he has found have made the deepest impact and evoked the most response from the reading public when they were first published.

In the English-speaking world Bhisham Sahni is still best known for his Partition novel *Tamas*, but the stories he has selected here demonstrate the breadth of his range. 'Paali' and 'Veero' deal in different ways with abductions during Partition, but 'Aham Brahmasmi' looks at the dilemma of an Anglophile Indian at the height of the freedom movement. In many of the other stories he focusses on the urban working and middle class of post-Partition India in the age before liberalization, portraying their ambition, greed, superstition, sorrows, adventures and misadventures, and the absurdity and crudity of the bureaucratic systems with which they have no choice but to interact. Several stories betray a keen sense of humour, particularly when he writes about his own circle—literary people and intellectuals.

Bhisham Sahni himself finds writing short stories much more demanding than novels, requiring greater precision of thought and expression. In his words, 'a short story is like lodging in a house one night and moving away the next morning, whereas a novel is like coming into a town where you have to bide for months on end. In a short story every word must have some eloquence, every utterance some significance.' Readers will be struck by the simplicity and of his style, which is deliberate and linked to his belief that life should be presented directly with as few embellishments as possible.

He writes in Hindi flavoured with Punjabi, and there's no surprise about this. After all he is Punjabi, born in Rawalpindi and educated in Lahore. As he explains, Hindi has the advantage of being the language of many different areas, and Hindi writers in these different areas still have strong links with their own local dialects, idioms and folk culture. I hope that in places the Punjabi lilt to these stories comes through. Ever since Premchand's time, Hindi short-story writing has had a strong social orientation. In this book, Bhisham Sahni comments subtly on many issues from Indo-Pakistan relations and the nature of war, to alienation and belonging.

I have thoroughly enjoyed translating these stories, and I hope that now that I hand them over to you, the reader, they will meet with your approval.

New Delhi
July 2001

Gillian Wright

DINNER FOR THE BOSS

The boss was invited for dinner this evening at the home of Mr Shyamnath.

Shyamnath and his wife hadn't time even to wipe away their sweat. She, in a dressing down, her uncombed hair knotted in a bun, oblivious to the rouge and powder smudged on her face, and he, puffing cigarette after cigarette, a list in his hand, were rushing from room to room.

Finally, as the clock struck five, the preparations approached completion. Chairs, a table, stools, napkins and flowers had all arrived on the veranda. The drinks had been arranged in the sitting room. Now all unnecessary domestic articles were being hidden behind cupboards and under beds. Suddenly an obstacle appeared before Shyamnath: What to do with Mother?

Neither he nor his capable wife had directed their attention to this matter. Mr Shyamnath turned to Mrs Shyamnath and said in English, 'What can we do with Mother?'

Mrs Shyamnath paused in her work and, after considering for a while, said, 'Send her to her friend's house at the back. She'll be sure to stay there all night and come back tomorrow.'

Shyamnath, a cigarette hanging from his mouth, regarded his wife through narrowed eyes, thought for a moment, shook his head and said, 'No, I don't want that old woman to start coming here again. It took enormous trouble to get rid of her before. We should tell Mother to eat early and go to her room. The guests will come about eight o'clock. Before that, she can do all she has to.'

It was a good suggestion. They both approved of it. But then suddenly Mrs Shyamnath spoke. 'If she goes to sleep and starts snoring, then what? People will be eating on the veranda just next to her room.'

'So we'll tell her to shut her door from inside, I'll lock it from outside. Or I'll tell her to go inside but not to sleep, to keep awake. What else?'

'And if she nods off? Goodness knows how long dinner will go on. You drink until eleven o'clock.'

Shyamnath became a little irritated. He flung up his hands and said, 'She was all ready to go off to my brother, and you went and interfered just to show how good you were!'

'Vah! And should I show myself in a bad light by interfering between a mother and her son? You know what went on, and so does she.'

Mr Shyamnath kept quiet. This was no time to argue; they had to find a solution to the problem. He turned towards his mother's room, which opened on to the veranda. Glancing along the veranda, he said, 'I have an idea,' and he walked over to the doorway of his mother's room. She was sitting inside on a wooden takht pushed against the wall, a dupatta wrapped around her head telling her prayer beads. Having watched all the preparations since the morning, her heart was thumping. The burra sahib from her son's office was coming. May everything go off satisfactorily!

'Mother, today you eat early. The guests will come at half past seven.'

She slowly unwrapped the dupatta from her face and said, looking at her son, 'I won't eat today, beta, you know that I don't eat anything when meat and fish are cooked in the house.'

'Whatever—just get all you have to do over with early.'

'Very well, beta.'

'And Mother, first we'll be in the sitting room. For that time you sit on the veranda. Then when we come out here, you go through the bathroom to the sitting room.'

His mother looked at him speechless. Then she said softly, 'Very well, beta.'

'And Mother, don't go to sleep early today. The sound of your snoring carries a long way.'

His mother said rather ashamedly, 'What can I do, beta? It's not in my control. Ever since I rose from my sickness, I can't breathe through my nose.'

Mr Shyamnath had fixed matters, but he was still not at ease. If the boss suddenly came this way, then what? There would be eight to ten guests, Indian officials plus their wives—anyone could go to the bathroom. He again began fretting in agitation and irritation. Picking up a chair and putting it on the veranda outside his mother's door, he said, 'Come here, Mother. Just sit on this.'

His mother took up her prayer beads, adjusted the end of her dupatta and slowly came and sat on the chair.

'Not like that, Mother. You don't sit with your legs up. This isn't a charpoy.'

His mother put her legs down.

'And for God's sake don't wander around barefoot. And don't come in front of anyone wearing those wooden sandals. One of these days I'm going to take them and throw them out.'

His mother said nothing.

'What clothes are you going to wear, Mother?'

'Whatever I have, beta! Whatever you tell me.'

His cigarette in his mouth, Mr Shyamnath watched her through half-closed eyes and began to consider her apparel. Shyamnath desired order in everything. The running of the entire household was in his hands: where hooks should be put, where the beds should be, which colour the curtains should be, which sari his wife should wear, what size the table should be. . . Shyamnath was afraid that if the boss should come across his mother, he might face embarrassment. Regarding her from head to toe, he told her, 'Wear a white shalwar and a white kameez, Mother. Go and put them on, so I can see.'

She slowly stood up and went into her room to change.

'She's going to be a problem,' he said again in English to his wife. 'People should speak only if they have something sensible to say. If she says something foolish and the boss takes offence, then the whole evening will be spoilt.'

His mother came out wearing a white shalwar and a white kameez. Rather short, swaddled in white, a small shrivelled body with cloudy eyes and only half of her thinning hair hidden by her dupatta, she appeared somewhat less ugly than before.

'There, that's all right. If you have any bangles or bracelets, then wear them too. There's no harm.'

'Where will I find bangles, beta? You know that I sold all my ornaments to pay for your education.'

This sentence pierced Shyamnath like an arrow. He said hotly, 'Why touch on that? Simply say that you don't have any ornaments, that's all. What does it have to do with my education? Whatever jewellery was sold, I have made something of myself, haven't I? I didn't come back a failure. Whatever you gave, take twice as much back.'

'May my tongue burn, beta. Can I take ornaments from you? It just slipped out. If I had any, I'd wear them a hundred thousand times for you.'

It was already half past five. Mr Shyamnath still had to bathe and get himself ready. Mrs Shyamnath had disappeared to her room long before. As Shyamnath left, he gave one more piece of advice to his mother: 'Mother, don't sit dumbly like you do every day. If the sahib comes this way and asks you anything, then answer him properly.'

'I've never been to school or learnt to write, beta. What can I say to him? You tell him that I'm illiterate, I don't know anything. Then he won't ask me.'

By the time it was seven o'clock his mother's heart was pounding. If the boss came and asked her a question, what could she reply? She was terrified even by the distant sight of an Englishman, and this was an American. Goodness knows what he would say, what she should reply. She wanted to go quietly to the house of her widowed friend who lived behind them. But how could she disobey her son? She remained sitting on the chair with her legs hanging down.

A successful party is a party in which the drinks are successfully served. Shyamnath's party had begun to touch the summit of success. The conversation was flowing as swiftly as the glasses were being filled. There was no let or hindrance. The sahib had liked the whisky. His memsahib had liked the curtains, the design of the sofa covers, the decoration of the sitting room. What more could they want? From only the second round of drinks the sahib had begun to make jokes and tell stories. He was being as friendly here as he was awe-inspiring in the office, and his wife, in a black gown with a string of white pearls at her throat and saturated in scent and powder, was the centre of adoration for all the Indian women. At everything she laughed and nodded, and she was chatting with Shyamnath's wife as if she were an old friend.

And in this flow of drinking and offering drinks, the clock struck half past ten. They had no idea where the time had gone.

Finally everyone drained the last drops from their glasses, rose for dinner and left the sitting room. Shyamnath was in front, showing the way, behind him the boss and the other guests.

Stepping on to the veranda, Shyamnath suddenly stopped dead. What he saw made him stumble, and in a moment his intoxication took flight. On the veranda, right in front of her room, his mother was sitting on her chair just as she had been. But both her feet were on the seat of the chair, and her head was lolling from side to side, and from her mouth issued loud snores. When her head fell to one side and stayed in the same position for some time, her snores became even deeper. And after she woke with a jolt, her head began to loll from side to side once again. Her dupatta had slipped from her head, and her thinning hair was dishevelled on her half-bald head.

The moment he saw her, Shyamnath was enraged. He felt like dragging her to her feet and shoving her into her room, but this was not possible; the boss and the other guests were standing nearby.

When they saw his mother, some of the wives of the Indian officials began to giggle, but then the boss said quietly, 'Poor dear!'

At once Mother hastily sat up straight. Seeing so many people in front of her she was so alarmed she could say nothing. She immediately pulled her dupatta over her head, stood up and began to stare at the ground. Her legs began to feel unsteady and her fingers to tremble.

'Mother, go and sleep. Why are you up so late?' asked Shyamnath and looked abashedly at his boss.

There was a smile on the boss's face. From where he was standing he said, 'Namaste!'

Hesitatingly, shrinking inwardly, Mother joined her hands together, but in one hand, inside the dupatta, she held her prayer beads, and her other hand was outside the dupatta, and she couldn't complete her namaste properly. Shyamnath was annoyed by this too.

Meanwhile the boss stretched out his right hand for Mother to shake. Mother was even more alarmed.

'Mother, shake hands.'

But how could she? She had the prayer beads in her right hand. In her confusion she put her left hand in the sahib's. Shyamnath began to burn inside. The wives of the Indian officers tittered.

'Not like that, Mother. You know you shake hands with your right hand. Give him your right hand.'

But by then the boss had shaken her left hand several times and was saying in English, 'How do you do?'

'Tell him, Mother, "I am fine. I am well."'

His mother muttered something.

'Mother is saying that she's fine. Go on, Mother, say, "How do you do?"'

She said slowly and hesitatingly, 'How do do. . .'

There was a peal of laughter.

The atmosphere became less tense. The sahib had taken control of the situation. People began to laugh and joke with one another. Shyamnath began to feel slightly less agitated.

The sahib was still holding on to Mother's hand, and Mother was cowering with embarrassment. There was a smell of alcohol coming from the sahib's mouth.

Shyamnath said in English, 'My mother comes from a village. She's lived there her whole life. That's why she's shy of you.'

At this the boss looked happy. He said, 'Really? I like village folk a lot. Then your mother must know village songs and dances?' He started to gaze happily at her, nodding his head.

'Mother, the sahib is asking you to sing a song, some old song. You must know lots of them.'

His mother replied softly, 'How can I sing, beta? When have I ever sung?'

'Vah, Mother! Can anyone refuse a guest? The sahib is so delighted. If you don't sing, he'll take it badly.'

'What can I sing, beta? What do I know?'

'Vah! Some really good folk song, "do pattar anaran de . . ."'

At this suggestion the Indian officers and their wives began to clap. Mother looked humbly sometimes at her son and sometimes at her daughter-in-law standing near him.

Meanwhile her son ordered her gravely, 'Mother!'

After that there was no question of arguing. She sat down and in a thin, weak and trembling voice, began to sing an old wedding song,

'Hariya ni maye, hariya ni bhaine, hariya te bhagi bhariya hai!'

Listen dear mother, listen dear sister, my son Hariya is truly blessed.

The Indian wives broke into laughter. After three phrases Mother fell silent, and the veranda resounded with applause. The sahib just wouldn't stop clapping. Shyamnath's annoyance turned into joy and pride. His mother had brought new colour to the party.

When the applause subsided, the boss asked, 'What handicrafts do you have in Punjabi villages?'

Shyamnath was swaying with joy, 'Oh, a lot, sahib! I will gift you a whole set of them. You'll be thrilled to see them.'

But the sahib shook his head and said, 'No, I don't want anything from a shop. What is made in Punjabi homes? What do women make themselves?'

Thinking a little, Shyamnath replied, 'Girls make dolls, and women make phulkaris.'

'What's a phulkari?

After an unsuccessful attempt to explain what a phulkari was, Shyamnath said to his mother, 'Do we have any old phulkari in the house?'

She quietly went inside and brought out an old phulkari of her own.

The sahib examined the colourfully embroidered cloth with great interest. It was old; in places the threads were breaking, and the cloth was splitting. Seeing this, Shyamnath suggested, 'This one is torn, sahib, I'll get a new one made for you. Mother will make it. Mother, the sahib likes your phulkari very much. You'll make one just like this for him, won't you?'

His mother was silent. Then she said softly and with trepidation, 'How much can I see now, beta? How can old eyes see?'

But interrupting his mother, Shyamnath told the sahib, 'She will definitely make it for you. You will be thrilled with it.'

The sahib nodded, thanked him and, swaying slightly, made his way towards the dining table. The other guests followed him.

When they had sat down and everyone's eyes had turned from her, the old lady slowly stood up and, avoiding notice, went into her room.

The moment she sat down there, her eyes flooded with tears. She wiped them again and again with her dupatta, but again and again they filled, as if a dam had burst after many years. She tried to control herself. She joined her hands, took the name of God, prayed for long life for her son, shut her eyes, but her tears like monsoon rain that would not cease.

It must have been the middle of the night. The guests had eaten and had left one by one. She was sitting leaning against the wall staring at it. The tension in the house had relaxed. The stillness of the surrounding locality had descended on Shyamnath's home too. Only the clinking of crockery was coming from the kitchen. Then suddenly someone knocked loudly on her door.

'Mother, open the door!'

Her heart sank. She hurriedly got up. Had she made another mistake? She had been cursing herself continually. Why had she fallen asleep? Why had she dozed off?

Had her son still not forgiven her? With trembling hands she opened the door.

The moment she opened it, Shyamnath stepped forward and took her into his embrace.

'Oh, Mummy! You really did wonders tonight! The sahib was so delighted, I can't tell you. Oh Ammi! Ammi!'

His mother's slight body crumpled and was hidden in his embrace. Tears again welled in her eyes. Wiping them, she said, 'Beta, send me to Haridwar. I've been telling you for so long.'

Shyamnath suddenly stopped swaying, and a line of worry began to form again on his brow. He released her from his arms.

'What did you say, Mother? What tune have you started on now?'

Shyamnath's anger began to build up, and he went on, 'You want to disgrace me so that the world will say that I couldn't keep my mother with me.'

'No, beta, now you live with your wife just as you like. I have done with fine food and clothes. Now what will I do here? The few days of life I have left I will remember God's name. You send me to Haridwar!'

'If you go, then who will embroider the phulkari? I agreed to give him a phulkari right in front of you.'

'I don't have the eyes, beta, to be able to sew a phulkari. You have it made somewhere else. Get one ready-made.'

'Mother, are you going to let me down and leave? Are you going to ruin my future success? Don't you know that if the sahib is happy, I'll get promotion?'

His mother was silent. Then, looking at her son, she asked, 'Will you be promoted? Will the sahib promote you? Has he said anything?'

'He hasn't said anything, but don't you see how delighted he was? He was saying that when you begin embroidering the phulkari, he'll come to see how you do it. If we make the sahib happy, I can even get a better job than this. I can be a senior executive.'

His mother's complexion began to change, gradually her lined face began to reveal a radiance, a slight gleam came to her eyes.

'So will you be promoted, beta?'

'Can it happen just like that? If I keep the sahib happy, then he'll do something; otherwise there's no dearth of people wanting to please him.'

'Then I'll do it, beta. However it'll have to be done, I will do it.'

And in her heart she again longed for a bright future for her son, while Mr Shyamnath, stumbling a little and with the words 'Now go to sleep,' turned towards his own room.

NANDLAL'S LEELA

The story is that my scooter was stolen. It was a brand new scooter, and I'd bought it less than two months before after waiting for a full four years. And then it disappeared in a blink of an eye. For years I'd been longingly anticipating its arrival, daydreaming about the day I would speed around the streets of Delhi, a silk scarf fluttering at my neck, my hair flying in the breeze, and my eyes protected by dark glasses. What was there to life in Delhi without a scooter? A young man in front, a girl behind, leaning over his back, her arms around his waist, her chunni or the end of her sari too fluttering in the wind and scattering romance over the thronging, unfeeling Delhi streets. But all my desires had come to nothing, and now I was standing dumbfounded on the roadside, staring wildly left and right, to see where, if the scooter had gone, it had gone. I wandered around the parking area behind the theatre where I had been watching a crude farce while my scooter was being stolen. My legs were filling with water, and my throat was growing drier and drier. And the crowd of theatre-goers was dispersing.

A crowd from a theatre or cinema is something unique. For a moment it seems as if a rose garden has burst into bloom, as if a town has sprung into existence, and a moment later owls are calling in the same place. I rushed to ask members of the departing audience for help, but all to no avail. Not one had any idea who had taken my scooter. They had all been sitting inside the theatre like I had. One light-hearted soul, still under the influence of the play, jested, 'It's a blessing that you weren't on it at the time, or the thief would have stolen you too.'

The indifference of the Delhi public in any case pains me. This uncouth pleasantry irritated me even more. In the end I restrained myself, stepped out on to the street, asked the way to the local police station and set off. Let me report the theft to the police, I thought, and we'll see what happens next.

When, after having been to the police, after having dragged myself along and after having been pushed and shoved in buses, I arrived home and told the story to my family. They were at first deeply shocked and then started making various comments. My father said, 'If you ask me, it was a mistake to take the scooter there in the first place. All kinds of pilferers hang around at theatres.' My wife said, 'I think you must have forgotten to lock it. If it had been locked, how could anyone have taken it?' Then addressing everyone, she said, 'I think that the scooter must still be standing there and he couldn't see it. Even if things are lying in front of him, he can't see them.' At this my uncle said, 'You always leave a scooter in someone's care. There must have been a parking man standing outside, but to avoid paying him ten paise, you went and left it goodness knows where.' In other words, it seemed to my relatives as if the main hand in the theft of the scooter must have been mine. Only my mother was repeating one sentence again and again, 'If there is justice in the house of God, my son will surely get his scooter back. When God has sent him something, it can never leave him and go to someone else.'

When I told them I had filed a report with the police, my uncle shook his head. 'Do you imagine the police are going to get your scooter back? If the police were that alert, your scooter wouldn't have been stolen in the first place. Now forget the scooter, and try to get your compensation from the insurance company. You did insure it, didn't you?'

At this my father lost his temper, and he and my uncle started arguing. It was my father's contention that every effort should be made to recover the scooter, while my uncle was saying, as if on the basis of centuries of amassed experience, that nothing would come of that, and I should collect my compensation from the insurance company as soon as possible. Finally it was decided that equal attention would be paid to both courses of action.

Accordingly I started doing the rounds of the police station in the mornings and the insurance company in the afternoons. The police appeared most disinterested. For the first two days they answered me politely, and then they started snapping at me. 'Have you found out anything about my scooter?' I would ask standing on the threshold like a supplicant. In reply there would either be silence, or some inspector would say coldly, 'We'll inform you if we find it. Don't come here every day.'

But one day when I rather fearfully stepped up to the threshold, the inspector got up from his seat and came towards me. My legs were shaking, but seeing the smile on his face, I fell into a quandary. Who knew? Perhaps he was smiling because he had found the scooter. He shook my hand, called me into his office, offered me a chair, summoned his orderly to bring me a glass of cold water and with the same smiling countenance said, 'Please relax. We are very concerned about your scooter. All possible efforts are being made to recover it. When we do find it, I will come personally to inform you.'

I returned home walking on air. Perhaps if the scooter had been found, I wouldn't have been as happy as I was with the inspector's friendly assurance.

'Why shouldn't he speak nicely to you? He must have had a shoe slap from his superiors,' said my Father. I didn't follow. Later I found out that ever since the scooter had been lost, Father had been writing letters, and having been written in all directions, one of them must have hit its mark. This particular letter had been written by my sister's husband's younger brother to his father-in-law, a senior police officer in Lucknow. Heaven knows where these kinds of letters were being dispatched.

But despite this assurance, the scooter nowhere made an appearance. The situation was exactly the same. Just the police's attitude towards me had changed.

On the other hand the people in the insurance company were not letting any water touch their feet. At least at the police station they had started talking to me, but here I would sit in front of the head clerk for a whole day, and no one took the slightest notice of me. If I raised my problem, he would mention various kinds of inquiries and then lose himself in his files again. An entire month passed in this way.

'Has any work in the world ever been done like this?' one day my father scolded my uncle. 'You'll never get your money if you sit around waiting for bureaucratic procedures.' Then he looked at me and said, 'If you want to get ghee out of a tin, you have to bend your finger. You can't take ghee out with a straight finger.'

The next day I went with my uncle to Ajmeri Gate. There a gentleman joined us, and we went to a large office in Asaf Ali Road. There a gentleman wrote a letter and handed it to us. The three of us then set off for Daryaganj, and a voice began to rise within me—something was going to happen, definitely something was going to happen. Whenever I hear that voice, something or the other always does.

After this we found ourselves sitting in another large office, and in front of us, behind a rather big desk, sat a rather fat man. This was Mota Nandlal, for whom we had brought the letter.

Mota Nandlal read the letter and then looked in front of him with his huge eyes. 'To hell with them. How can they not give you your money!'

His tone was such that my heart sank. Mota Nandlal reached for the telephone, but my uncle at once pre-empted him. 'If you would take the trouble of coming with us rather than speaking on the phone, it would be better. You know these insurance people . . .'

'To hell with them' Mota Nandlal repeated, and my heart sank again. But he put down the receiver and said to me, 'Come to me tomorrow. I will take you to the insurance company office.'

The next day Mota Nandlal was in front of me climbing the stairs of the three-storey insurance-company building, and my heart was pounding at the thought of the scene that would take place, afraid my good case might be destroyed. This man seemed rough and uncouth, and on their side the company officers exhibited much ill will.

We arrived upstairs. Whereas I had spent whole days sitting and pleading before the head clerk, Mota Nandlal walked straight to the office of the director, opened the door, went in and, planting both palms of his hands on his desk like a bear balancing himself before an attack, pronounced, 'What sort of performance do you call this? His scooter has been stolen. The whole matter is clear. Why don't you give him his money?'

The director rose from his chair. But before he could open his mouth, Mota Nandlal said, 'I give you five lakhs of business every year, and here you are harassing my brother for a whole month.'

The cheque was made out there and then. Mota Nandlal still hadn't sat down and hadn't had time to reply to the director's insistence that he have either a hot or cold drink, either tea or coffee or sherbat or lime juice, when the same head clerk who had made me sit in front of his desk for whole days, came in with the cheque, form and register. Precisely ten minutes after we had entered the office, Nandlal and I were going back downstairs. The cheque was in my pocket and Mota Nandlal was saying, 'To hell with them. How could they not give the money. . .'

His words stimulated me. Gazing at his fat neck and huge buttocks and long bear-like arms, I thrilled with devotion.

That day at home we discussed Mota Nandlal for hours on end.

'You get things done by looking after people,' my father was saying. Then he began to sing the praises of those three men one by one: first, the man who had come with us from Ajmeri Gate to Asaf Ali Road; second, the one who had given the letter; third, Mota Nandlal. Among these Mota Nandlal stood out as a god incarnate.

At this my uncle said, 'But the man is crooked. Goodness knows how he got it done.'

'It is all the sport of Nandlal,' said my mother, 'his frolic'.

'Mota Nandlal's or Lord Krishna's?' I asked.

But my mother was so carried away that she paid no attention to me and went on. 'It is all the sport of the Lord. When he wanted to give my son money, he sent Nandlal as his instrument.'

As I was descending the steps of the insurance company, watching Mota Nandlal's neck and big fat hands, covered with rings, every pore of my body was tingling. Such a thrill must excite the hearts and souls of devotees only when they behold God.

My mother was right because whatever happened next could only be called the sport or leela of Nandlal.

Several days passed very comfortably. I had money in my pocket. My spirits were high. Before I'd had to wait silently for four years for a scooter. Now, thanks to Mota

Nandlal, I could buy a new scooter the next day. But the people at home were not in favour of my doing so.

'Anyone who can have one scooter stolen can have another one stolen too. You just come and go by bus. That is what you're fit for,' said my father.

I myself was not in favour of taking a second scooter. Just one scooter had wiped all the romance from my heart. You get pushed and shoved in buses too, but looking at the blows you suffer when you lose a scooter, it's better to go by bus. But my wife was miserable. Whenever I suggested we go somewhere in the evening, she would heave a cold sigh and say she didn't feel like going anywhere. I realized that she had tasted the blood of scooter transport, and now it seemed idiocy to go by bus. Wives generally reveal what is in their hearts in the darkness of the night. Once she sighed and said, 'Ever since I stepped into your home, my condition has gone from bad to worse.' Then she made an excuse of a headache and turned her back towards me.

It was six months since the scooter had been stolen, and I was again dragging my feet along the streets of Delhi.

Suddenly I received a rather strange letter from the police station. It read, 'Your scooter number DL———— has been recovered. At present it is being kept in Dayaram's compound in Shyamnagar, street number four. Please go identify it, and inform us if you wish to take it back or not.'

The corners of my mouth curled into a smile. It was amazing; they'd found my scooter. I had not felt as upset over losing it as I felt joyful at its being found. What fun was there in Delhi without a scooter?

When my family heard, there were mixed reactions. My mother joined her hands in prayer beneath her dupatta and said, 'There is delay in God's house, but not darkness. I said from the first that my son would get his scooter back.' My wife chirped up too. She looked at me as if my value was somewhat restored in her sight. But my father was not in the least enthusiastic. He said, 'Now it's stolen property. Once a thief lays hands on something, it's no longer auspicious. Then you are getting it back after six months. What will there be left of it? Its ribs and bones will have been shaken.' At this my uncle nodded in agreement, and my heart skipped a beat. My father and my uncle were agreeing; this was not a good sign. When they kept arguing, life seemed to proceed at its natural pace.

'How can you take the scooter back? You have already taken compensation from the insurance company?'

'What does that matter? It can be returned.'

'And if they refuse, then?'

'Mota Nandlal is there. With him around they won't refuse,' I countered bravely.

In the end it was decided that first I should identify the scooter and have someone take a good look at it. We would decide later whether to take it back or not.

The next day I was setting off for Shyamnagar with the letter from the police in my pocket. I had already started dreaming of sightseeing by scooter. My wife would be happy too; the gloom that had loomed over the house since the scooter had been lost would be lifted.

I spent a long time kicking up the dust of the streets of Shyamnagar, but I still couldn't locate the compound whose address the police had given me. What was the logic of keeping a scooter in a compound? Why hadn't they put it in the police station? Then I thought that the compound itself might perhaps belong to the police, where they kept recovered property. They must have made a kind of warehouse.

Finally I set foot in the compound. It was a rather large yard at the end of which stood a rather small bungalow. In the yard were seven or eight motor cars and four or five scooters. Were they all recovered property? Had I come to the wrong place? This looked like the house of a wealthy man. Where was I? I took out the police's letter to look at it carefully, and then I saw a gentleman wearing a white nylon shirt and terry-cotton trousers approaching from the bungalow.

'Excuse me, I've made a mistake. I was looking for another compound.'

I automatically handed him the letter from the police.

He looked at it briefly and then, gesturing to one side with his hand, said, 'The scooters are there. Please identify which one is yours.'

I examined this gentleman from head to toe. Was this a police officer keeping recovered property at his own bungalow? 'Senior officers don't wear uniforms at home,' I thought to myself. 'That's why he's in civvies. But police officers don't wear as many rings on their fingers as he does. But, who knows, perhaps they do. He could take them off when he puts on his uniform and put them on when he takes it off.'

I was eager to see my own vehicle. Without saying anything, I turned to the scooters.

I took in all five with one glance, but I couldn't see mine among them. Then I began to look at them carefully one by one. One scooter looked a little like mine, but it had a high quality mirror, and a radio aerial was sticking up above the handlebars. There really was a speaker installed in it. How could this be my scooter?

Then the gentleman came up to me.

'Recognized it? This is yours, isn't it!' he said, stroking the handlebars. 'I have taken special care of this one. It has never been in the least damaged.'

'You have taken care of it? What do you mean?'

'I kept this scooter solely for my own use. I enjoyed riding it very much.' Then he touched the aerial with great affection. 'I had this aerial fitted. The mechanic said, "You can't fit an aerial on a scooter." I said, To hell with you. Let's see how it doesn't fit.' He was speaking in the very same tone I had heard Mota Nandlal use. Do all people who have rings glittering on their fingers talk in the same tone? Do they all go round sending people to hell?

After all, who is this man? How is he speaking about my scooter with such authority?

'Is this all recovered property?'

'What else?' he said with a touch of arrogance, as if to say, 'If I am going to steal scooters, do you think I would only steal one?'

'Did you yourself . . . ?' That was all I managed to say. In any case, I stand in awe of anyone in a suit and boots. Here the fingers of both his hands were glittering with gems, and there was a gold chain beneath his nylon shirt.

My head was spinning. How could this man be a thief? He didn't have a knife under his arm or shining, bloody teeth behind a beard and moustache, but he was telling me in broad daylight that he himself had lifted my scooter. Is this what thieves are like? Ali Baba's brother Qasim went into the thieves' cave and never came back alive. I am standing in his compound, I thought, and he is talking to me like I'm his cousin-brother! What is this all in aid of?

'Were all these scooters and cars, by your sleight of hand . . . . ?' I inquired informally.

'What else . . .' he replied with great self-confidence. Again stroking my scooter he said, 'I had this mirror fitted later when I was going on a pilgrimage to Vaishno Devi. It's a hill area, you see. You have to keep an eye on who's coming behind you. Very tight bends. My family kept on saying, "We won't let you go on a scooter," but I didn't listen. I said, "By the grace of the goddess, nothing will happen".'

'You went on a pilgrimage to Vaishno Devi?' I babbled.

'I go every year. Whether I go anywhere else or not, I always go for a darshan of Vaishno Devi.' He was moved, like a devout soul. 'Once a year one should take prasad of the goddess.'

'Undoubtedly,' I said. 'Did you make any other pilgrimages on my scooter?' But he made as if he hadn't heard and again began stroking my vehicle.

'I have kept it very lovingly. Only for my own use . . . although I'm not that fond of travelling by scooter.'

'Undoubtedly,' I said again. 'Why should anyone who has so many cars go by scooter?' I felt as if I had begun to flatter him. 'The police have asked me whether I want to take my scooter back or not. What do you think?'

'Take it, take it. It's engine is good, and I have kept it very safely,' he advised like an elder brother.

'But how can I get it back now?'

'The police will hand it over themselves,' he replied. 'You have taken compensation from the insurance company, haven't you?'

'How do you know I have?'

'That much a man keeps track of, doesn't he, bhai sahib?' he remarked with a guru-like smile.

Returning from the compound, I was thinking to myself, 'Yaar, what is going on? This man from his own mouth is saying that he stole the scooter. The police send me a letter and send me to his house, but it doesn't cause a wrinkle on his forehead. Do thieves ever admit to people in front of them that they are thieves?'

The next day when I went to the police station I couldn't restrain myself. I asked the police inspector, 'Please explain one thing to me, Inspector Sahib. The man in whose compound my scooter was kept not only admitted to me that he had stolen it himself but that he had stolen many more cars and scooters. So why hasn't he been caught?'

The police officer looked at me as a father looks at his little son when he hears him asking a childish question.

'He told you himself that he had committed theft?'

'Yes.'

'Do you have any evidence?'

'But I am telling you he told me himself.'

'You are telling the truth. But do you have any evidence?'

'You know that he has stolen cars. Otherwise why did you send me to his compound?'

'We have recovered vehicles from his place.'

'Then why didn't you arrest him?'

'He was arrested, but then he got out on bail. Now the case will proceed.'

I listened in silence. He explained, 'The police can arrest people but not punish them! That's the court's job.'

'Then will he be punished?'

The inspector burst out laughing. 'You seem to be an educated man. You drive a scooter. Does the law ever work like that? The law is the law, sahib. Under the law a man is innocent until he is proven guilty.' Then smiling and drumming his fingers on the desk with profound self-confidence, he began to assess the effect of this amazing statement on my expression.

'You will be summoned to the court. Not only will you give evidence, but you will have to produce your scooter there as well. The court will investigate the matter, and from their side the police will conduct the prosecution. The law is the law, sahib. This isn't the rule of Nadir Shah when the emperor can cut off the head of whomever he likes. The law is the law.'

When I came out of the police station, I felt as though I was leaving a temple. My head bowed, both my hands behind my back, it was as if the music of righteousness and democracy was playing in my head. A man is innocent until proven guilty. Vah, vah, I began to exclaim in appreciation. But as I walked along the street the face of the devotee of Vaishno Devi came to mind, and I was again confused. What was going on? The police recovered goods from him and said he was a thief, the thief himself admitted in private that he was a thief, but the court said prove that he has done it.

Anyway, after a few days I returned the compensation amount to the insurance company and brought the scooter home. Again I tied a silk scarf around my neck, put on my dark glasses, sat my wife on the pillion and set out to tour the streets of Delhi. I didn't give a damn. Let the father of the law understand the law! I had my property back, and now the law could get justice done. The scooter was flying beneath my thighs after a gap of about six months. There was no particular difference in the music of its engine. The pilgrim really had looked after it well. It really was running in a more natural, calm and stable way, as if it had found peace, as if it were almost floating. My status had begun to rise slightly in the eyes of my wife, although sometimes I felt that now my status was not so much that of a scooter owner as her driver, as if I was driving it just to take her somewhere. Now when she put her arms round my waist, it was not out of love, but to sit comfortably, and when she spoke, it seemed like she was issuing orders.

But what happiness is that which can last for more than two days in Delhi without impediment?

Another letter came. This time it was from the court to tell me to report on a certain day, at 10 a.m. at Tis Hazari. I also had to bring the scooter. By now about nine months had passed since I had brought back the scooter. I was vexed. In the days before the scooter had been found, I was interested in the thief, the courts and justice, but now even the scooter had forgotten the climb to Vaishno Devi. What did I care about it?

But still I went. Even if I wasn't interested in justice, the court was.

When I reached the court, there were people everywhere—people on the steps, stuck to the walls, sitting, sprawling, half lying on the floor. In doorways, windows, people upon people, and, as if creeping among them, black-coated lawyers—one creeping lawyer behind every ten men. I had never seen that many people at any festival, fair, function or meeting. And they were all watching and waiting for someone or something. What were they waiting for? Justice?

When I walked past a courtroom, I heard a rather loud voice from behind.

'Moolraj, son of Hukum Chand!'

And some Moolraj sitting leaning against the wall stood up in a panic, cut through the knot of humanity at a run and entered the courtroom. The knot of humanity joined again, and some other Moolraj sat pressed against the wall in the place where the first had been sitting.

I jumped up and down in order to read the room numbers and finally arrived outside room number ——. A list of the day's cases was right next to the door. I read it carefully. My name was not there. At first I felt stunned. Whenever my name is excluded from a list, I feel stunned. It's as if I wasn't considered worthy of being included. When I moved to Delhi, the desire to see my name in lists increased progressively; even in a list of robberies my name should be there. Then the thought arose that the list must be of thieves' names. Why should mine be there? But my heart couldn't accept this. What was the harm in giving the name of the person whose scooter was stolen? Was he a person of lesser importance? The names of thieves and robbers could be given, but not mine?

I wasn't even called. After loitering around for a while, I began to run my eyes over the crowd. That gentleman thief must be here somewhere. After all he was the bridegroom of this particular marriage party. But I couldn't see him anywhere. Summoning my courage I cut through the knot of clients and plaintiffs and arrived in the courtroom. There, on a raised wooden platform behind a broad, long table, wearing a black coat and thick spectacles, sat the magistrate sahib. Below him stood a dozen or so men among whom two or three were black-coated lawyers, and two or three uniformed police. The thief was not there. A stack of files stood on the table.

'Who is this man? Why is he wandering in here?'

The magistrate's voice was harsh and directed at me. I went and stood before him.

'Your Excellency!' I said. 'My scooter was stolen, and I have been summoned here today on that account.'

I did benefit from using 'Your Excellency'. Once upon a time a wise old man had advised me never to address a constable as constable, but as havildar, and to address a havildar as thanedar. This makes those in authority soften. When I called the magistrate 'Your Excellency', his face muscles relaxed.

'What is this case?'

'Your Honour,' the government lawyer replied, 'this is a case of vehicle theft. But, Your Honour, this case will not be heard today. The accused's lawyer had requested another date.'

'Why?'

'The witnesses could not be produced, Your Honour!'

'Yes, yes!' the magistrate said, and then turned to me. 'Please go home today. You will be informed of the next date.' Then he turned his attention to the case in hand.

I breathed a sigh of relief. When something is put off, I breathe a sigh of relief, especially when it's something official. But then it occurred to me that I would have to present myself in court again on the next date. What was the point of it? After hanging around for a while longer and thinking that it was possible that the magistrate had made a mistake, I went before him again. The magistrate's face muscles tightened.

'Your Excellency, the fact is that it is my scooter that was stolen. There is no case against me. Therefore . . .'

'I know,' replied his Excellency, 'but you too will have to record a statement in this case.'

'I have already given my statement, Your Excellency. I had the police write it out on the very first day.'

'That was given to the police. You have to give one to the court.'

'Your Excellency, if my statement could be recorded today . . .'

'Should I leave my other work?' said the magistrate angrily. 'This case will not be heard today.'

I was about to say something when somebody tugged my sleeve. A tiny, fairish man was standing next to me. He beckoned me to one side. 'You do not cross-examine the magistrate. Come on the next date. I'll see that you get away quickly.'

I went outside, kick-started my scooter and set off for home.

The next date came three months later. I took leave from the office and sped over to the court. That day too the gentleman thief was absent. I found out that today he had to appear in some other case. If he turned up in time, my case would be heard; otherwise a new date would be set.

I wandered over to stand in front of his Excellency. My legs had begun to tremble because I was afraid he would tell me off again.

'Your Excellency, my scooter was stolen, and I am here in that connection.'

He looked me up and down.

'What case is this?'

The government lawyer again referred to the case and said that the accused was appearing in another case today.

But the magistrate remembered my case, and he gave permission for me to record my statement. The defendant's lawyer was standing right beside me. Here I made a mistake. I called the thief a thief. In my statement

I also went so far as to say that the thief himself had told me that he had stolen my scooter.

At this the thief's lawyer rose in anguish. 'Your Honour, how can this man call my client a thief?'

The magistrate sahib pointed at me and ordered me to be quiet. 'You can call him the alleged thief.'

'Your Excellency, I'm not making this up. The thief really did tell me. He even went to Vaishno Devi on my scooter.'

The thief's lawyer shrieked, 'My lord, this is contempt of court!'

At this the magistrate himself lost his temper. Now he pointed his finger at my chest as if it were a pistol and said, 'I can lock you up for the offence of contempt of court. Record your statement in a straightforward manner.'

At that moment someone shook my elbow. It was the diminutive, fair-faced clerk. 'Record your statement, sahib, or you'll be the one in deep trouble.'

I panicked, and in that panic I forgot the date my scooter had been stolen.

'I made my statement to the police that very night. It must be in the file here. The date is written there.'

'You cannot refer to the file,' the lawyer shouted. 'Your Honour, the witness cannot be shown the file.'

The diminutive clerk pressed my elbow again.

'Record it, sahib. Record it,' he whispered. I was scared that if I gave the wrong date my whole statement would be spoilt.

Anyway, somehow or other I managed it, but the experience made me break into a sweat. I was beset by the constant fear that if I made any mistake, I would be put in the lock-up. Finally I signed the statement and heaved a sigh of relief. Well, that was over. Now I would never have to see the court again.

I bowed and said with great respect, 'Your Excellency, I have recorded my statement.'

'Have you brought the scooter?'

'Yes, it's outside.'

'Bring it to the next hearing.'

'The next hearing? Why, Your Excellency? I have recorded my statement.'

At this the magistrate again pointed at me and said, 'It is necessary to produce the scooter at each hearing.' Then, in a slightly softer tone, he added, 'If you can't come yourself, then send it with a driver.'

'My lord, scooterists don't have drivers. Only motorists have drivers.'

'It is necessary to produce the scooter here,' he said gravely. 'And listen, until there is a decision in this case, you cannot sell the scooter without the permission of the court.' Then the government lawyer suggested, 'Tell him the date of the next hearing now. In fact, have him note it down that his scooter must be sent here.'

The next date set was 11 June.

Eleven June came. I arrived in court. Then 15 October came. I was present in court with the scooter. Then 3 February, and I was in court. After that there came a never-ending series of hearings. There was one every three or four months. Once I arrived in court, and the magistrate had changed. The next time the court had changed. Instead of Tis Hazari, cases were being heard at Parliament Street courts. But I only managed to see the alleged criminal on a couple of occasions. Once I found that he had gone to give evidence in some other court. Another time I discovered he wasn't in town; he'd gone on a pilgrimage to Vaishno Devi! The diminutive clerk told me that it wasn't as necessary for him to stay here as it was for his lawyer, or for my scooter.

The case is still continuing. In the meanwhile my hair has turned grey at the temples, and my wife has become the mother of two children. The magistrate hearing the case has changed four times. Two governments have fallen, but the man who stole my scooter has still not been properly identified, and inquiries are proceeding.

Everything is going on at a regular pace, just one thing is not the same as before: Now the scooter is not what it was, it has begun to grow old. As it drives through the streets, it has begun to cough and sneeze. Sometimes it comes to a dead halt. You can kick the starter again and again, but it shows no sign of life. Now I no longer go to take the air with a silk scarf at my throat. My wife has given up riding it altogether.

The day before yesterday there was a hearing. The scooter refused to go. I kicked the starter for a whole hour and made two neighbours push it, but it was so obstinate that it wouldn't even budge two yards. When I took it to the mechanic, he said, 'Sahib, the vehicle needs overhauling. I told you before. What's the point of tinkering with it every other day? Even if I repair it now, you can't rely on it.' I put the court argument to him. If I didn't arrive on time, the proceedings couldn't begin. At this he laughed, 'Sahib, you say that every time.'

I arrived at the court in the nick of time. I mean, both I and the scooter arrived. Even though it refused to use its engine, it would move unmounted. Accordingly, from the Filmistan Cinema to the court, we decided to walk together.

I greeted the magistrate, wiping the sweat from my brow.

'Have you brought the scooter?'

'Yes!'

This is the fifth magistrate who has been looking after the case. As I am always coming to court, he has started to recognize me and so treats me considerately. Within an hour of my arrival, he calls me and gives me the next date.

As I was receiving the new date, I meekly submitted, 'Your Excellency, my scooter is not in a condition to reach the court.'

He looked up. 'Today I have pushed it here,' I said with all humility.

The magistrate fell into thought. Then he shook his head and said, 'Bring it on a cart or tonga from now on. A scooter can easily be loaded on a cart,' he added, giving a date three months hence.

I fell silent. What could I say? That day I had seen a dead buffalo being taken away in a cart. If you could load a dead buffalo on a cart, you could load a scooter.

But still I plucked up courage and said, 'Your Excellency, I am worried about one thing: If my scooter completely packs up, then what will happen to this case?'

The magistrate pondered for a moment and then replied, 'It will continue.'

I came out. I wiped my scooter's nose and face, patted it and kicked the starter. No reply was forthcoming. Then I kicked it again. Still no answer. Then one kick after another. Sometimes I opened the choke; sometimes I closed it. No reaction.

In the meanwhile, the court had adjourned for lunch. A car sped past me. I looked up, wiping away my sweat. It was the magistrate's car. He was in the back seat, and he turned and looked at me. A little while later a station wagon passed. That too was going at a fair old lick. Its passengers turned to look at me too. It was a police vehicle. I caught sight of the inspector and the diminutive clerk. The clerk waved to me.

Then I started kicking again. I thought of pushing it away, but in the heart of every scooter owner there always remains a hope that the engine will start at the next kick.

Then a car passed and pulled up ahead of me. It was a shiny black Fiat.

'Tell me, bhai sahib, isn't it starting? Is it troubling you?'

Arré, this was Dayaram! The thief who stole my scooter! No, no—the alleged thief. In these years I'd caught a glimpse of him once or twice in court. From inside the car he commented, 'What a state you've let it get into, yaar! It was such a great scooter.'

He looked at it as if it were linked with very happy memories.

'That scooter climbed the whole way up to Vaishno Devi. But after all, it is a machine. If you don't take care of it, it won't look after you.'

I was panting. I was profoundly irritated by his admonition but when my eyes fell on the rings on his fingers an idea suddenly began to glimmer in my mind. I left my scooter and went up to him.

'I have a problem, Dayaramji.'

'Tell me. Your wish is my command. What's the matter?'

'I have to bring the scooter for every hearing. This is the sixth year. It's very difficult for me to carry its corpse here now.'

'Vah, you're bothered about such a little thing? Why didn't you say before? Don't you worry. It'll be done. We'll find some way out. To hell with them . . .' He patted me on the shoulder, innumerable rings glinting on his fingers. 'It will be done,' he said, and the car started and swiftly drove off.

I stood where I was, rather overwhelmed and unable even to express my gratitude properly.

MOTHER OR STEPMOTHER

There were just one or two minutes before the 15 down was due to depart. The green light had been given, and the signal was down. The passengers had already taken their seats in their compartments when suddenly a scuffle broke out between two shabbily dressed women. One woman was trying to grab a baby from the other's lap. The woman with the baby held the infant tightly to her breast with one hand and, fighting off her assailant with the other, tried to climb into the train.

'Let me be, may death eat you, let me alone, the train's leaving . . .'

'I won't let you go, even if I die, I won't let you . . .' said the other woman snatching at the child again.

A short while before, both women had been standing talking to one another. Passers-by were astonished to see them fighting, and a crowd began to gather. A uniformed havildar of police on the platform saw the argument as he was going for a drink of water at the tap and made his way over, swinging his baton.

'What's the matter? What's this row about?' he inquired with authority.

At the sight of the havildar, both women suddenly stopped fighting. They were both panting and staring at each other like animals.

Noticing a few more passengers climbing into the train, the woman with the child again rushed towards it, but the other woman pounced on her and pulled her into the middle of the platform. The black, rather skinny baby, its limbs dangling, was asleep against the woman's shoulder. As the women fought its thin, rather long neck jerked, and its head lolled from one side to the other. But still it didn't wake.

'Don't make such a noise! What's going on?' the havildar shouted, forcing his baton between the two women in an attempt to separate them.

The woman who was trying to grab the child looked at the havildar with great big, timid eyes and said in anguish, 'My baby is being taken away, I will not give it to her.' And then she leapt to grab the baby again.

'The train is leaving, naspitti, let me go!' screamed the woman with the baby, and again began heading towards the carriage. The havildar stepped forward and blocked her way.

'Why are you taking her baby?' he said sharply.

'How is it hers? It's mine.'

'She says its hers. Tell me, whose is it?'

'It's mine,' said the other, younger woman, bursting into tears. Her face, surrounded by dry, dishevelled hair, was flushed, and there was still fear in her eyes. Bewildered and distressed, she went for the child again.

The havildar wanted to have done with the argument as soon as possible. To the woman with the child he said, 'Hand her the child.'

'Why should I? It's mine . . .'

'Did it come from your stomach?'

The woman holding the child was silent and began staring at the other woman.

'Speak up! Did you bear this child?' the havildar asked angrily.

'It wasn't born of me, but I have fed it. I have been feeding it for the last seven months.'

'You've fed it, and it becomes yours? You are taking it away by force.'

'Why should I take it by force? May my own children be safe and sound. Ask her. The witch is standing in front of you.' Then she addressed the other woman. 'You blackface, why don't you speak? Am I grabbing this child and taking it away? Havildarji, she herself put the child in my lap. She gave birth to it and was going to throw it on the dungheap. I said to her, "Give it to me. I will bring it up." Since then I've been looking after it. She brought me to the station. Then when she got here, she went back on her word.'

The havildar turned to the other woman, 'Did you give her the baby yourself?'

The young woman's great big, confused eyes stayed on the other woman for a while, then lowered.

'I gave it to her, but the child is mine. I will not let her have it.'

She began to look helplessly at the other woman. The tears which had welled in her eyes immediately dried in her distress.

'If you gave her the child, why do you want to take it back now?'

She turned her timid gaze suddenly upwards, and her whole body began to tremble.

'She is taking it far away . . .' she said, beginning to cry again.

'Am I to stay with you for ever?' the woman with the child asked and, stretching out her arms, appealed to the crowd, 'All the people of my camp have left. This woman won't let me go. She would say, just stay for ten more days, then leave. Stay for five days more, then leave. It's been going on for a whole month. How can I lie around here? Today my train was about to leave, and the blackface went back on her word.'

'She's a relative of yours?'

'How could she be, ji? She's from Kathiawar, and we are Banjaras.'

'Where are you going to?'

'Firozpur, ji.'

'What do you have there?'

'We are Banjaras, havildarji. First we took land here and ploughed it for a full two years. Now we have found land in Firozpur. All our people have gone, but she doesn't let go of me.'

The havildar was in a quandary. One of them gave birth and threw the baby away, the other fed it and brought it up. Whose was the baby?

'Don't you have any home of your own that you gave her your own child? Where do you live?' the havildar asked the baby's natural mother.

'Where will she live, ji? The huts of grass near the bridge, she lives there. We lived there too. She was my neighbour, ji; she works as a labourer. I cut the baby's umbilical cord myself.' The baby's natural mother was looking timidly at her baby as if she were hearing nothing.

'Where is her husband?'

'She doesn't have one, ji. She runs after men, but no one sets up home with her. If she had a home, why would she give birth and throw the child away?'

The guard blew his whistle.

The crowd thinned, and people began to head for their compartments. The Banjarin too turned towards hers. The child's natural mother rushed forward and clutched her feet.

'Don't go, don't take my child, don't go!'

Several of the people watching were moved to pity. The havildar stepped forward gravely and said, 'Give the child back. If the mother doesn't want you to take the child, you can't take it.'

There was finality in his voice. The Banjarin had not expected this decision. She rushed forward. 'Why should

I, ji? Does anyone give up her child? Whom do I give the child to? She has no home, belongs nowhere . . .'

'The train's about to go, hurry up, give the child back to its mother, or I'll throw you in the lock-up,' the havildar barked.

The woman was bewildered and stood, uncertain what to do, looking at the people standing watching her. Then she turned to her companion and shrieked, 'Haramzadi! Bitch! She has come here and changed her mind. Take the baby, you shameless woman. Take it and care for it! If you ask me to feed it again I shall poison it. It and you too. For seven months I denied my own child and fed yours.' Suddenly she dumped the baby in the other's arms and broke into sobs.

It was a strange scene. Both the women were weeping, both each other's enemies, both the child's mothers. Homeless people know neither how to laugh nor how to cry politely. And the cause of the trouble, the weak little jaundiced-looking child was still asleep with clenched fists.

The Banjarin climbed into the train, cursing, crying and complaining.

'You have got your child. Get out of here at once . . .' threatened the havildar, resting the end of his baton on the sleeping infant's back. 'Get away from here immediately.'

The mother retreated, the baby pressed to her breast. The crowd dispersed. From the door of the compartment the Banjarin was still screaming, 'Whore, haramzadi, why didn't you kill it the moment you gave birth? When you kill it, only then will my heart find rest, naspitti!'

Perhaps because the child recognized its mother's breast, or perhaps because of the pressure of the policeman's baton, it awoke and began to grind first its nose and then its eyes with its tiny little fists, and then it put one fist in its mouth and began to suck it. The woman was standing back, rather confused, against the wall at the side of the platform.

The infant kept sucking its fist but when it realized it wasn't getting any milk, it awoke fully and began to cry and kick its legs. Its mother shifted it from her right to her left shoulder. But the child began to cry even more loudly.

Its mother was alarmed. She turned the child from side to side, from one shoulder to the other. Hearing the baby wail the Banjarin began to scream again from the door of the carriage. 'Murder it, you just murder it! May you be ruined! Why don't you feed it poison? It hasn't had a drop of milk since morning. Do you think it won't cry?'

The havildar had already walked away waving his baton. Apart from a couple of coolies there was no one in front of the carriage. Far off behind them the blue-uniformed guard was waving the green flag.

The engine whistled and began to pull out.

The baby was crying unceasingly. Its mother took a few peanuts from the pocket of her torn kurta and began to shove them into its mouth.

'Naspitti, what are you putting in its mouth? Will you kill my child? Butcher, whore . . . !'

She turned round and threw first a small tin suitcase and then a small bundle on to the platform and, swearing and cursing, jumped down from the train. 'Haramzadi, you made me miss my train. May death eat you! Naspitti!'

The train departed. One by one the coolies made their way out of the station. Silence enveloped the platform. By then the havildar had already reached the far end of the platform on his beat, but when he returned, swinging his baton, the same two women were sitting in a corner against the wall.

The Banjarin had lain the child in her lap and, covering it with the end of her headcloth, she was breastfeeding it, while its mother sat close by stroking its hair.

SALMA AAPA

One thing leads to another. When you mentioned intuition, I remembered a story of my own. I don't know whether there's such a thing as intuition. It's impossible to say anything definite about the subtle perceptions of the mind, but occasionally your understanding is right on target, and you begin to wonder yourself how it happens. Till today I still haven't been able to unravel what happened to me that night.

I was coming back to India from Zambia. The flight was via Karachi, and I thought, 'Why not spend two or three days sightseeing there?' My family was with me — my mother, my wife and two children. But I thought that I didn't get such opportunities every day, and now I was bidding farewell to Zambia to return home, and after I reached India, I was unlikely ever to visit Karachi. Now was my chance, and I should see it on my way. So, before we set off, I sent a telegram to an editor friend in Karachi to let him know when we were arriving. He used to publish my stories in his magazine, and we used to correspond as well. We were on pretty informal terms.

In those days it was quite risky going to Karachi. Tension was on the rise between our two countries, and anything could have happened at any time. And afterwards it did. It would have been sensible not to break our journey and reach home in good order. But when a melody fills your mind, what can you do? My mother was elderly, and my youngest child was unwell. But I can't help my nature. The moment a ripple stirs my mind, I pick up my belongings and set off wherever I feel like. If I had taken every step in life after due consideration, then things would have been different. But I'm not logical. Once a thought has taken hold of me, I lose all my balance. I can't control myself; all moderation is thrown to the winds.

This is precisely what happened in Zambia. In one day I kicked away ten years of permanent employment. And for what? Just because someone I met on the road, with whom I had only a nodding acquaintance, told me, 'Now, sahib, you've come to belong in Zambia, and you are going to stay right here,' and then laughed.

At the time I laughed too, but afterwards my heart began to prick me, and that night I couldn't sleep. I kept tossing and turning, and the next day the country began to seem alien. After that I wasn't happy, and within a week I had resigned from a permanent job where I'd served ten years and was packing my luggage.

What haven't I had to endure in life due to this nature of mine? And then the hand of fate—on that day I had to meet that very acquaintance. Couldn't I have met any other neighbour? Dozens of families lived in our locality. If I hadn't met him, who knows, I might still be sitting in Zambia, and I might never have met you in all my life. The man didn't even say anything exceptional. Obviously, in my subconscious, I must have already been uneasy, and this was raked up by his remark. And when I left Zambia I never thought of what I was going to do next or where I would live when I returned to India. There was no one holding a job open for me. But none of this concerned me. I just packed my bags. When that's your nature, what can you do?

Now when I think about it, there was more to it than that. It was not just a matter of living abroad. The seeds of my disquiet were pressed layer beneath layer, who knows how many layers deeper, and there somewhere they had germinated. It's said, isn't it, no one can plumb the depths of the heart? For years I'd longed to be an author, to sit down in peace and write novels and short stories. I'd been tossing this ambition about for years, but I never could fulfil it, and at every turn in life, whenever my environment changed, I turned a deaf ear to its suppressed voice. I did write a little in Zambia, but not as I wanted. How can anyone write anyway, sitting away from one's own country? For that, you need to smell the earth of your own land.

Whenever the seasons changed in Zambia, I felt an odd pang in my heart. In fact the same longing was stirring within me when that neighbour made his remark. And this time when I felt that pang, it was as if a storm had broken within me. And without knowing whether I was coming or going, the next day I went to the office and put in my resignation. And the very next week, as I said, my elderly mother, my wife and my two children, and a third child too—who is now studying engineering but at that time was in his mother's womb—were sitting in an aeroplane.

Years before when I'd set off for Zambia from Ludhiana, I had felt a similar wrench when I'd bade farewell to my family. And now when I was returning after ten years, I felt the same.

But who knows if even the urge to write wasn't just an excuse and there was really another reason motivating me to return home. If someone really wants to write, he can do it anywhere. A jailed poet used to scratch his verses on the walls of his cell with his nails; he didn't feel that he could write only if he were released. Who knows if I

wasn't throwing dust into my own eyes by claiming that
I could fulfil my desire only by returning to my own home.
I was already writing in Zambia, and my stories were
being published in various places. They had also been published in Karachi in the magazine to whose editor I had
sent the telegram.

Now where have I got to? I started telling you a story
about intuition and then gave you my life history!

Well, I was sitting in the aeroplane with my family, and
had set out from Zambia without any plan for the future.
The plane headed steadily towards Karachi airport, and I
was sitting imagining what the city would be like!

I had never seen Karachi, and I was really enjoying
visualizing it. Situated next to a blue ocean, bright, bathed
in sunshine! Masts, sails and the towers of buildings
gleaming in the sun! This was the picture that rose before
my eyes, and in order to behold it, I had informed my
editor friend that I was arriving on such-and-such a flight
and that my family and I would break bread with him for
two days.

Now look at the twists of fate. The flight was due into
Karachi at five in the evening, and it arrived at half past
two in the morning. Not that half past two is morning;
it's the dead of night, which God shouldn't even show
His enemies. Because of some technical or other snag, on
the way the plane had stood for hours on some runway.
Now when we deplaned, sahib, the place was pitch black
and deserted—there was no sign of my editor. On top of
that was a fiendish cold, fog and a biting wind. Goodness
knows how the plane had managed to land! A handful of
people were wandering around the airport.

Now what were we to do? Where were we to go? My
wife suggested we stay the night at the airport and we'd
see in the morning. If we couldn't make any arrangements,
we'd catch the next flight onward.

I had the address of the editor's office, but I had no idea where he lived. I was angry with him as well. He must have been at home snoring in bed when we were shivering under an open sky.

At first I thought that we should head straight for the editor's office. There would be some chaprasi there, and even if he opened the door for us, it would be something. We could pass the night sleeping on the desks. But then I collected myself. My friend was the editor of a literary periodical, and what did a literary periodical need a chaprasi for? In such organs the editor is all in all—he is the chaprasi, the manager and man who brings you water to drink.

Then a thought occurred to me: In Zambia one lady acquaintance had told me on a couple of occasions that her brother lived in Karachi. Talking about the city, she used to become quite emotional and would say that she found great peace there. In front of her brother's house there was an open park where she used to stroll gently in the late mornings, and when she grew tired, she would sit on a bench in the shade of a spreading tree and watch the children playing.

She'd also told me that her brother lived in a housing colony known as the 'Society', and that it was very clean and new with beautiful, detached bungalows. Now this woman was also fond of writing short stories, and she had wonderful powers of description. As I listened to her I could clearly see the Society. Clean, bright, bathed in sunshine!

Standing at the airport I resolved to set off for that lady's brother's house. After all, we had come to see Karachi, not to shiver at the airport. Every moment was precious, and if we left, at least we would see something. It is my nature to roam; I just can't sit idly.

We walked out of the airport building, loaded our bags into a taxi and ordered the driver to head for the housing colony called the Society.

Soon the car was out of the airport and speeding along a deserted road. God's power is great. As soon as you leave your home, a road opens up in front of you.

Perhaps you've had this kind of experience too! When I reach a new road I've never seen before in an unfamiliar locality or town, I feel a sense of romance, a thrill of delight. At that moment there was nothing special to see outside; there was an open plain on both sides of the road, swathed in fog, and there was a forbidding silence. Trees rising out of the mist looked like masses of darkness. The whole scene was unearthly. Time and time again my mind surged—I was in Karachi, was seeing it for the first time. I kept on telling my wife, 'Look! Behind the mist it looks like there's some jungle, but really it can't be. It must be the ocean, which will be spread out in the daytime like a clean, blue sheet.'

My wife was silent. For her, this was the most terrifying night of her life. She was highly alarmed. My mother was also silent. She was sitting holding her knees as she suffered from rheumatism, and the cold air was exacerbating the pain.

Then gradually we left the field behind, and rows and rows of houses began to emerge from the fog swirling all around. In places dense filaments of mist, like torn rags, were blown high into the air. Sometimes we seemed to be in an immense cemetery—there was the same desolation, forsakenness and the howling wind.

The scene was made even more strange, more otherworldly, by the fact that it was a moonlit night. I was observing it fascinated. I was trying to engrave on my mind the darkness before the dawn; I wanted a clear impression of this scene so that afterwards I could use it in a story. Later I realized that my wife was by then extremely upset. She had seen the brutality at Partition, and she was terrified that anything might happen in this deserted place. The driver must have realized who we were, where we were from. If he had wanted, he could have done anything to us. But you may call it my weakness or a natural strength that, even at times of adversity, I cut myself off from my family and observe my situation like an outsider.

This has its own pleasure, its own flavour. I become as eager as a child; I wait impatiently for whatever's going to happen next. The veil lifts from one thing after another. As we turn each corner, new sights meet the eye. At that moment I was wondering what that lady writer's brother would be like, whether he would resemble his sister or not, whether he'd have a beard, what his home would be like, what colour his lampshades would be, and so on and so forth. Whenever my wife is angry with me, she calls me selfish, but in fact I'm not. It's just that my nature is such . . .

'This is the Society, sahib. Now where do you want to go?'

It was the driver. The taxi had slowed down. It was as if I'd been startled from sleep. I looked outside attentively. On the left a long row of houses faded into the distance and disappeared into the mist. In front of them was a wide open area dotted with trees.

'Salma Aapa's house!' The words slipped from my mouth, but I couldn't even complete my sentence. What had I done? I didn't even know the lady writer's brother's name, and there were rows of hundreds of houses here. How could I knock at anyone's door? I didn't even know the house number.

I had never seen her brother, I couldn't recognize him, I'd never even seen his photograph. All I knew was that there was a park and a bench beneath a tree, and it was very sunny, and somewhere there lived Salma Aapa's brother. I didn't even know whether it was her elder brother or her younger one. What had I done? Oh, my nature!

'This is very difficult, bhai. What can we do? Is this a very big locality, or can we ask at someone's house?'

At this the driver said with some irritation, 'Sahib, if you didn't know the address, you could have told me at the airport. I wouldn't have brought you here. No name, no address, where can I take you?'

'I'll just find out. Why are you getting angry? Yaar, there's nothing to get angry about,' I replied very confidently and climbed out of the car. Now standing in the road and casting a look around, on the left there was a row of houses about a mile long that disappeared into the mist. And on the right, across the open land, there were houses too. Houses and mist, and fog and mist!

I crossed over and headed towards the houses. At that point my wife lost her patience and shouted out, 'Where *are* you going? I'm not letting you go anywhere. Come back!' And in the same tone she said to the driver, 'If there's some hotel nearby, please take us there. Otherwise please take us back to the airport.'

'Look, I'm just going to find out. Don't get upset!' I said and then turned to the driver. 'Bhai jaan, how big is this colony?'

'This isn't a colony. It's a township. Thousands of people live here.'

'So why are you getting upset? Yaar, we'll go back. We won't go to Salma Aapa's brother's home. If Aapa ever complains about it, we'll say that we went there, but we couldn't find her brother's place. Why are *you* getting worried? We'll pay you the entire fare.'

I climbed back into the vehicle a little embarrassed. I'd brought him so far and couldn't even tell him the address. Well, no matter, everyone makes mistakes. In the circumstances my wife's suggestion was the best. We should go to some nearby hotel, and if there wasn't one, then back to the airport to spend the night.

The driver muttered something and turned the car round. I was feeling defeated. What was the harm in knocking on someone's door?

The vehicle picked up speed again. The driver kept muttering and shaking his head.

'Slow down, my good man,' I told him. 'We've come to your country for the first time. The way you behave will give us the impression that the people here are either welcoming or unfriendly!'

The driver muttered something more which could have been a curse or him bemoaning his fate.

The car drove on, and we were making our way out of the Society area. My swimming eyes were losing themselves in the mist all around, the shrubs and trees rising out of it, the walls of houses, the open spaces and parks. My mind had begun to roam the unearthly city of Karachi.

Then suddenly a thought struck me hard. I felt that we'd reached our destination, that this was the place we had to go to. A scene came before my eyes as motionless as a picture. A large tree in a park, and beneath the tree a bench and directly opposite across the street Salma Aapa's brother's house. This was the place, this was Salma Aapa's brother's house!

'Stop, driver, stop. This is it,' I said confidently. 'Get out everyone, we're home.'

Everyone was silent. The driver did stop the car, but he was staring at me. My wife said nothing either, nor did my mother nor my elder daughter. It seemed as if all the exhaustion of the journey was falling away. I felt totally self-assured, and I opened the door and got out.

'How do you know that this is the house? Why don't you ask first? Who knows, it might not be the right place,' my wife called out.

But I recognized the entire scene before my eyes. This was the house, the place . . . a tree and a bench beneath the tree, and a bungalow across the road . . . 'Get down. Unload the luggage. Don't waste time now.'

I crossed the road and walked up a slight slope to the gate. It was just as Salma Aapa had described it. I gently opened the gate and, crossing the courtyard, reached the veranda. The house was sunk in stillness; not even a dog barked. I didn't feel that this was a stranger's house; it all looked so familiar. The wide veranda, two doors opening on to it, which at that time were closed. Behind those closed doors lived Salma Aapa's brother. I stood there very contentedly and then stretched out my arm and rang the doorbell. It was as if the button came to my finger of its own volition. Far within the bell rang. Meanwhile my elder daughter arrived on the veranda. My younger one was standing near the gate coughing. My wife was near the taxi, perhaps waiting to have the luggage unloaded only if I told her to do so.

The second time I rang the doorbell there was a sound from inside. The glass in the upper portion of the door suddenly lit up. There was movement indoors. The sound of footsteps. Then suddenly the veranda light was switched on. By now my younger daughter too was on the veranda but was still coughing continuously. And my mother, perhaps to prevent herself from shivering, had made her way slowly there, bent nearly double, her hands on her knees, and had sat down on a takht.

The next moment the door opened, and before us stood a white-bearded, lean old man. He was wearing a long jacket, and on his head was a small skull cap.

'Please forgive me, we have come from Zambia,' I began. 'Our plane arrived late, and that's why we're troubling you. Salma Aapa told us that you live in the Society . . .'

The old gentleman with the white beard was looking at me through watery eyes. It was extremely chilly, and the cold gusts of wind through the open door were making him shiver too. My little girl was still coughing.

'I had sent a telegram to an editor friend of mine, but our plane arrived late. No one came to collect us. Then I thought we might disturb you . . .' I continued with a smile.

For an instant the old gentleman's eyes rested on me, then his watery gaze turned to the other members of the family. Then a slight smile came to his face, a smile of recognition and sympathy, and he opened the door. 'Please come in!'

This was the only answer he could have given. No other was possible. It was as if I'd heard it before he'd even said it.

We stepped indoors. The sitting room seemed rather familiar—small and comfortable.

The children sat down. My mother sat on a swing that hung on one side of the room. I went to bring the luggage and pay the taxi driver. He helped me with the bags, and I also gave him a good tip on top of the fare.

When I came back inside the old gentleman was gently stroking my little girl's head and asking about her cough. 'Now it will get better. It'll get better by lying in a nice warm bed. Now, let me make arrangements for you to sleep first . . .'

And he stood up and went into the room behind.

'He's a very good man,' murmured my mother. It was the first time she'd spoken, and she surprised me. He was Salma's brother. How could he be indifferent to us? The moment I'd mentioned her name he'd immediately opened his door.

Salma's brother was quick to return and standing in the doorway said, 'Let the little girl go to sleep first, then I'll make arrangements for you all . . . Come, beti.

With this he took her hand in his and led her inside.

The old gentleman quietly went about his work. There seemed to be no servant in the house, and even if there was, then perhaps he wouldn't have woken him at that time of the morning. After my little girl was asleep, he came to my mother.

When all the other members of the family were comfortably in bed, he came to me in the sitting room.

'We were really fortunate in finding you at home. Your sister Salma never tired of talking about you. Today when the plane was late, I at once thought of you. I have troubled you.'

A light smile played on the old gentleman's lips. He nodded, 'How is Salma?'

'She's fine, in good health. She's so good-natured, just like you. When she finds out that we met you on our way home, she'll be extremely happy. She used to talk about you a lot. She's fond of short-story writing as well, and so am I. That's how we got to know each other. Look how strange it is. I didn't even know your exact address, but Salma had described the house in such detail that I had a clear picture of it in my mind.'

He was smiling, a distant sort of smile that plays on the face of every good soul. Then he nodded and said, 'It's night, and you're tired. Take some rest.'

Now tell me, what do you say about intuition? There were hundreds of houses in the Society, dozens of roads and alleys, but as soon as I passed by that tree I at once knew that we had reached our goal. There were dozens of trees there too, and benches beneath them, but that very tree, that very bench, that very house . . .

We left the next day. I spoke to the editor on the phone, and he came to pick us up. That was our first and last encounter with Salma Aapa's brother.

It's years since I returned home, life has taken so many turns, but Salma's brother's face still comes before me again and again. He wasn't a man, he was an angel. The impression he left in my heart is so fine that I want to cherish it, unchanged. I fear anything happening to cause even a fine crack in the picture.

You may find this difficult to accept, but I still haven't mentioned in my letters to Salma Aapa that we stayed the night with her brother just in case she may write back and say, no that was not my brother. And it appears that the good-natured old man hasn't written to his sister about the incident either. Why should he? To tell her about it would in a way be to show that he had put her in his debt by giving her friends shelter in his house.

AHAM BRAHMASMI

In the winter holidays I used occasionally to set out for long morning walks. Leaving the narrow lanes of the town, I would cross the bridge over the river that separates it from the cantonment. Then, once over the bridge, I would either head towards Queen Victoria's statue or turn left and cover two or three miles to reach the dense break of trees where the English used to play golf or ride or stroll arm in arm with their girlfriends. It felt very satisfying to wander on these roads after the suffocating urban alleys. After a substantial circuit of eight or ten miles, I would end up at Bhatia's house in the cantonment, an essential part of my morning's programme. Pleasantly tired after the walk, with my shoes thick with dust, my eyes heavy and my body slow, there was a particular enjoyment in taking breakfast in Bhatia's neat, clean, well-ordered flat. If I felt so inclined, I would lie around there until lunchtime, take in a film and then go home in the evening, or if I saw Bhatia was very busy, I would stop for a brief chat and then head back to the town.

Bhatia considered me a child, but Jeetendra was his firm friend, and Jeetendra was related to me. He was older than I was, but we were walking companions. That day too we arrived at Bhatia's about eleven o'clock in the morning.

Bhatia ran a bookshop and lived in the two or three rooms behind the shop. A khansama wearing a white uniform and red cummerbund opened the door and greeted us very courteously. He was in fact Bhatia's shop assistant, but in the mornings he would come to help the cook and, the moment he arrived, would don his uniform.

'Come in, Jeetendra, come in,' Bhatia's voice issued from within.

The drawing room was gleaming, and Bhatia was sitting on the sofa holding out his hands in greeting. As I slipped inside, Bhatia cast a fleeting and embarrassing glance over my dust-covered shoes. Smiling to reveal all his thirty-two teeth, he said, 'Don't worry about it. As long as you don't put them on my table, I won't object.'

Bhatia sold English books and lived in the cantonment where the English lived and where white soldiers walked the streets, so his ways had become just like those of the English. In any case, shopkeepers selling English books are different from ordinary shopkeepers in that they naturally develop an intellectual posture. They know the names of the latest authors and can talk about all kinds of issues. Bhatia was a darkish, rather ugly-looking man, but there was a strange acuteness in his expressions and mannerisms. He would suddenly turn to speak, smiling to show off his sparkling teeth. He would bow in an odd, crooked way before his English customers, then at once change his stance and put a dozen books down before them in a blink of an eye and discuss them as if he had read entire libraries. In any case, his interests were tinged with the intellectual. Those days he used to talk a great deal about spirituality, and he was also taking an interest in Vedanta because Aldous Huxley had just published a book that had praised Indian philosophy highly.

After we'd been sitting on the sofa for a while, Bhatia, as he generally did, invited us into the dining room. It seemed that he had been waiting for us.

Near the doorway, as was his habit, he stopped and said very politely, with all thirty-two teeth revealed, 'First you, Jeetendra, beauty before the beast!'

This was his catchphrase, and there was some truth in it as, compared to him, Jeetendra could have been called handsome.

I always felt somewhat shy sitting at Bhatia's table as I often forgot which hands to hold the knife and fork in. Bhatia sat in his place at the head of the table and tucked his serviette under his chin, as was the fashion in those days. All the English used to do it. Silver plates were placed before Bhatia while the bearer placed simple china crockery in front of us. This too was one of Bhatia's whimseys. He always ate off silver plates while his guests were given simple china ones.

The bearer swiftly served the breakfast. Bhatia took two boiled potatoes from a silver dish and put them on his plate. Then adding a little mayonnaise, he cut them up with a silver knife and ate them with a silver knife and fork. He ate very little, measuring each bite. Thankfully, in keeping with our taste, we were brought omelettes. If we were only going to eat potatoes after such a long walk, there would have been no reason to come to Bhatia's.

We took full advantage of Bhatia's Anglomania. In the winters there would be a fire in his room, and we would sit in front of it sipping port wine and chatting. His every habit was English. On Sundays, wearing a sports jacket with leather patches on the elbows, he would smoke a cigar and take his dog for a walk. In the summer he changed his shirt four times a day and his vest ten, and three times ordered his bearer to prepare his bath with the command, 'Ghusal lagao!' Despite so much cleanliness when he fell ill once and was rambling in delirium, the nurse at the hospital ran out with her hands over her ears, exclaiming, 'Oh my God! Never did I realize that a bachelor could use such coarse language!'

Now I think that this lifestyle and Anglomania must certainly have been a burden to him, because the times were changing and people like him were beginning to look confused in the new atmosphere, and even the attitude of his English customers towards him was not much different from their attitude to other Indians. One day, in front of me when I was standing in the shop, an Englishwoman was giving him a real scolding for sending her an old bill with a sticker, saying 'Please pay' on it. The woman had erupted when she saw that sticker and Bhatia just kept saying, 'Yes, madam. Yes, madam.' He must have been even more upset because I was present. After she'd left, he kept remarking in a low voice, 'Horrible woman,' and then smiling with all his teeth and admitting his mistake. 'She was right in what she said. Sending a bill means "pay it" — there's no point in putting a label on it as well!' He was annoyed because there was one way of working — the English way — and in this he had been found wanting.

After eating his boiled potatoes, he introduced the topic of spirituality as he sipped his black coffee. 'Jeetendra, do you know how Huxley has translated "aham brahmasmi"?'

'No, how?'

'The translation is "I am the divine flame"! It's a wonderful translation, isn't it?'

Then Bhatia repeated in a soft, deep voice, 'I am the divine flame! There really is enormous power in that mantra. Whenever I repeat it, I always feel strength being set in motion within me.' Then as he sat there, he clenched his right hand into a fist and announced this mantra in a deep, loud voice, 'I am the divine flame! Aham brahmasmi!' This time his voice was trembling more than before. He kept on repeating the mantra. Each time he emphasized the word 'I' more. Each time his voice rose higher. After repeating the sentence three or four times, it seemed to me that he'd reached a kind of ecstasy and was oblivious of the world around him. Behind his spectacles his eyes too seemed to deepen. 'I am the divine flame! For I am the divine flame! Aham brahmasmi!'

After some time he fell silent, as if intoxicated, and sat with his eyes closed. Then gradually he opened them and his clenched fists.

'There's brilliance in this mantra. Jeetendra, whenever I'm worried or upset, say that sentence over and over again, and it's as if I begin to fill with energy, confidence and strength. It feels like my individuality is spreading, and I am lifting up. I begin to feel myself to be a part of the entire universe. It's as if I am the centre of the moon and stars and thousands of circling planets.'

And again Bhatia repeated two or three times, 'I am the divine flame! I am the . . .'

'Now try doing it just in Sanskrit!' suggested Jeetendra.

'No, it's not the same in Sanskrit. There's a gleam of great power in the word flame. Aham brahmasmi!' he announced. 'No, it's not the same. It seems whispery. But there is great life force in this mantra, enormous brilliance. Pronouncing it clears away all weakness, fear, all anxiety, distress. I begin to be a part of the power of the world. My existence begins to touch the heights of the heavens.' Then, as if swaying in ecstasy, he said, 'This is the fibre that joins me with the spirit of Bharat. I have searched out this fibre for myself . . . I will discuss it with Dick in detail. He's very interested in this too.'

The words 'Dick who?' escaped my mouth.

'Dick! You don't know Dick? You should be ashamed of yourself.'

I flushed. In fact Dick, Dicky, Dickinson were all the names of one man who was the British deputy commissioner of the town. When Bhatia talked about him in front of us, he always called him Dick or Dicky, but whenever he was face to face with the deputy commissioner it was always 'Mr Dickinson'.

'He's also fascinated by Indian philosophy,' Bhatia said.

In those days, perhaps all of us enjoyed reading European authors who praised Indian culture and philosophy. They rid us of our sense of inferiority. The times were changing and, to maintain their equilibrium in the new situation, everyone was shifting slightly from their previous position. In the cantonment itself, the shopkeepers who used to send baskets of gifts to the British officials had also begun, on the quiet, to give money to the Congress party. Jeetendra had begun to wear clothes that could be seen from a distance to be made of pure khadi. The feeling of pride in India's ancient culture was a part of this process. Perhaps because of this, even Bhatia had visions of the spirit of Bharat. Although he did regard the British raj as a boon for India, and every day of his life he praised the British sense of justice, their discipline, their democratic spirit, to the skies, still, who knows, Vedantic philosophy might really have quietened some inner hunger, some inner turmoil.

Then from somewhere far off came the sound of drumming. Bhatia's ears pricked up. He was afraid the drumming was coming from inside the cantonment. Those days there were Congress meetings held every day, and the volunteers would take drums into every lane and alley to announce them. The moment the drums were heard, people would gather on rooftops, at windows and balconies to listen to the announcement. There was a particular beat to this drum that could not but appeal to one's heart. But this was the first time it had been heard in the cantonment, and immediately it made the small hairs on our arms and neck stand on end. Who could have the temerity to make a proclamation in the cantonment?

'It's the announcement of some meeting,' said Jeetendra. 'There were arrests in Bombay yesterday. Perhaps that's the reason.'

'But what's the point of making an announcement here?' asked Bhatia. 'Are you going to spread the Congress word among the English?' he continued excitedly.

The drumming was drawing closer.

'Come on, let's go outside to hear,' I suggested.

'No, no. We'll go upstairs and watch from the window. We'll be able to see everything,' replied Bhatia.

I was anxious to go outside, but Jeetendra persuaded me that it was better to go upstairs, and so we did.

The moment we reached the window, a tonga turned from the crossroads and headed towards Bhatia's shop. A tricolour fluttered above it. Against the background of the clear blue sky and the green of the cantonment it looked bright and beautiful. From that tonga came the drumming —dhum, dhum, dhum, dhum. The people on the street began to stop and stare—bearers, small shopkeepers, even some Anglo-Indian girls in skirts and a couple of white soldiers too. Perhaps all of them were astonished at the insolence and rashness of someone who could come to the cantonment to spread Congress propaganda.

The tonga drew to a halt right in front of Bhatia's shop, and immediately he stepped back a little.

Then a thin man stood up in the front seat of the tonga. He had a pale, almost yellow face and wore white, crumpled khadi obviously washed at home and not by a dhobi. A film of sweat was shining on his face. He stood up and put one foot on the shaft that harnessed the horse to be directly beneath the fluttering flag. From here he began his address. He recited a couplet, which might have been about martyrs, then rather emotionally began in a loud voice, 'Friends, you must have heard that yesterday our leaders in Bombay were caught one by one and sent to jail. All Indians should raise their voices against this shameful action of the government. Today all markets, all shops will stay shut. I also appeal to our shopkeeper brothers in this bazaar to keep their doors closed, and this evening at six o'clock there will be a public meeting in Company Bagh . . .'

Then he gazed directly at Bhatia's shop. No assistant had come out on to the pavement. As no one was there, he looked up to where the three of us were standing at the window. Seeing us, he joined his hands and appealed to us to close the shop. From where he stood, Bhatia motioned him to move along with the same gesture he would have used with a beggar. But when the man kept speaking, Bhatia retreated to remove himself from his sight

A short while later, the drum again began to sound, and the tonga set off. The few bystanders dispersed and went their way.

'What enormous stupidity,' Bhatia said as the tonga left. 'The army officers will shoot him to smithereens. Making a Congress proclamation in the cantonment, that is no joke! And then he's telling us to shut our shops!'

Afterwards we discovered that the man who made the announcement had insisted on bringing the tonga into the cantonment even though he knew that to do so would be to run into the face of death. I also found out that he had embraced his companions in the town saying that he didn't know whether he would ever meet them again. And, in fact, he never did meet them again because the same night he died after his skull had been broken by police lathis. But all this we came to know later. At that time the tonga had headed towards the Massey Gate with its flag flying and the drum drumming. The surging electric thrill of his arrival there still stirs me.

'It's a very courageous act, to come and proclaim in the cantonment like that,' said Jeetendra.

'It's not courage, it's insanity. Who is going to listen to you here? Are you going to spread your message among the white military? Are the Indian shopkeepers, who are dependent on the British for their living, going to be influenced by you and close their shops? In the end, what have you come here for?'

A discussion began between Jeetendra and Bhatia. The subject shifted from the proclamation to ahimsa, then to Gandhiji's philosophical views, and in this way layer upon layer of principles began to be exposed.

Meanwhile the sound of the drum passed from earshot. Perhaps after the tonga crossed the Massey Gate, the sound had become very faint. Gradually it was lost in the air, and its throbbing was silenced. Later we came to know that there, a little ahead of the Massey Gate, where the main cantonment bazaar began, someone had stopped the tonga, then someone else had come forward and slapped the message bearer in the face and grabbed him and pulled him down from the tonga. Then all at once the police arrived and, in order to get to the bottom of the disturbance, took the thin young man into custody, and then no one in our town ever saw his pale face again.

After the beat of the drum had died, the discussion between Jeetendra and Bhatia continued for a long time. Jeetendra was a disciple of non-violence, while Bhatia would make fun of it along with the spinning wheel and khadi. According to him, they had made the country impotent. Jeetendra found a new experience in ahimsa, while Bhatia called it the obsession of an old man and impotence. Watching them, I felt that man was essentially a discursive creature, that this was his sole natural strength.

We had lunch with Bhatia and stretched out on his sofas. Evening drew in. The time came to shut the shop. The head clerk locked up and sent the keys to Bhatia. Bhatia drank sherbat from a silver tumbler, while Jeetendra and I sipped tea from high-quality English china.

It was then we decided to go to the cinema. One of the two cinemas in the cantonment was showing a Greta Garbo film, which it would have been foolish to miss.

To go to the cinema on that day was a mistake. Even an experienced man like Bhatia overlooked the fact that after the proclamation, tension would have permeated the cantonment, and that a drum and the tricolour had the potential to cause unrest.

During the interval Bhatia felt the need to use the lavatory. Generally he didn't use the toilets in the cinema because they were always full of British, and there was no separate facility for Indians. They had to relieve themselves quietly on the ground or behind the trees or in the bushes of the cinema garden, which was shrouded in darkness by the time of the interval.

But Bhatia went into the white man's loo. The toilet was a circular room with small partitions between the many urinals. The white soldiers raced to the lavatory at a run to empty their beer-filled stomachs the moment the interval bell rang. It's not easy to express what happened to Bhatia there. The white men streamed into the toilets. Some of them had opened their trouser buttons even before they got inside. At once the whole round room was filled. Seeing a black-necked Indian in a white shirt and trousers in front of him, one of them immediately shoved Bhatia aside and took his place.

'I beg your pardon!' Bhatia said, and showing all his teeth to the Englishman, with great politeness retreated to stand before the empty urinal on his left. The soldiers were still pouring in, and no one had the time to wait even a moment. Bhatia was elbowed from this place too and rushed to a third urinal that was free, but the same thing happened to him there. By now he had become a joke. The white men were pushing him around on purpose—first in one direction and then another. Bhatia was no longer in his right mind, and he didn't even have the courage left to run.

When he came to his senses, he was standing in the middle of the cinema's garden. In his hand was a sodden handkerchief with which he was wiping his face again and again. I don't know what state his mind must have been in, what emotions were churning inside him—remorse, self-disgust, anguish or rage.

We heard the whole story later. At the time we were sitting in the cinema hall. When Bhatia failed to return, I went to look for him outside, but by then he'd already left the park.

By the time I tracked him down in his home, he was standing on the flat roof of his house beneath the open sky. He was in the centre of the roof babbling in a soft, deep voice, 'Aham brahmasmi! I am the divine flame! I am the divine flame!' Gradually his voice rose, his fists were closing, and his neck and chest was slowly straightening. 'I am the divine flame! I am the divine flame!'

He didn't see me. As I stood there, his voice grew louder and louder. It was clear that strength was flowing within him. Perhaps even before I reached there, the evening's incident had already fallen from his consciousness like a dry leaf in its insignificance, and he had long risen above the lowest point of insult, disrespect, remorse and anguish. And he was rising still, still rising.

Now if I consider it, perhaps at that very time, two streets away in the Massey Gate police station, under a shower of lathi blows a half-dead young man was murmuring, 'Bharat Mata ki jai! Mahatma Gandhi ki jai!' And when Bhatia's spirit was touching the heights of the universe, when he had risen above the gross world around him, to become one with the moon and the stars, at approximately the same time, blood was starting to flow from the mouth of the pale, thin young man who'd made the proclamation and, still murmuring 'Bharat Mata ki jai', he collapsed on the police-station floor.

PAALI
(for Shashi Anand)

Nothing ever comes to an end. One shore of life never meets the other, neither in fact nor in fiction. We merely live in hope that one day they might meet, and occasionally we suffer from the illusion that they really have.

Once Manoharlal and his wife too were under the illusion that they'd managed to pass through a crisis, and that the knot that had bound them had opened. But such knots never untie so easily either in fiction or in reality. As one opens, another closes. The story never really ends. The blessing is that life goes on and keeps posing us new questions.

One part of Manoharlal's and his family's life was left behind in a distant small town when the country was partitioned, and, with hundreds of others, they too packed up their belongings and set off in a refugee column, the atmosphere filled with the dust of their feet. Just as different rivers flow separately towards the ocean, the columns of refugees too travelled towards the dividing line, which those days had been drawn to cut one land in two.

Manoharlal was with his wife and two children—the younger one still at her mother's breast, and the elder, four-year-old Paali, walking behind his father. Every refugee with his bundles of belongings was scanning the road with strained eyes; each one's ears were turned to everything said by passers-by in case they could suggest a way out, could tell them what was happening all around and what was going to happen.

And on that last day, the refugee camp in the city began to empty. The refugees again picked up their bundles and began to leave. On the road outside, a long line of lorries was waiting to take them to the partition line. Manoharlal, a bundle on his head and holding his son by one finger, and his wife Kaushalya, a bundle on her head and her baby at her breast, were walking towards the lorries into which refugees were throwing their boxes and bundles before climbing up themselves. When Manoharlal felt his son Paali's hand had parted from his, Kaushalya was already in the back of a lorry, and he had handed his bundle to her. Then he noticed Paali wasn't there. At that instant, though, Manoharlal wasn't too perturbed as he imagined the boy would be somewhere close by. He could still feel the warmth of his hand in his own. There were commotion and crowds all around. The camp chaudhuris were shouting for people to get quickly into the lorries as they had to cross the border before nightfall. The drivers were sounding their horns; the refugees were screaming at one another.

When he couldn't see Paali anywhere, he began to worry and turned back calling his name, but there was no reply. Then he panicked and began shouting for his son at the top of his voice, running unthinkingly.

The lorries were driving off one after the other, and the one in which his wife was standing with her infant child was also crammed full, and its driver too had his hand continuously on the horn.

'Paali! Paali!' shouted Manoharlal, his throat growing dry, his legs shaking and his head spinning. People who lose their homes behave like this. He stood on that jam-packed road feeling as if he were screaming into an empty desert.

He was still searching for Paali when his lorry began to move off. His terrified wife—whose eyes were fixed on her husband in the crowd and who was losing sight of him—suddenly lost control of herself and began to weep and scream, tangled locks of hair scattered over her face, her infant swinging at her breast, and her breath heaving.

'Stop! Stop! Lorry! Hae! Stop the lorry!'

But who was going to listen? Everyone was shouting. It wasn't just her family leaving home. Half of one refugee's luggage had been loaded, while his charpoys were still lying on the road; an old mother couldn't manage to climb into the lorry; everyone was being shoved from all sides. As the lorry slid forward, Kaushalya's eyes sought only one form, that of her shouting, searching husband. Then, when she wailed and wept—like a bird would whose nest is destroyed—her voice did reach someone's ears, and someone else in the lorry raised the cry, 'Stop the lorry! Stop the lorry!' Then a few more joined in, and the lorry lost speed.

Who knows whether matters are determined by circumstance, or human beings themselves or fate. Incidents keep happening, and the ironies of life peek through them and make faces at us. Kaushalya had even thrown down one of her bundles and was about to hand her screaming baby to a refugee standing on the road when Manoharlal ran back. His son was not with him. He didn't know what whirlpool had swallowed him.

Some voices were addressing Manoharlal. 'The child, he must be here somewhere!' They waved their hands to beckon him. 'Come on, come here! He must be in another lorry!' Other voices were angry and impatient. 'Will you keep this lorry here just for the sake of one child? If you want to look for him, get off!' Several points of view had changed. If Manoharlal hadn't arrived at that moment, perhaps Kaushalya would have climbed down from the lorry, crying and sobbing, and the other refugees would have thrown her belongings down after her. They were right; they did have to cross the border before sunset. The lorry couldn't be kept waiting just for one child!

Mercy had dried in their hearts. When the same Paali once got lost in his own small town, everybody had turned out to look for him. And here someone kept on shouting, 'Get off the lorry. If you want to look for the child, get down!'

The husband and wife couldn't decide whether to get down or not. There was no sign of Paali. They stared at the road as if insensible. Gradually the city was left behind; the screaming ceased. Then trees, fields and green plains came before their eyes. Paali, lost among the city crowds, was left further behind. Kaushalya kept sobbing for a long time in that column of lorries, and her agony expressed itself first in insane weeping, then silence and then in deep, heart-rending despondency. The column of lorries jolted along. Gradually, as the shadows descended from the skies and the occasional star began to glitter beneath the unknowable heavens, Manoharlal began to comfort his wife, 'We'll find him. We will. He must be somewhere close by. He can't disappear, can he? Some kind person must have put him into another lorry.' Then he looked at Kaushalya's stony eyes and the mute anguish etched on her face and said, 'If we don't find him, then what can we do? By the grace of God, we still have one child. Lekhraj saw all of his three children killed in front of his eyes. When God ordains something, what can we do?'

Kaushalya's desolate eyes were fixed on the road.

In fact there was nothing exceptional in one small child being lost. There was no sense in making such a hue and cry about it. The homeless refugees in the column gradually began talking amongst themselves. The women too. Here and there you could even hear laughter.

By the time they approached the border, it had begun to grow dark. When the lorries stopped, Manoharlal leapt down on to the road and began shouting 'Paali! Paali!' in front of every lorry. He peered into each vehicle but received no reply. His voice returned like an echo in an empty desert. There was no sign of Paali anywhere.

Close to the border, the refugees climbed out of these lorries and into others that set off in the darkness towards Amritsar. Studded with innumerable stars, the sky looked unfathomable and mysterious. The refugees had fallen silent and were looking out into quiet nothingness. Suddenly Manoharlal's wife began to scream. Such a howl came from her that the other people in the lorry thought she'd gone mad, but then, after shrieking for some time she began to whimper. Then they were reassured that she was not insane but grieving, that she couldn't forget her child. Finally, when she leant her head against his shoulder and went to sleep, Manoharlal resolved that, as soon as they found somewhere to stay, he would come back, and, no matter what, he would trace his son.

The column of lorries, sunk in darkness, was forging ahead. Nobody was able to consider what would happen next; their minds were numb. Fate had thrown such a black curtain before their eyes that they couldn't see as much as a flickering oil lamp behind it. There were just jolts, pushes, strained eyes, dry throats and the terrifying canopy of countless twinkling stars.

That night when, after crying and grieving for hours, Paali fell asleep against Zainab's bosom, his sobs sank deep into an ocean of affection. The greatest shelter for the human race, the greatest source of affection, is the bosom of a woman. Zainab's arms held him in an embrace. For the first time in her life she was feeling the joy that can only belong to a woman who has never been able to have children. The sweet-smelling young body was clinging to her as if he had been created to lie in her lap. For the first time, Zainab felt as if at any moment milk would come to her breasts. A restless motherhood was surging through her body.

'You're not saying anything.' her husband said.

Lying on the charpoy next to her, Shakur had been staring for a long while at the sky. The countless stars that studded it reminded him of Zainab's deep blue chunari, which she had worn when she stepped into the courtyard the first time after her marriage and which was covered with sparkling silver sequins. When she peeped out from beneath the chunari, the way her face shone really made him feel that the moon itself had come down into his courtyard.

Shakur sold china crockery. His basket of dishes on his head, he went from lane to lane, street to street. He had spent years walking round the streets of the town shouting his wares, and today as the afternoon was drawing to a close, this boy, tossed out of the crowd, was standing at the end of the lane crying 'Pitaji! Pitaji!' when Shakur saw him and stopped. He sat down next to the boy and began to pat him and wipe his tears, and when he saw that being comforted calmed the boy's sobs, he said, 'Come, I'll take you to your pitaji,' and, holding him by the hand, led him away. First they went to the place from where the refugees' lorries had left. By then all the vehicles had gone, and the dust they'd thrown up had mainly settled. Even the refugee camp was empty. When that night Shakur set foot in the doorway of his ramshackle home, Paali was sleeping against his shoulder.

Shakur was a God-fearing man; he lived his life in apprehension. Ever since the riots had started, he kept a distance from them. When the market was set on fire and one or two people in the town were killed, he kept on murmuring just one thing: 'It is the wrath of the Almighty!'

'You're not saying anything,' Shakur repeated.

'What do you want me to say?' Zainab replied lazily and then fell silent again. She felt immersed in the affection of that dear little body. She felt as if all the obstacles in her life were crumbling before her, and she was growing more and more relaxed, but still she didn't want to tell her husband that she'd found a treasure, that a tide had risen within her just by putting a strange child against her breast.

'All the Hindus and Sikhs have left their homes and gone. The camp's empty. Now no one's going to come back,' Shakur murmured.

Still Zainab kept her silence. The child stirred in his sleep and then sighed deeply and went back into a deep slumber, his hand on Zainab's breast.

Looking at the sky above, it seemed to her too as if the heavens were glittering at her good fortune. But she spoke in the same tone Shakur had used, 'Go and put him back where you found him. Why should we be the cause of some unfortunate woman's distress?'

'Why should we be? We've given him a refuge,' said Shakur. 'If we hand him in at the police station, they're not going to take him to his mother and father.'

Each was testing the other's heart.

Rubbing her cheek against the child's forehead, Zainab whispered, 'What's his name?'

'How do I know? When I asked him he just said "Paali, Paali".'

'What odd names these Hindus have. What sort of name is Paali? I would have called my son Altaf.'

They both lay in silence for a while. Zainab was floating in joy while Shakur was considering many things. If no one made any inquiries, then Zainab would have a child of her own. He would play in the courtyard. Now no one would come to inquire. Mahmood the tailor had abducted a Hindu woman and was keeping her in his house, and no one had come to ask about that. Mir Zamaan had taken all the things from the tailor's next door and hidden them in his house, and no one had said anything. I am providing shelter, supporting a crying, lost child . . . but still, despite all this, from time to time he felt doubtful.

The next day when the child awoke and, finding himself among strangers, started crying again and shouting for his pitaji, Zainab held a bowl of milk to his lips and kept stroking his head and back. Little Paali developed hiccups from crying. Zainab kept raising her eyes to the closed door in case someone might hear him and come into the house. She now had a child all right, but it was a stolen one! If someone found out, then what? For some days they would have to keep him hidden.

When he stopped sobbing, Paali chose to be silent. He sat in a corner of the courtyard looking here and there with lost eyes and sighing. Every sigh made Zainab feel something she couldn't express. She had begun to be disturbed herself by the child's arrival.

Shakur was outwardly confident that the child would begin to feel at home in a couple of days and get accustomed to them. But he was not so sure in his heart. Who was to know if the boy's parents weren't around somewhere nearby and might not come to the house in search of him? Not every single one of the refugees had left yet. Who knew? Perhaps the police might find out! This might turn into a disaster.

They managed to get through two days, and on the third the child began to open up a little. When a white cat came from somewhere and sat on the courtyard wall the boy broke into a smile. And when it jumped down into the courtyard, he ran after it shouting, 'Pussy cat, pussy cat!'

Now Zainab came back to life, and it was at this moment that there was a knock on the door. Both husband and wife were startled; both their hearts began to pound.

'They're here—the people whose child he is.' The words escaped Zainab's mouth, shock in her eyes.

'I hope it's not the police,' said Shakur and looked at the door in bewilderment.

Someone rained blows on the door, as if with a lathi.

'Open this door,' came a voice from outside.

'Open it,' appealed Zainab. 'We'll have to see what happens.'

Shakur walked forward hurriedly. 'Take him to the back room.'

Zainab rose and picked up the child.

Outside the door there was no havildar of police or even the child's parents. A rather fat, bearded maulvi sahib with a stick was standing there. Two men armed with lathis were with him.

'Who brought that son of a kafir here?' the maulvi shouted at the top of his voice as he entered the courtyard. The two men with lathis followed him into the house.

'Have you hidden any other kafirs here?'

Shakur retreated from him and picked up a stool in self-defence.

'I swear by the Qu'ran Sharif, I have hidden no one here,' said Shakur. 'I have just given shelter to an orphan boy.'

'Where is the boy?'

'Ji, he's asleep inside.'

The maulvi looked suspiciously at Shakur and then, thumping the ground with his lathi said, 'Bring him before me! Who is he?'

At this Zainab herself brought the child out.

'Are you giving shelter to the child of a kafir?'

'I have adopted a child. I haven't committed a sin, maulvi sahib!' said Zainab steadily.

'Have you had him circumcised? Taught him the kalma?'

Zainab took heart. The maulvi hadn't come to seize the boy but only to make him a Muslim. Still she said nothing.

'Why don't you speak? You put the unclean child of a kafir in your lap? Feed it your milk? You are raising a snake!'

Zainab was embarrassed by the maulvi's argument. She was amazed that she had never thought of it like that. The child had never seemed unclean to her or the son of a snake. She was about to say something when the maulvi banged his lathi on the ground and announced, 'Bring this child of a kafir to the mosque tomorrow morning. Otherwise things will go very badly for you.' And he turned towards the door.

After he'd left, Zainab tossed her head and smiled. The maulvi wanted the boy to recite the kalma, to be circumcised, didn't he? Why tomorrow, why not today itself? He won't take the boy away from us, will he? So what is there to be afraid about? She threw off all her worries, took the child in her arms and covered him with kisses.

The next day he was circumcised. When he saw the knife, little Paali was frightened and went and hid behind Zainab's legs.

The maulvi began to caress him the moment he'd been circumcised. Now when Paali shrieked in pain for his pitaji, even the maulvi didn't find it objectionable; in fact he was laughing and smiling. The neighbours had also arrived and were congratulating them. The maulvi had brought him a fez with a black tassel and placed it on his head. Zainab had dressed him in a new muslin kurta. The maulvi himself picked up the child and placed him in her lap.

'Take him, now he's yours and no child of a kafir. He's now a child of the faith.'

And the child's name was changed from Paali to Altaf.

For Zainab and Shakur radiance brightened their courtyard. When they distributed sweets around the whole neighbourhood, Zainab went from house to house with the child in her arms.

Gradually little Paali grew accustomed to his new environment. Within a year he became known as Altaf Husain, son of Shakur Ahmed the crockery seller. Now when he played in the courtyard, he called out like his father did when he was selling his wares. He would put the household's dishes into a basket, lift the basket on to his head and walk round the courtyard shouting, 'China dishes! Cups, jugs, plates!' When Ramadan started, he would stand in the centre of the courtyard, banging a tin can and shouting 'Get up, Muslims, keep the fast . . . Oooh . . . Eeh!' And Zainab and Shakur had been quick to put him in the mosque's madrasa where with the other children, sitting on the mosque veranda, rocking back and forth, he began learning the verses of the Qu'ran by heart. They now had a focal point, one axis around which their life began to revolve very happily. They began to weave their dreams of the future about little Altaf. Shakur, the man who'd spent his life hawking crockery, began to dream of the day he'd open a shop, and he and his son would run it together. They would be beholden to no man, would sleep freely and wake freely. And Zainab began to dream of the day when Altaf's bride would step into the courtyard with the jingling of anklets, spreading brilliance and light.

Two years passed in this state of intoxication.

One day the crockery seller was not at home. Little Altaf was away at the madrasa. Zainab was alone, sitting in the courtyard behind the sackcloth curtain, grinding wheat, when there was a knock on the door. Zainab replied from where she sat, 'The man of the house is not at home. Come in the evening.'

There was a moment's silence outside the door and then came a voice, 'There's a summons for Shakur Ahmed. He's called to the police station.'

And Zainab left the grindstone, pulled her chunari dupatta fully over her head and came to stand behind the curtain. A tingling wave of fear passed through her from top to bottom.

'What is it, ji?'

'Send him to the thana tomorrow morning. It's important.'

'What is important?' Zainab asked apprehensively in a trembling voice.

'They've come from Hindustan to take a child back. A letter's come.'

Zainab shook from head to foot. Her throat grew dry.

'Send him to the thana tomorrow morning. Don't forget.' And there came the sound of retreating footsteps.

Some shocks merely wound you, and as time passes, the wounds heal. But there are also the shocks that become obsessions and eat at you, completely beyond your control. When Kaushalya reached India with her husband, she had no child in her lap.

That day, if the line of lorries had reached the border safely and if Manoharlal and his wife and child had crossed it safely, then gradually the dust of time would have fallen on their memory of Paali and the sorrow of his loss would have grown fainter. But that did not happen. After they had left the city, there had been one more incident. The lorries were driving on when suddenly some people appeared out of the field next to them screaming and ran on to the road. They had the same covered faces, were armed with spears and were shouting slogans and curses. Many of the lorries had already passed, but the last three fell into their grasp. In the darkness came again the same screams and shrieks, the spears and knives, the same pain-filled cries that had forced Manoharlal and Kaushalya to flee their home town. Blood sprayed in all directions. Kaushalya didn't know when she was pushed from behind and fell. All she heard was Manoharlal's voice saying, 'Here, give the child to me,' and then even that disappeared, and she was shoved from behind and fell face down. When she came to, there were whistles being blown somewhere, and there was pitch darkness, and there was the sound of people moaning nearby. Beneath her hands on the floor of the lorry she felt something wet, which could have been water or blood. Then the lorry moved off. Looking up at the stars, it was as if they themselves had begun to move. Her mouth was dry, and she needed water. Then it seemed as though the stars were going round and round, and she again lost consciousness.

When they reached Delhi, it sometimes seemed to Manoharlal as if he was still being stifled beneath a pile of corpses. He was struggling to get out. He felt that if he couldn't, he'd be crushed. As he tramped the streets of Delhi, he knew that if he spent all his time sitting mourning his children, he and his wife would die of starvation. Hundreds, thousands of refugees were roaming the lanes of Delhi looking for shelter. If he was going to manage to get two meals a day he would have to turn his back on the past. This hadn't just happened to him; it had happened to hundreds of thousands of refugees. Some people gave him a helping hand, others averted their eyes, but finally he had a handcart and became a street trader. But when he came back home after standing in the dust all day and found his half-mad wife sitting desolately, or when she began to whimper or cry out in her sleep, his courage failed him. If she went mad, how would he look after her? Whatever was left of life would just be a torment. Manoharlal would stroke her, hold her hand in his and explain, 'Look, dear, if God wills it, we will have other children, take hold of yourself.' But just at the mention of children she would begin to tremble and moan so that his heart ached.

So, despite spending all day standing at his handcart, in his spare time he would knock at the door of courts and offices and important people's houses. The government had opened large offices to recover women, girls and property and to locate missing people. And the people employed in these offices—government servants, social workers, men and women—generally used to go to and from Pakistan for their work.

Manoharlal had begun running around, but he had no support. Month after month passed, and nothing concrete emerged. There was no trace of Paali anywhere. In a city full of hundreds of thousands of people, to find one lost child was no easy task. When he started searching, he was hopeful, and he began to think that if he could just go back to that city, then he would run to the locality where Paali's hand had lost hold of his, and Paali would be standing at the end of some lane waiting for him, and he would at once pick him up, bring him back to Delhi and deposit him in Kaushalya's lap.

But there seemed no end to the search. For two whole years Manoharlal's case just hung in the air. When parties of officials and social workers working on recovery went to Pakistan, sometimes he would also pick up a bundle of belongings and go with them. But every time he returned beating his head in frustration.

The day the havildar first brought the summons to Shakur Ahmed's home, Zainab began to flounder like a fish out of water. Snakes seemed to slither round the light-filled courtyard, and her dreams were crushed. But by evening she began to regain her composure. Shakur came home. When he heard the news, his face also turned pale and his legs shook, but then the other people in the area heard. Several sympathizers arrived. When the maulvi sahib found out, he too came over with his lathi.

'To hell with them. You don't worry. No one would dare lay a finger on the child. Now that he's accepted the faith, do you think that I would let him be handed over to kafirs?'

Peace returned to Zainab's soul. The maulvi was right. Altaf was no longer the same child who had slept in her arms on the first night. If anyone had wanted to take him then, they could have done so. Now who could?

The elders held a meeting. The decision was taken that maulvi sahib himself would persuade the police that the havildar who came with the summons would in his own hand write on the summons that Shakur Ahmed was not at home, that he'd gone out of town and that it was not known when he would return. And if the summons came repeatedly, then the couple really would take the child away for some time. 'To hell with them. I'll see how any kafir can remove the child from here,' said the maulvi banging his lathi on the ground and leaving.

Then began a strange game of hide-and-seek. Although the leaders of governments make policies, these are put into practice by smaller people. From above comes the order that a certain boy should be recovered, and the constable from the police station follows his nose and arrives at the correct house. He knocks on the door, frightens and threatens the people inside, and returns with money pressed into his hand and writes on the summons that the door is locked from outside, that the occupants of the house are out of town and that there is no saying when they will be back.

Here it was not just a matter of a small bribe. It was not even a matter of returning an adopted child. It was turning into a matter of religion. Not to return the child was serving the religion, was a matter of faith and of earning merit.

Then months and years passed.

Once a whole recovery party did actually turn up at Shakur Ahmed's house, but the door really was padlocked. The night before the family had received advanced warning of the visit and left. The party found that Shakur Ahmed had gone to visit his brother in Sheikhupura. It wasn't known when he'd be back. When the party reached Sheikhupura, they discovered that only the previous day Shakur Ahmed with his wife and child had left for Lyallpur. 'Yes, the child was with him, but we don't know his address there. He didn't tell us.'

Three years passed in this game of hide-and-seek. Manoharlal's face had turned almost black, deep lines were etched on his cheeks, his hair was turning grey. The dust of doubt constantly flew in front of his eyes. He no longer knew how to tell truth from lies. As an eagle tears its prey with its beak, life was tearing Manoharlal to pieces.

Now whether it was the effect of the strength of Manoharlal's resolve or the sighs of the unfortunate Kaushalya, a whole five years later Manoharlal was sitting in Shakur Ahmed's courtyard. With him were other members of the recovery party. There were a female and a male social worker and government officials. From the Pakistani government side there were a magistrate and two policemen. In fact, this was the result of a request made by a well-known connection of Manoharlal's to a senior government official who had raised the issue with a senior Pakistani official and thereby had it carried forward to this point. Today legal action was being taken as a result of which, if it were proved that the child was Manoharlal's, then Manoharlal would be given custody.

The tension in the courtyard was mounting. On one side, away from the officials, sat the maulvi sahib. Outside the house between ten and twenty men from the locality had gathered, and on the veranda behind the sacking curtain sat Zainab. Her face was yellow as a flame, and her eyes were like those of a great bird from whom someone had come to steal the eggs. Nine-year-old Paali— now Altaf Husain—was nestling up to her, confused and frightened, and Zainab, restless, was repeatedly hugging him close.

The maulvi was making all kinds of statements before the proceedings started. 'No one can take this child. No kafir can lay a hand on him.' The party from India was repeatedly requesting the magistrate to instruct the maulvi to be silent as his remarks were adding to the tension.

Since Partition the drops of blood on the roads had dried, but the marks they had left had not been rubbed out. The fire in burning houses had died, but their black skeletons still stood here and there. The madness of the time of Partition had to a large extent cooled, but what was left of its effect had not been erased from people's minds.

'Call the child here,' came the magistrate's voice.

At this Zainab called out in agitation, 'We haven't stolen anyone's child, why should we send him to you, ji?'

'Call the child here,' repeated the magistrate, and Shakur Ahmed went behind the sacking curtain to fetch him.

Manoharlal's heart was pounding. A decisive moment had come again, a moment which would decide his fate. He was longing to see his child again, but doubt and fear also gripped his heart.

The child came forward. Seeing the crowd in the courtyard, he became even more disconcerted, clung to Shakur and stared at the people standing near with his finger in his mouth.

'Beta, come here. See who it is. Do you know anyone here?' asked the magistrate. At this the police officer added in a loud voice, 'No one is to say anything. Let the boy do the identification himself.'

Manoharlal couldn't recognize his own child. A nine-year-old boy, tall, wearing a fez and a muslin kurta and shalwar. Manoharlal's own eyes were deceiving him. For a long time he gazed at the boy; then as recognition dawned, his throat filled. He longed to shout, 'Paali! My son Paali!' and with difficulty restrained himself.

There was no change in the boy's expression even when he looked at his father. He was already scared, and he became even more so at the sight of all the people there. Manoharlal was standing gazing at him. The boy had filled out, grown taller; he was looking very fair and beautiful.

Manoharlal began to feel as if the decisive moment was passing, and nothing had been achieved. Now again he would have to trudge through the dust of the desert of life.

Breaking the silence all around, the maulvi spoke. 'Did you see! The boy didn't recognize him. If he'd been his, he would have run to him. And they've come to take the child!'

The woman social worker was perturbed. Addressing the boy she said, 'Beta, come here. See who it is.'

At this the police officer again shouted, 'No one will speak. I've told you, let the child make the identification himself.'

Inside Zainab was sitting holding her breath. Who could imagine what she was feeling?

The woman social worker turned to Shakur. 'You accept the child is not yours, that you adopted him?'

Shakur was about to respond when the maulvi banged the ground with his lathi and said, 'That I also accept that the boy was adopted. But how can anyone say that the child is a Hindu or the son of this man?'

The magistrate nodded. He was watching first the boy and then Manoharlal most attentively. Manoharlal was losing hope. The child was in front of him, and Manoharlal was just looking at him as if uncertain what to do. The moment was slipping through his fingers.

'The child is upset,' remarked the woman social worker. 'Please be quiet.'

'There, it's over, what more do you want to see?' shouted the maulvi. 'Please get out of here.'

Then the woman social worker addressed Manoharlal. 'Where's that photograph you showed me?'

Manoharlal could find nothing to bring with him as proof but a small photograph. At Kaushalya's insistence, he'd had one taken of himself and Kaushalya with the little boy at the Baisakhi mela. In the photo little Paali was sitting in his mother's lap. But now, what was the purpose of it? The child had grown so that you couldn't make out it was him if you tried.

He took the photograph from his pocket and handed it to the magistrate.

'The child in the photograph, sir, is this child. Please see for yourself.'

At this Shakur Ahmed grew excited and said, 'What does a picture prove, sir! We have a picture too.' And, stepping inside, he came out dusting a framed photograph with his sleeve and put it in front of the magistrate.

Manoharlal's photograph was still in the magistrate's hand.

'Come here, son!' the magistrate said, calling the boy and holding the photograph in front of him. He said nothing more. He knew that the child would never be able to recognize himself.

Finding himself faced with the photograph, the boy regarded it carefully for some time. Then putting his forefinger on the picture, he said in a loud voice, 'Pitaji!' He moved his finger to Kaushalya's face and cried out in the same tone, 'Mataji!'

An unfamiliar restlessness stirred within him.

Manoharlal began to cry, and to stifle his sobs, he kept stuffing the end of his turban into his mouth.

The magistrate put the second picture before the child. The child burst into a smile and said, 'Abbaji! Ammi!'

A wave of joy rose in Shakur's heart.

Behind the curtain, Zainab's eyes overflowed.

The maulvi was still frowning, but his face relaxed a little at the boy's answer.

'Now he is the son of a Muslim, not the son of a kafir. Now he knows the kalma.'

'You shut up,' shouted the lady social worker.

'Why should I? This gentleman threw his son away. We raised him,' the maulvi shouted back.

At the maulvi's words, the boy first clung to Shakur Miyan's legs and then ran behind the sacking curtain.

The noise inside must have been audible outside the house as voices cried out 'Allah-o-Akbar!'

The female social worker and both the Indian government officials were earnestly arguing that since the child had now identified his father, he should be handed over to them. But the situation was deteriorating. Tension was mounting again. And behind the sacking curtain, the child lay frightened with his head in Zainab's lap, holding on to her with both arms.

Whose the child was, or who had raised him had become secondary; the question had become a Hindu–Muslim one.

Manoharlal could think of nothing else to do. He went quietly up to the sackcloth purdah, joined his hands in pleading, and said, 'Sister, I am not begging for the child, but for my wife's life. She has lost both her children. Without Paali, she is going insane. Night and day she is in agony. Please take pity on her.'

There was silence behind the sacking curtain. The officials also stopped speaking and turned towards it. The maulvi too rose to his feet. He expected that the only thing the man would hear in response from behind the curtain was curses.

Then a rather broken voice came

'Take your child back. I don't want any unfortunate woman's ill will on me. How were we to know that you had lost both your children?'

Manoharlal felt like rushing behind the curtain and touching the woman's feet.

About an hour later the child was being bade farewell. Tears rolling down their cheeks, Zainab and Shakur dressed him in the smart white clothes which they'd made for him for the coming festival of 'Id. They put his fez on his head, and as they sent him from the house, Zainab's voice came from behind the purdah. 'But I give the child on one condition. You will send him back here every year for 'Id. He will stay with us for a month. Tell me, do you agree? Promise me.'

Manoharlal was trembling with emotion. As he had done before, he joined his hands and said, 'He is your treasure, sister! You have taken care of him, brought him up. I promise. I will remember your kindness to me from birth to birth.'

Life began to motor along again. The same crooked roads, the same turns, the ups and downs. If the matter had ended here, then the entire documentation would just have been a story, but it didn't. Nothing really comes to an end.

The female social worker and the officials drew a line through another name on the list of people to be recovered and added a name to their list of successes.

The government jeep was speeding forward. On the front seat with the driver was an armed policeman and with him a police officer. In the back on one side the father and son sat close to each other and opposite them sat the woman social worker, the man social worker and an official from the Indian government. The child was still in a state of confusion, but he was gradually leaning closer and closer to his father, and the warmth from his body was again warming to Manoharlal's blood. The fibres of parental love had begun to join them again.

Around midday they crossed the dividing line. They all got down from the Pakistani jeep, and the Pakistani officials handed papers to the Indian officials standing on the other side of the line and left in the same jeep.

Manoharlal, his son and the other members of the party climbed into another jeep, which set off towards Amritsar.

The jeep had just entered the plains when something came into the lady social worker's head, and she stretched out her right hand, took off the boy's fez and tossed it out of the jeep. The red fez, with its black tassel, flew on to the side of the road and fell in the dust.

'My hat,' the boy put his hand to his head, 'hae, my hat!'

At this the woman social worker leaned forward and said, 'If you're the child of a Hindu, why should you wear a Muslim hat?'

To throw the hat away like this seemed to Manoharlal very out of place. She must have hurt the boy. He said patiently, 'How does the child know that it's a Muslim hat? Why did you throw it like that? Stop the jeep, and I'll fetch it.'

The child was tearful, and with his hand still on his head was crying for his hat.

'He's a child. How does he know?' he repeated softly, 'Look, he's crying.'

'Let him cry. It doesn't matter. You're not going to give him any more fezes to wear, are you? He'll shut up in a little while.'

And the jeep plunged on throwing up dust.

Far off in a small town, where a good many refugees had settled, the news spread like lightning, as if the impossible had happened, that Kaushalya and Manoharlal's son had returned. Hae! There was delay in God's house, but never darkness! He'd come back after a whole five years! He was very lucky. The women kept kissing his head and giving their blessings and joining their hands in thanksgiving to God. 'Fate draws a long line for some . . . Look, behen, the child she kept at her breast was killed, and the one who was lost and helpless, he survived and came back. Whosoever's in God's keeping . . .'

When he arrived here, the boy was just as lost as he had been the first day in Zainab and Shakur's house. He just kept staring at his mother from a distance; there was nothing of the old mother left in her. One child went missing, and the whole of her youth collapsed. In the boy's mind, very slowly the faint memories were reviving, disordered, upside down. He remembered his young sister in his mother's lap, then the buffalo that used to be tied outside their house and on whose back he used to climb. Then he remembered the wooden takht outside their door. Then the house filled with noise. And his mother's awareness gradually returned. She couldn't believe that the boy standing staring at her with his finger pressed in his mouth was her own Paali. Something was gathering within her, and her agitation was increasing.

Three or four days passed in this way.

It was Sunday. A dholak was being played in Manoharlal's courtyard, and women from the locality were sitting singing to its beat. Two small durries had been spread in the courtyard. There were two or three stools, one or two charpoys. By now Kaushalya had to a large extent collected herself and begun to laugh and talk a little. Her son too now came and sat beside her from time to time. Kaushalya had a red chunari wrapped about her, a gold-fringed red chunari, intimating the greatest good fortune.

Manoharlal was telling first one neighbour and then another, 'They looked after him with tremendous care. I'll never forget their kindness as long as I live.'

'Certainly, certainly, there is no shortage of good people in the world,' they nodded in agreement.

The courtyard was full of people, and to celebrate this auspicious occasion Manoharlal was about to distribute laddus from the tray he was holding when the boy—Paali

—did something very strange. At that moment he was sitting close to his mother in front of the woman playing the dholak. He was watching the dholak attentively when he suddenly quietly got up and, going into the room on the right, quickly picked up a mat, spread it out on a side of the courtyard, knelt on it and began to say his prayers.

Many of the men and women in the courtyard watched this with great curiosity. They were dumbfounded to see him saying namaaz.

'Hae! What is this, Kaushalya? What is your son doing?' one woman asked.

At this Manoharlal said to a man standing next to him, 'He says his prayers at this time every day. He knows himself that it's the time for prayer.'

He said this, but he felt ashamed that his son had started saying namaaz in front of so many people. Before he'd arranged this function, he'd forgotten that this would be the time his son would start to pray.

'Don't you stop him?' someone asked.

'He's a child. What does he know? Gradually he'll understand on his own.'

At this one gentleman, who was the chaudhuri of the locality, said loudly, 'If you put a stop to it now, he'll stop; otherwise he's going to stay a Muslim.'

As long as the boy kept praying, the people nearby kept on turning to look at him. Manoharlal kept on saying, as if defending his son, 'They had no child of their own. But they kept him with great affection for five years. I will never forget what I owe them in this life or the next.' This made the chaudhuri scream, 'They've turned him into a Muslim, and still you're defending them?'

The boy was kneeling with the palms of both his hands raised towards heaven repeating the words of worship which he had been taught by heart. Then the chaudhuri of the locality who had been standing next to Manoharlal strode up to the boy.

The child had just finished his namaaz and stroked his face with both hands when the chaudhuri grabbed him by the wrist and pulled him into the centre of the courtyard.

'What were you doing?'

The boy was frightened but said softly, 'I was saying namaaz.'

At this the chaudhuri said severely, 'You can't do that here. We'll not have any namaaz-vamaaz here.' Addressing the people standing around him he said, 'The louts have poured the poison of fundamentalism into his brain even at this age.'

Then, in the same loud voice, he called out to one of his companions, 'Call the pandit and the nai. Get the boy's head shaven now, and give him a topknot. To hell with them. They've sent him here a Muslim.'

The boy was panic stricken and tearful.

'What is your name?'

Looking up at the huge figure of the chaudhuri, he replied in a frightened voice, 'Altaf! Altaf Husain son of Shakur Ahmed!'

The chaudhuri felt like slapping him hard on the face. The boy felt the pressure of the chaudhuri's grasp on his wrist, but he was still trembling and looking at his face.

'No, your name is Paali—Yashpal.'

The boy was silent, and then softly said, 'Altaf!'

'If you say that name again, I'll tear your tongue out!'

He turned to the people watching. 'Have you seen what those bastards have done? This is what they call tabligh.'

At this point the pandit and the nai arrived. There was another man with a hearth for a fire ceremony on his head, and behind him another one with tin of ghee, a bag of sacred herbs and some kindling.

The boy was made to sit down on the same mat and the nai, stropping the razor on his palm, began to shave his head according to the instructions of the pandit and the laws of ritual. As long as he was being shaved, the sound of low sobbing came from beneath his bowed head. Once he stood up in panic and shouting 'Ammi! Abbaji!' ran to the wall of the courtyard and stood pressed against it. He looked at the chaudhuri with his huge eyes like a frightened deer looks at a hunter. This time Manoharlal went to fetch him at the behest of the chaudhuri and, holding him by the wrist and coaxing him, brought him back to the mat.

Soon, right at the top of his shaven head hung a topknot. Then Paali was bathed and dressed in a dhoti and kurta. According to religious law in the midst of mantras, he was invested with a sacred thread.

'Son, what is your name? Repeat five times Paali, Paali, Paali, Paali, Paali....'

A short while later the child Yashpal, dressed as a young brahmachari, was standing with joined hands by the door next to his father, bidding farewell to the friends and relations who'd come, and the friends and relations were stroking his head in blessing as they left. Manoharlal was distributing laddus.

At that moment hundreds of miles away, sitting in their deserted courtyard Zainab and Shakur were considering what had happened. Zainab was saying, 'He's taken all the light of the house with him. This was the time when I used to go and search the neighbourhood for him. Sometimes he'd have gone one place, sometimes another. What do you think? He will come at 'Id, won't he? They will send him here, won't they? Can't we go to see him? . . . You used to say, didn't you, that you had a relative in Bareilly. We could go to stay with him and visit our son. What do you think?' And she kept wiping the tears from her eyes.

GENESIS

The director of the radio station had just sat down on his chair when a commotion broke out on the veranda. Someone was shouting at the top of his voice. The director paid close attention to the nature of the commotion. He stood up and was about to go out when he paused and rang the bell to summon his stenographer. Then he turned his ears again to the voices outside. Light began to dawn.

The steno appeared.

'What is that noise about? Is the ten o'clock recording over?'

The steno smiled slightly. 'That is the noise of the ten o'clock recording.'

'It seems that the programme assistant has slipped up again. Who is that shouting?'

'Some Shivanand, sir!'

'Which Shivanand?'

'A writer. He writes short stories. He'd come to take part in the discussion too.'

'So why is he shouting?'

But the moment he asked the question, he already knew the answer. His face relaxed, he sat down, and he smiled. 'He couldn't have given out the cheques in sealed envelopes. I've told him several times, but you people. . .'

The commotion was now situated directly outside his

room. It sounded as if someone were about to push open the door and start a rumpus in his office.

Precisely this happened. The director was about to rise from his chair when the door opened and a gentleman entered, flushed with anger and holding up an open envelope. 'This is a total insult! They call you here just to insult you!'

The director stood up and said very patiently, 'Why, has there been some mistake?'

'You call four writers for a discussion and give them all different fees! If this is not a dishonest trick, what is?'

'Please put your point calmly. There are certain rules in All India Radio. I can explain them to you.'

'What will you explain? Look at this cheque! Forty rupees! You've given other people one hundred and me forty . . .'

'There must have been a reason, please sit down.'

But Shivanand was enraged and went on, 'In the whole discussion Devraj couldn't have spoken two sentences, and he gets a hundred rupees, and I blather on throughout and get forty!'

The director's guess had been correct. The programme assistant had slipped up. He was a new man and didn't know how to deal with writers.

'Please sit down. I will inquire into the matter,' requested the director, and he very humbly moved forward to draw the chair next to the desk back a little so that the respected author could sit down comfortably.

But Shivanand's temperature was still high. 'You people insult authors on purpose. If I had known that everybody would get different fees, I would never have come.'

At that point the writer's glance fell on the programme assistant, who had followed him into the director's office.

'Why didn't you tell me before the recording? You made me sign the contract. You didn't tell me then either! Whatever is in the contract, this is a matter of principle,' continued Shivanand and turned towards the director. 'I do not object to the fact that I am being paid forty rupees. I object to the fact that everybody is not paid the same fee.'

It was very unbecoming for there to be a row in the station director's office. The director was losing his temper with the programme assistant for allowing this man into his office. He felt like telling Shivanand to send in a written complaint and get out, but a radio station is a public relations department of the government. Restraining his ill will, he said, 'Please do sit down. I will inquire into the matter. Please take a seat!' And then to the programme assistant he said, 'Come with me!'

And they both left the room.

Shivanand was still agitated. After the director left, he addressed himself to the steno.

'What is there to inquire into? I have seen Devraj's cheque with my own eyes. It is a matter of principle. You people are discriminating between greater and lesser writers, causing divisions among them.'

'It looks like someone has made a mistake. The director sahib has gone himself. He'll just find out about it.'

'What will he find out? What is there to find out? What mistake has been made? Does this look like a mistake to you?'

The steno was listening in silence. He said gently, 'You're getting upset over a very little thing. It's not such a big thing.'

'To be insulted is a minor matter? And that, too, when it's done on purpose.'

The director was swift to return, looking very satisfied. He gestured to the steno to leave and sat down on his seat of office behind the desk.

'Forgive me. I have asked for the file. We will soon find out where the mistake is.' Putting both hands on the table, he clasped his fingers together and smiled softly.

To the writer, his smile seemed somewhat poisonous.

'You have ruined my whole day with this nonsense. There was no point in my coming here at all.'

The director gazed steadily at the writer and then said gently, 'I will explain everything to you. Please relax. And wherever the mistake has been made, I will try my very best to see that it is corrected.' Then he remarked a little informally, 'Would you like some tea, or shall I order some cold drinks?' Lifting his right hand slightly, he went on, 'I won't even take much of your time. I know that all writers work in the morning.'

The writer was sitting dejectedly with a long face.

'I know,' began the director, 'that if you weren't sitting with me now, you would be creating another story like "Genesis".'

The writer looked up. His eyes widened slightly.

The director pressed the bell for the chaprasi and said to him, 'Bring a half set of tea.' Then he addressed the writer. 'That was a very rare piece of creative writing, sahib, "Genesis".'

Shivanand was still sitting rather lost holding the cheque for forty rupees, uncertain whether to put it on the director's table, or in his pocket, or keep it in his hand.

'Well, this is at least an opportunity to spend a few moments in your company. Humdrum official work goes on here all the time.'

Shivanand looked up to find the director gazing at him with enormous reverence.

'I have had a great desire to meet you ever since I read "Genesis".' He paused before continuing, almost stammering with emotion, 'These days mountains of short stories are being written, but you see very few which leave a deep impression on your heart! When I read "Genesis" I wanted to write to you.'

The tea arrived. Two beautiful cups of tea, full to the brim, on a shining tray. Sugar separate.

'How much sugar do you take?'

'One please,' Shivanand replied distractedly.

'Do you write better in the morning or at night? Rakesh used to say that he could sink more fully into his work at night.'

'Everyone develops their own style,' replied Shivanand quietly and picked up his cup of tea.

'Are you writing a novel at the moment?'

'Yes, I am doing something.'

'This will be your first novel after *Free of Attachment*, won't it?'

Shivanand was pleasantly surprised by the director's knowledge.

'Yes, this is indeed my second novel.'

'How far have you got? Of course you shouldn't ask authors. Mostly they don't like to talk about these things.'

'No, there's no such difficulty.'

'Oh, but there is. Some authors imagine that if they talk about their work beforehand their creativity will be blasted by the wind,' said the director with a guffaw.

The writer nodded.

'Look at this happy coincidence. This very day I took out a copy of *Free of Attachment* from the bookcase, and this very day I have met you.'

'You seem fond of reading. Generally station directors have no interest in literature.'

'To start with they all have an interest, but you can say that there are some who retain it.'

Shivanand felt like asking the director how he liked *Free of Attachment*. But he realized that he hadn't yet read the book, he had just taken it out to read it. Still he did remark, 'If you had read it, I would have asked you what you thought of it.'

'How can I tell you, sahib? I read to save myself from dying. Government work is like a bog—you just get sucked down into it.'

'No, no, you seem a very cultured man to me.'

'Keep on writing, sahib, keep on writing. You are blessed with your pen. God has given you talent.' Carried away on a stream of emotion he said, 'Creation is itself a miracle, sahib! I am amazed by it. It can be a simple story taken from everyday life. But the imagination of the author metamorphoses it. Invents new life for it. Turns dirt into gold. This too is nothing less than magic. Do you compose poetry too?'

'I do, occasionally.'

'I was right. When I read "Genesis", I sensed a special kind of musicality. Please write poetry, lots of poetry. Poetry most definitely is born of sorrow.'

Shivanand had begun to experience the same sort of excitement as he had once felt during a rail journey when "Genesis" had just been published and he had found a young woman in his own carriage reading it. Then he had felt a thrill. His heart had filled with enthusiasm, and he kept looking at the girl's face to discover what her reaction to the story was. The girl had begun to doze as she read and had fallen asleep with her head leaning against the window, and the magazine had fallen from her hand on to the floor. But Shivanand was so inundated by his unexpected good fortune that, despite the fact that he had not been able to find a seat and had had to stand half the night in the packed carriage, all the while he was in a state of intoxication, all the while, all the way. He felt as if he had been rewarded for his entire life's work.

The director was saying, 'I don't know that much, but it seems to me as if your work will bring a new direction to the Hindi short story. When I read "Genesis", I felt as if I was hearing a new voice.'

A gentle smile began to play on Shivanand's lips. There was humility in it, and the perception of divine joy and a feeling of 'I've got it', of satisfaction, of the fullness of life.

Not letting the director see, he put the cheque in his pocket.

The director was saying, 'It's a matter of real regret that in our country writers still do not find true recognition.'

At this Shivanand remarked lightly, 'There was a time when you used to get only eight rupees as fees for a story. We used to be content with that.'

'Vah! And still you kept on writing!'

'Even if I'd earned nothing, I would still have kept on writing, sahib. If I didn't write, then what would I do?'

'It's true, the true devotees of Sarasvati never even put their foot into the courtyard of Lakshmi. Please write, sahib. Write a lot, lose yourself in your devotion to your art. You must of course know that Premchand had sold the manuscript of 'Prem Ashram' for seventy rupees. Only seventy rupees! Vah, there's nothing like an author, sahib! In this world, people in every business weigh their work on scales of money. It is only authors who live solely to write, vah!'

The chaprasi came in carrying a note, which he silently placed on the director's desk before standing to one side.

The director glanced at the chit and pushed it away.

'Tell him to take a seat.'

The chaprasi bowed in respect and went outside.

Shivanand felt that he was taking up an unnecessary amount of the time of a busy officer.

'Do get on with your work, sahib. I have taken a lot of your time.'

'No, no, it's my good fortune to have had the opportunity to sit with you for some moments.'

'Please look into that matter when you're free. It's not such a big thing. What's a few rupees here and there? I was in any case a little agitated . . . ' and he stood up.

The director made to rise from his chair, 'I must have a long talk with you some time. When we are free, we'll sit and enjoy ourselves.' He rose to his feet and, walking to the door, said, 'I've asked for the file. I'll inquire into the matter today.'

'Please don't worry. It's not that important.'

'Not for you, but it is for me. I need your cooperation,' said the director, opening the door.

'Please, please, do sit down, don't come out. I've taken such a lot of your time.'

With this Shivanand folded his hands in a namaste, bowed his head and almost floated out.

Sitting down at his desk, the director rang his bell and summoned the programme assistant.

'Don't make that mistake in future. Always hand out cheques in sealed envelopes so that no one finds out what the others get.'

'I got him to sign the contract at the time, sir! At first his name wasn't down for the discussion. Dayanath's was. When he didn't turn up, I called Shivanand.'

A light smile ran over the director's lips. 'You were very timely in telling me the names of his works. What was the name of his short story—"Genetics"?'

'No, "Genesis".'

'And the novel?'

'*Free of Attachment.*'

'If you find copies of them anywhere, bring them here. I'll see how he writes. And look here . . .'

'Sir!'

'Keep that villain at a distance for a while. He can still pick a fight any time. And never get in a tangle with a writer!'

The programme assistant was going to say something in his defence, but the director turned his attention busily to the papers on his desk.

TOYS

'Yaar, I agree to helping my wife, but this isn't helping. I can't call this helping. What you can call helping isn't acceptable to my wife.'

At that moment he was in the kitchen peeling onions, and his wife was standing beside him stirring the dal.

'To help means to share the work in the kitchen. She does some, I do some, and we both get on quietly with our own work.'

'What does Bhabhi say?' I asked.

'She wants to issue the orders in the kitchen and me to carry them out. If she says peel potatoes, then I should start peeling them. If she says pick up the tongs, then I should run to pick them up. This I don't accept.'

At this his wife wiped her hands on a cloth and laughed. 'I have to do all the work, ji, whether I share it out or not. This man is absent-minded, he does less than he messes up. If he does do what you tell him, then it's something really exceptional.'

'Well, listen to that. Is that the reward I get for helping?'

At this she laughingly began to placate her husband.

'Are you angry? His face swells up at the slightest little thing.' Then she said coaxingly, 'No, ji, he does help me a lot. If he wasn't here, I wouldn't be able to do anything.'

'This is what I can't accept,' said Dilip. 'Do all the work and then have her say that I only help her.'

'Women run the house. However much work you do, in the end it will only be help,' I teased and, putting my hand on Dilip's shoulder, went on, 'This will always be your position, mister. Peeling onions isn't cooking, and you will always be peeling onions.'

There had been no electricity in the house for about half an hour, and they were both cooking by the flickering light of a candle. My wife and I were standing outside the door laughing and chatting with them.

'You go, ji, go and sit outside, and sit them down too,' said Dilip's wife taking the knife from his hand. 'I'll look after everything. There's only a little bit left to do.'

'We are also always competing to see who gets the credit for work and who doesn't. Now if I stop peeling the onions, she will take all the credit for this meal herself. She'll say she cooked all the food.'

'It's the same with us,' I added. 'Women want to retain their authority in the kitchen. Even if the husband does all the work, they'll say he helped them just a little.'

At this my wife, who was standing next to me, at once spoke up, 'What do you do? You spend all your time at home reading the newspaper. Here Bhai Sahib *does* help.'

'Say it again, say it again, Bhabhiji,' Dilip said with glee, 'I have also started making chapattis. If you like, I'll make them for you this evening.'

'Don't boast too much, ji,' said his wife. 'If you just knead the dough, that will be a lot. He makes chapattis that are just like wood. Burnt on both sides.'

It seemed to me that Dilip's wife was really getting annoyed. Within their laughter they had both begun to flare a little. I was afraid that they might start fighting in front of us. After all, how long does it take for a husband and wife to start arguing? On top of that it was a hot summer night, and there had been no electricity for a while. Veena, standing in front of the stove, was in bad shape. The landlord had extended a brick wall to half its height to make a kitchenette in one corner of the open terrace and covered it with a tin roof. Roast in the day and roast at night.

'Come on, let's sit outside,' I said, seeing the deteriorating situation and taking Dilip outside.

'You both sit outside, and I'll help Veena,' said my wife slipping into the kitchen.

It was a great relief to come out on to the open terrace. A slight breeze was blowing beneath the stars. Though to call this a terrace was an insult to terraces.

We sat on beds on the far side of the terrace facing the oppressive, high wall to which the kitchen from which we had just emerged was attached. Here too, behind us, was the wall of the adjoining house, which was four and a half storeys high. So Dilip's terrace was between two high walls. But still there was certainly some sense of openness.

'It's really pleasant here,' I said. 'At least there's a breeze, and the stars are shining above.'

Dilip laughed at this. 'At the moment there's no electricity, so that's why it feels good to you. Just see what happens when the electricity comes.'

'Then what will happen?'

'Then this will happen: the streetlights in front will come on, and higher up on the other side of the street is a cinema hall. Its dazzling lights will shine in your eyes and will continue to shine in your eyes the whole night. And if you lie with your face towards this wall, you feel scared. Veena tosses and turns all night.' Dilip mopped his sweat and said, 'Forgive me, yaar. You arrived, and here we hadn't even prepared dinner.' Then to defend himself he said, 'There's not just one problem with living in Delhi. Once you miss one thing, the rest of the day gets spoilt. Has a guest ever arrived when we're still only peeling the onions?'

'We are not guests. Why worry? Just make sure we catch the 10.30 bus, we don't want any more than that. If we miss that bus, then we will be in trouble. But there's still a lot of time. There's no need to be bothered.'

'If I hadn't made one small mistake, all the work would have been done in good time. But what can I say, I got caught.'

'What happened?'

'Today when I left the office it was all of 4.30. This is my routine every day. I leave the office at 4.30, and I get a bus at 4.40. It goes from just there, near the office. If I get late for the bus, then everything gets upset, and I arrive home out of breath. Today that happened again. I stepped out of the office door and met Tilakraj. He was walking right past the office, and I couldn't stop myself—I called out to him. Now, I can't find a friend in front of me and turn my face away. In the first place, here you get no time to visit people at their homes. Someone had told me that Tilakraj had been unwell. I thought that at one and the same time I could ask after his health and put an end to any complaint of not meeting him. But the moment I called out, I sensed that I'd made a mistake. This was not a day for meeting people. We had guests coming, and I should have gone home as soon I could. But it was too late. When you leave your office, there should be no friend in front of you. You should go straight to the bus stop with your eyes shut. You shouldn't look right or left. But, knowing all this, I still went and called out to him.

'In a confused way I imagined I would shake hands with Tilakraj, make my apologies and then go on ahead. But the moment the fellow met me, he hugged me to his chest and started sobbing. It was as if he were full to the brim with emotion. The moment he hugged me, my heart filled too. I thought, to hell with the bus. If I miss it, I'll take a scooter. I haven't met Tilakraj for years. Can I leave him for a bus? It was as if Tilakraj needed something.

'Then he told me that his wife had died. I had never heard. Now what could I say? I was staring at him, and he was standing in front of me weeping, and there was the bus about to leave. Years pass here without meeting people, and when you meet them, life has taken yet another turn. The last time I'd met Tilakraj his second daughter had just been born; today it was already four months since his wife died. To tell the truth I'm nervous of meeting anyone I know now. I want to slip shyly away. I feel that if I do meet anyone, yet another burden of duty will land on my head to bother me. Even as I was standing in front of him a thought struck me: There was still time, I could get away, catch the bus . . .'

'But what was all the trouble for, yaar?' I said. 'We're like members of your own family. If you were late, what did it matter?'

'Where was I thinking about you, yaar? I was thinking about Pappu. After he comes back from school, he wanders around the road. It takes Veena until six o'clock to reach home.'

'Then?'

'Then what? It just escaped my mouth. I said, "I'll come and see you soon Tilakraj, I really had no idea." "You're going?" he asked, as if he were about to faint. He had never expected me to display such disinterest in his grief. So I was helpless and stood beside him while the bus left right in front of me.'

'You worry for nothing. People get late now and again. Where is Pappu?'

Partly because the electricity had been down and partly because I had been listening to Dilip, I'd forgotten about Pappu. We had bought a toy for the child and wanted to give it to him, but not seeing him in the house, we'd also forgotten the toy.

'He's at a neighbour's. If we get late, he goes there. Once the food is ready, I'll go and fetch him.'

The sound of hot oil and spices being poured over the dal came from the kitchen. At the same time Dilip's wife Veena said from the doorway, 'I am thinking, ji, if you can, bring rotis from the tandoor. It's getting very late. If we make chapattis at home, it will get even later.'

In a little while both women came out of the kitchen chatting with one another. Veena was saying, 'Today I have prepared the spices for the dal separately; otherwise I don't do it at all. Who is going to go to all that trouble? When I put the dal on the stove, I put chopped onions in at the same time, and ginger, tomato, whatever is to be put, I put it in all together at the same time. Nowadays who is going to sit down and fry spices separately? Who has the time?'

Women can chatter. Men spend all their time fretting and complaining. They will talk about politics, insult politicians, in their eyes the world is falling into a chasm. Women can pick particles of happiness from even the smallest things. If they stop talking about cooking, then they will take up the subject of children. If they stop talking about children, then they will start discussing saris. And then criticism and praise and stories and gossip—women know how to stay happy.

When she came outside, Veena looked at her husband and said, 'Oh no, ji, you have forgotten all about Pappu. Aren't you going to fetch him?'

'How could I forget him? I thought when you'd finished the cooking, I'd go and get him.'

'If it gets late, won't he go to sleep?' said Veena in agitation. 'He's sitting there without having had anything to eat all day. In any case, who leaves their child with neighbours every day?'

'He just sits in their house and watches television. What else does he do? He'll be sitting there quietly. You have tutored him so that even if anyone offers him food a hundred thousand times, he won't eat. He doesn't even take water.'

Dilip stood up. 'Come, give me the bowl, I'll bring the rotis and Pappu.'

When Dilip went towards the stairs, Veena said, 'If he's asleep don't wake him. It's very late now. I will give him a little milk to drink as he sleeps. There's a small bowlful of milk in the house.'

As Dilip descended the stairs, Veena began to tell us, 'Once we were late coming home like this before. Where the school bus drops Pappu, just near there is a shop, Paris House. I have told Pappu that if his Papa gets late, he should sit on the raised platform at the front of the shop. He shouldn't dare to move an inch one way or the other. That day we arrived four hours late. The shadows had lengthened, and lights had been switched on. He was worrying where on earth Pappu could be. But I said to him, "Ji, I know my child, he won't go anywhere." Pappu really was standing right there. Just like a statue, hungry and thirsty, he was standing in front of the shop. In fact the shopkeeper told us, "Ji, your son is a real yogi. I gave him a cold drink, and he didn't even touch it. The whole afternoon children were playing in front of him. He stood watching them from the platform. He didn't even go near them."'

'If he is hungry and thirsty, then what does he do?' I asked.

'I give him everything to take with him in the morning. Three sandwiches and one banana. I give him a separate bottle of water. He has two sandwiches at school; he leaves the banana and one sandwich. He eats them when he comes back from school. I have taught him never to take anything from outside and never to go with anyone.'

'He really is a yogi.'

'That much you have to teach them. There is no alternative to it. Your daughter is still small. When she starts going to school, then you will have to do all this. It's even more difficult to take care of girls.'

'What class does Pappu study in?'

'He's hardly studying. He's only in class one.'

'He's very mature,' I said. 'My brother's son is a calamity, a total calamity. He doesn't listen to his mother or his father.'

After a short while Dilip came up the stairs on to the terrace carrying Pappu against his shoulder. In his other hand was the bowl of rotis. Pappu was fast asleep. Seeing him, Dilip's wife stepped forward and held out her arms to take him.

'Shhhhh!' Dilip whispered, 'He's gone to sleep.'

'I was afraid of this,' Veena remarked in irritation.

'He's just dropped off,' said Dilip softly as he held the child. 'Vermaji was saying that he sat with his eyes glued to the television. The family got up for dinner, but he sat just where he was watching the TV.'

'I'd like to know if neighbours ever tell anything straight,' lamented Dilip's wife. 'I don't want him to go there, but what can I do? If he goes there one day, they are certain to tell me the next, "We weren't watching TV, but your son was".' Then turning to my wife, she said, 'The old widow is so vain she's still having jewellery made for herself, but her heart is as small as a bird's.'

My wife signalled to me to take the toy out of the bag. I hesitated. It wouldn't have been right to have given the toy now. As we were going home we would quietly put the toy by the head of the child's bed. Then the mother and father would know that we had brought the toy and the child would see it when he woke in the morning.

But suddenly the boy woke up. It was Dilip's wife's fault. Dilip was laying him down on his bed, and his wife couldn't resist stroking his hair. As soon as she put her hand on his head, the child recognized her touch and opened his eyes.

'See? You woke him up,' Dilip whispered. 'If you want to make a fuss over him, do it on holidays. On other days, let him lie in peace.' Then patting Pappu he said, 'Go to sleep, Pappu, go to sleep. It's late and you have to go to school tomorrow.' And Dilip gestured to his wife to retreat into the deeper darkness.

But at that moment the electricity returned, and the light above the staircase came on, and outside the street lights burst into illumination, spreading light across the entire terrace. Partly because of the light and partly due to his mother's touch, the child opened his eyes again.

'Pappu!' Dilip said firmly, 'Shut your eyes.'

'Now he's woken up. Let him stay awake, ji. He can at least eat a couple of mouthfuls of roti.'

'Shhhh!' said Dilip again, putting his finger to his lips, and turning the child over and patting his shoulder.

Pappu had woken up, but out of fear of his father, he was lying with his eyes shut. Partly out of curiosity to meet us and partly because of the desire to be with his parents, he began screwing up his eyes as he lay on his cot. After a while he asked, 'Papa, can I open my eyes?'

'Oh the poor little thing,' my wife blurted out.

'Shhhhh!' hissed Dilip once more. But the child was truly awake. Now there was no point in patting him. Dilip was annoyed.

'Now you put him to sleep. I can't do it.'

'He's not had anything to eat all day, ji. Now that he's woken up, he can have something to eat.'

'You're spoiling him.'

'No, no, how is he spoilt? He's a very sweet child.'

At this goodness knows what occurred to my wife. She said in front of everyone, 'Give it to him, ji, that toy, the one we brought for Pappu.'

At the word toy Pappu's eyes opened wider.

'Now you've ruined everything,' remarked Dilip in irritation. 'Now he won't sleep until eleven.'

'It doesn't matter. Nothing will happen if he doesn't go to sleep on time one day.'

'You don't know his sleep, yaar. His eyes just don't open in the morning. If his mother starts trying to wake him at six, then he finally wakes at seven. He only gets up if we sprinkle water on his face.'

'It's all right, it's all right,' I said, taking the toy out of the bag. What was the toy but a motor car attached to a long wire. If you kept the other end of the wire in your hand and pressed the button, the motor car stopped, and if you pressed it again, it started to move.

Seeing the motor car, Pappu's eyes opened wide.

Veena took the car from me and said, 'Take it, beta, see what Uncle has brought for you. Just touch it once and then give it to me. The toy is yours, I will put it by the head of your bed. Take it in the morning when you get up.'

Pappu's eyes were on the toy, but out of fear of his father, he didn't put out his hands to take it.

Veena gave it to him.

Pappu sat up. Taking the toy in his hands, he looked at us again and again and then hugged the car to his chest. His eyes were still full of drowsiness.

'No Pappu, I have told you once. You can only touch it once, not more than that.'

But Pappu clung to it more tightly than before.

'Give it to me, beta, now give the toy back to me. Good boy, Pappu is a very good boy,' Dilip said in a soft but very firm voice.

'Can I keep it by my bedside, Ma?' asked Pappu rather weakly.

'No, Pappu,' Dilip scolded him. 'I will give it to you tomorrow myself. Now you lie down.'

Into Pappu's eyes, which a moment earlier had been fixed lovingly on the car, came a remoteness, as if the shape of the toy had begun to appear indistinct. Something like a sob convulsed his whole body, and he removed his hands from the toy.

We moved away from his bed. Veena brought a small bowl of milk and held it to his mouth. Dilip turned out the light. The light from the street was quite sufficient for us to sit and have dinner.

'Wouldn't it have been better to put the toy by Pappu's bedside?' my wife asked gently. 'Pappu would have contentedly gone off to sleep touching it.'

'No, behenji,' Veena replied. 'He wouldn't have been able to sleep because of it. Pappu starts talking to toys, and then he can't sleep for hours. All his sleep disappears.'

The little child looked very innocent and meek lying on his cot in a white kurta and pajama. His little body took up hardly one third of the bed.

'You really have taught him well.'

'If we didn't, how could we manage?' said Veena and several stories about Pappu came to her mind. 'To start with, he used to be really mischievous, how can I tell you? He didn't let you sit in peace. Wherever you went, he hung on to you to take him with you. At every single thing he would start being stubborn. If we had been soft with him, then he really would have been spoilt.' As she said this she remembered a story. 'You don't know, behenji, how naughty he was. In our old flat, where we lived before, there was a tiny room. That is when he was very small. We would put him in his cot and tie a string across it so that he couldn't get out. And this little thing would untie the knots and get out. Once Dilip must have tied no less than fifteen knots, and he undid all fifteen of them and climbed out. That's how he was. But now he doesn't bother us.'

Then Dilip said softly, explaining to his wife, 'Don't praise Pappu in front of him. I've told you before. It makes him stubborn.' Then, looking at me, he said, 'Now he'll make an uproar in the morning again. Now my princeling will wake up at 7.30.'

'Don't worry about it, ji. If he doesn't get up then I'll wake him by telling him about the toy. That will get him up early,' Veena comforted her husband.

It was about 9.30 when we sat down to eat. We ate hurriedly, then rose and set out for home in haste. Our eyes on our watches, we forgot all formalities and rushed towards the stairs. Dilip came with us up to the bus stop. When we were sitting in the bus, my wife asked me, 'Did they say anything to you? What were they saying? Why did they invite us for dinner?'

'We didn't talk much. There was no time. But still as we were coming here, Dilip put one thing to me.'

'What did he say?'

'He said that Veena wants to do a B.Ed. course. If I spoke to my uncle and got her admission, she'd be able to get a B.Ed. in one year.'

My wife paused, then said gently, 'Why did they call us to dinner for such a small thing? They could have written to you or phoned you in the office.' Then looking at me she asked, 'What did you say?'

'I said that I'd try.' My wife was again silent.

'Dilip himself wants to put his name down for a banking course. It has evening classes. He will go after work. For that too he was saying that I should speak to Uncle on his behalf and have it arranged so that he gets admission.'

'If both of them go to the office and do courses as well, what will happen to Pappu?'

'I asked Dilip that. He said "Pappu's not an infant any more. He's grown up, and slowly he'll become more grown up. Now we can't ignore our careers for Pappu's sake. These are the years when you can really improve your prospects."'

The bus thundered along in the darkness.

THE WITCH

My mother is very sharp-sighted, ji. She can look at a man strolling up the street and guess his intentions, who he is, why he's there. Her eyes can bore through ten layers to uncover a secret.

We have a shop in Kalkaji, selling lentils and flour. Early in the morning after saying his prayers, my father sits there. After she's returned from the temple and washed the pots and pans, my mother follows him, spreads out a piece of jute matting and sits down behind him. She sits there for hours. She keeps an eye on every customer and every passer-by.

My bapu is a very simple man. He keeps watching the street in front of him, but if you ask, 'Bapu, what are you looking at?' he just shakes his head and says, 'Nothing at all. What is there to see?'

At this Ma tosses her head and says, 'If a cobra raised its hood in front of him, he wouldn't see it.' With a frown, she continues, 'What use is such a simpleton? He's an absolute cow. Anyone can put a halter pin through his nose and lead him wherever he chooses.'

Bapu just listens. Sometimes, when my mother's remarks are very harsh, he smiles and says, 'All right, a cow of a man may not be of much use, but this cow of a man used to just have a hawker's box, and now he has a shop and behind the shop, he's built a brick house. You, good woman, think before you speak.'

My mother can't resist passing comments. 'He built a brick house because I sat on his back all the time. If I'd left it to him, he'd still be a hawker today.'

We actually enjoy our parents' squabbling, ji, but when there's some problem at home, then it's disturbing.

We are three brothers, ji. My elder brother has a small government job, and I drive a taxi in the Shimla hills. From Kalka to Shimla, Kulu, Manali, Dharamsala—I go everywhere. Thanks to your kindness, my work is going well. This is the third time I've taken a loan and bought a car. The bank people give loans you have to return in three years. I pay them back in just two and apply for a new one.

There is one principle in taxi driving, ji: punctuality. If you tell a passenger the car will be there at eight in the morning, then the car should be outside their house on the dot of eight. If you say the journey to Manali takes seven hours, then it shouldn't take one minute more. You should fill up with petrol the night before. Everything should be done with proper preparation.

My elder brother is also a very straightforward soul. Rather like my bapu. He also keeps quiet, not a word out of him. But it's not his fault, ji. He's in the power of a witch. Whatever she wants, he does.

Yes, a witch. My sister-in-law, my brother's wife, is a witch. She really is, ji. You can't tell it to look at her. I didn't even realize it when she married and came to our house. But Ma found out even before the wedding. She really is a witch—a wide-bodied, sallow-coloured woman. Big broad hands, big broad feet. Ma would say, 'Look at the witch's eyes. Even in the dark, they glint blue.' She came from Ajmer, ji. It was when she was sitting in Ajmer itself that she bound us. Ma used to say that if your father had listened to me, the witch wouldn't have been able to cast her net. But Ma began to cut through her net only after we were all caught in it.

The root of the whole mischief was Kubara the shopkeeper. We didn't know him from Adam. One day early in the morning he was loitering in front of our shop. Ma had just arrived when her eyes fell on him, and she stopped in her tracks. It struck her that he was a bad omen; just his being there was a bad omen.

'Who is that, ji? Where's he from? Why is he standing here?' she asked nervously.

At that moment, old Kubara approached and very humbly addressed my father. 'Lala, I have a barrow on the back street nearby. I sell slippers, Rajasthani slippers. But now the police won't let me stand there. If you agree, can I put my barrow on the pavement in front of your shop?'

Sitting behind Bapu, Ma also heard this. She whispered, 'Tell him, ji, not here. Take your barrow somewhere else.'

But my father is a very soft touch. He never grasps all that you tell him. He just listens and nods, and then he suddenly makes a decision without any consideration.

My mother was just about to say something more when Bapu spoke.

'The barrow is yours, and the pavement the government's. Why are you asking me? But just stand it a little away so that my business doesn't suffer.' My father had pronounced on the matter, and my mother bit her tongue and kept shaking her head.

Even today when Ma remembers that morning, she shakes her head from side to side in the same way, bites her tongue, rubs her hands together and says, 'A lost moment never returns. But that was the moment our luck changed for the worse.'

On that day, though, she could only say, 'What are you doing, ji? You have no idea who he is. Who is he to us that you've invited him to sit here in front of you?'

Ma says that day had started badly. Coming back from the temple in the morning she had stumbled on some sorcery. Someone had cast a spell right at the crossroads. There was a square of four bricks, a flickering clay oil lamp inside it, a rag doll with its hair pulled out and blotches of red on its limbs, and scattered about the broken clay saucers you put on top of chilams. My mother does everything very carefully, but on that day she didn't take care, and her foot knocked against the brick on which the rag doll lay. She was taken aback and tried to move away, but at that moment she shivered as the shadow of the spell fell on her, and her foot touched the head of the hairless doll.

Ma bathed again as soon as she got home. To remove the shadow of the bad omen, she dropped burning embers into a metal dish, and sprinkled harmal and chilli powder on them, and holding up the dish, she went to every corner of the house until everyone was coughing and sneezing from the smoke of burning chilli and harmal. Ma said that after fumigating the house with harmal she was sure she had warded off the evil, and she came and sat very contentedly in the shop behind Bapu. But the shadow had not passed. That very day that Kubara arrived.

Then Ma became certain that some affliction was coming on our house, that it had found a way of gaining entrance. Whenever Ma looked at Kubara, she recalled the black-magic doll made of rags.

Sometimes my mother gets annoyed with us and says, 'Fat has grown over your father's eyes, but even though you have eyes, you don't see.' She's right. If there's going to be a storm, she feels it coming. There is a tall tree in front of our house. Crows have nested in it and parakeets too. During the day striped squirrels climb up and down its trunk, and doves come and perch on its branches. Beneath a cat keeps watch for the moment when it can pounce on a bird. And often at night sitting in the kitchen, Ma suddenly says, 'The cat has caught a dove.' And the next day under the tree we actually find the scattered feathers and spots of blood.

That day when Bapu told Kubara to park his barrow in front of our shop, Ma fretted and fumed all day. But Bapu, as always, nodded his head without a care, 'Good woman, what have I done wrong? He's an elderly man. He'll manage to earn two meals a day, and he'll bless you for it. How will that harm you?'

But it hurt her eyes just to look at Kubara, at the ugliness of his old age, his dry, flyaway hair, and salt-and-pepper beard. No one knew his background or where he was heading. Why had he just landed up there?

Well, ji, the next day Kubara stood his barrow outside our shop. He sold different types of Rajasthani slippers. They don't wear well, but they're bright and attractive, especially the women's slippers. Some are embroidered with small gold stars, some with flowers in gold thread. Customers began to flock to him, his business took off, and he began to earn good money. Not only that, he became a friend of my father's. When there were no customers, they chatted and laughed with one another. Ma sat behind Bapu frowning. 'That wretched Kubara, wretched Kubara,' she kept repeating, but my father's nature was such that he never could see into another's heart.

Even before the year was out Kubara brought that witch into our house. He played the most important role in arranging my elder brother's marriage to her.

The truth is, ji, that Kubara brought us the engagement proposal. When our mother gets upset, her face flushes, and she screws up her eyes and claps her hands together. Ma was beside herself when Bapu repeated, 'I haven't promised anything. He said, "Come with me to Ajmer

Sharif, I'll introduce you to her family, and you can see them for yourself." That's all.'

'And you agreed!' replied Ma writhing in anguish.

'I said, "All right, we'll see her".' Then Bapu looked at me and said, 'If she's not acceptable, then we won't have the engagement. We'll refuse. It's not as if anyone can force us.'

At this, I looked at my mother. Her face, which had been red a little earlier, had now turned yellowish, and she was staring at Bapu slowly shaking her head. Then she said decisively, 'I am not going to let you go. Leave alone Ajmer. I wouldn't let him take you to the houses next door.'

Bapu's patience was still intact. Just as before, he said very evenly, 'I agreed to go to Ajmer Sharif with him. What is the harm in meeting them? I *am* arranging my son's marriage. I will be seeing girls for him after all.'

'I'm not letting you go anywhere,' Ma repeated, but her voice was trembling. On occasions when Ma can't defeat Bapu, first she loses her temper, and then she becomes plaintive.

Bapu decided to go to Ajmer the following Saturday. At the time Ma kept quiet, but when Saturday came and Kubara stood waiting with his bundle of luggage in front of our shop, Ma stepped outside. 'I'm coming too,' she said.

Kubara was somewhat taken aback, but he nodded his head in agreement. After all, what could he say? He couldn't tell her not to come. It's women who arrange engagements; it's women who examine future brides. How could he refuse?

I remember that day, ji, when the three of them—our father, Kubara the shoe seller and our mother—crossed the street in the direction of the bus station. My elder brother was standing next to me. The three of them were going to look at a bride for him. Just then—and it's a strange thing—it seemed as though the whole street was deserted and a dust was blowing in all directions. I am very fond of my brother. I felt that when he was engaged he would be separated from me. I don't know why I felt that when I believed that my mother's decision would be final. My father was a soft man; he would do what Ma told him. But when I saw them going far away down that deserted street, I felt very odd, ji.

Before she left, Ma had sprinkled oil on the threshold, poured oil into a bowl and dropped a silver rupee into it, and then put her hands together and prayed for a long time for God's favour. She even wrapped the end of her dupatta around her neck, as she does only when she is deeply disturbed.

The three of them disappeared from sight. I asked my elder brother, 'Bhaiya, how do you feel? Will you get married in Ajmer or somewhere else?'

At this he smiled, 'Wherever Ma says.'

There was no line on his face or any confusion or shadow of concern. In fact he looked very happy.

Three days later we were standing on the veranda of our house when we saw my father and mother approaching from the direction of the bus station. Kubara was not with them. Bapu came first, his head bowed, his eyes fixed on the ground, as if he had been humiliated in Ajmer. And Ma was drenched in sweat, with one bundle on her head and one in her hand.

'What happened, Ma?' I asked as soon as they came close.

'Wait, I'll tell you. Let me get my breath.'

Both were drained. On the street and sitting on his cot, my father kept his head lowered and his eyes on the ground. Even this angered her.

'Now he won't say anything, but there he roared at me like a tiger,' she said, and then, as was her nature, she rubbed both hands together. 'Your brother is engaged to be married.'

'Why are you talking like that, Ma? This is very good news.'

But Ma was silent and wiped away her sweat. Meanwhile Bapu rose, went indoors, washed, came out and went to his seat in the shop.

'There, in those people's place, they had just started discussing the proposal, when I whispered to him to tell them that we'd consider it and reply when we'd spoken to our family members. And he agreed to say that. He even said that they looked poorly off. They lived in a mud house.'

'Then how did the engagement happen?'

'At that point that witch came with glasses of sherbat. I told her, "Today is my fast. I will only have a glass of water." But your father went and took the sherbat, and at that very moment my heart stopped. It took only as long as one gulp of sherbat for your father to change his mind.'

Ma was rubbing her hands and shaking her head. 'The moment I sat down in that house, I began to feel uneasy. The kitchen was just behind where we were sitting. I could see that witch in the gloom of the kitchen. She was hanging around by the window. As soon as I laid eyes on her, I knew this was the girl whose proposal had come, and I started to shake inside.' Ma was becoming increasingly upset.

'First your father agreed that we would not confirm anything there, but one gulp of sherbat changed his mind. First he sat there lost and quiet. Then he started laughing and talking with them. And when that witch came to take the empty glasses away, your father put his hand on her head and said, "Now she will be the Lakshmi of our home." The second I heard it, my heart trembled. The witch was standing in front of us, her face half veiled by the end of her sari. In her sallow face I saw her pointed white teeth. She had put something in the sherbat.'

Listening to the driver's story I didn't notice when we reached the Shivalik hills. The air became cool. On one side of the road was mountain, and on the other a steep drop. But the driver was driving very determinedly and telling his story.

Suddenly he stopped the car. There was a waterfall on the right by the side of the road.

'I'll cool off the engine at bit here, ji,' he chuckled. 'After all, it is a car, ji,' and he got out and opened the bonnet. 'When the engine says, look after me, then I do.' And he looked at the car with great affection. Then he took out an empty can and fetched some water.

'I can feel the pulse of my car, ji, just like a doctor. Just a small noise will tell me where the fault is and what it is.' Having disposed of the water, he rolled up his sleeves and said, 'You wash your hands and face too, ji. This water is coming straight from the locks of Shiva. It's very pure.'

I was not surprised at this devotion. Even on the way as he was telling his story, whenever we passed a roadside temple, he would keep his forearms on the steering wheel but bow his head and join his hands in respect.

When we set off, he talked for a while of his plans. 'By your blessings, if I ever get a bank loan, I'll set up a factory. I know everything there is to know about engines. If I ever get the chance, I'll go to Japan, see new kinds of engines . . . nothing is difficult, ji. Take an entire engine apart, and I'll put every bit of it back together again. All you have to do is love your car and understand it.'

When the car had begun to take the tight bends on the mountain road, I reminded him of his story. 'Your mother thought that girl was a witch. It was just that she didn't like her, wasn't it?'

At this he instantly replied, 'She was a witch, ji. I couldn't see it, but Ma realized it the first day.'

I watched his face carefully for some time as he drove the car with great dexterity.

'Then what happened?' I asked.

'The witch came to our house.'

'If your mother knew she was a witch, why did she let the marriage take place?'

'Bapu had put his hand on her head! What could she do? How could she go against him in public? But at home she lamented.'

'How old was she?'

'Who? The witch? How do you ask the age of a witch, ji? No one can tell their age. But through her spells she came to our house. She looked young. She was broadly built. Ma said we had been caught in her net. Who would have known that she could take Bapu into her power with a mouthful of sherbat.'

She came to our home, ji, and she took my brother into her power just as she had done my father. You could see him become a puppet in her hands. If she said it was day, it was day. If she said it was night, it was night. He spent all his time on his cot, staring at her, until he didn't even remember to go to work.

Bapu built another room at the back of the shop, and she spent her time there.

One day, very early, even before the crack of dawn, Ma woke me up. My mother gets up at first light, sits cross-legged on her bed, covers her head and face and prays. That morning she came over to me and whispered, 'Get up, get up, go and see what she is doing in the storeroom.'

I sat up. 'It's still dark, Ma. How do you know she's in the storeroom?'

'Get up, get up, go and see and tell me if I'm lying.'

Bhai sahib, to set my mother's mind at rest, I got up and softly opened the door to peep into the storeroom.

The witch really was standing in front of the cupboard where we kept our cooking pots. In the darkness she seemed shadowy. Watching her gave me the creeps. She was hovering in front of the cupboard like a ghost. Ma used to say that witches are fond of cooking pots. Through them they put spells on the family. At that point the witch looked to me like a shadow and not a creature of flesh and blood. Who knows if it's true that at night witches wander like shadows but at first light they change to bodies of flesh and blood?

Then I had to go away for some days. That's what a taxi driver's life is like, ji. I had to take customers to Shimla. I take customers to Shimla every day, sometimes twice a day. It only takes two and a half hours. I would have gone in the morning and come back in the afternoon, but that day when I reached Shimla, I found customers for Manali. When I got to Manali there was a group waiting to go to Dharamsala. What is a driver's life, ji? You go where your customers want.

When I came back after a full two weeks, it was as if the house was in mourning. Bapu's health had begun to fail, his face was yellowish, and Ma took me aside and told me that sometimes as he was sitting in the shop, his head would loll to one side.

'The witch has started her work,' she whispered to me. 'Now she's made her way into the house, she'll eat each of us one by one.'

'But, Ma, why should she eat Bapu? He put his hand on her head.'

'Only when she sends your father to the next world, will her path be clear.' Then she sobbed and said, 'I warned you, but no one listened.' And her face began to flush and her eyes to screw up.

While I was away my brother had called vaids and doctors. Bapu was being treated. If you asked Bapu what was wrong, he had one answer: 'Nothing has happened to me. I'm perfectly all right.'

I was even more astonished to hear him. As if someone had put it into his head that he was well.

My father's health was really failing fast. One day around noon he collapsed in the shop. His eyes turned upwards, and a rattling noise came from his throat. I ran and fetched the doctor. Bapu did regain consciousness, but from that moment, it was as if he was fixed to his bed.

Three days afterwards Ma stood up and said in anguish, 'My husband will not be saved. He's possessed by a witch. She will devour him. My fate is blighted! I brought that witch into this house!' She created an uproar in the house.

All day she was disturbed. As she sat at the foot of Bapu's bed, her face would suddenly flush. She would get up and sit on the floor, rub her heels on the ground, shake her head from side to side, and cry for mercy for her bad deeds. We couldn't control her. After raging like this, she stood up and went to the head of Bapu's bed.

'I will not let you go like this, ji. I will pull you out of the witch's clutches. I will not let you die.'

The next day when I got up, Ma was not at home. God knows where she'd gone. The sun had risen by the time she returned. The moment she set foot in the house she said, 'I am going to Ajmer. Come on, drop me at the bus station.'

'Why are you going to Ajmer, Ma?' I asked. She instantly replied, 'I'll tell you later. This is not the time to say.' She quickly tied her bundle for the journey.

How could I let her go alone, ji? I had never seen her so upset. I thought, 'Why don't I take Ma in my car? How will she manage all by herself?' But when I suggested it, she went quiet and then said gently, 'You stay at home. Look after your father.'

'Your other daughter-in-law is at home, Ma. She will look after Bapu.'

'Her?' she exclaimed, shaking her head. 'No, no. You stay at home.' It was as if Ma was afraid of something. But I didn't agree. I didn't want her wandering around on her own.

She said, 'Behind the Shiv temple is a place where they exorcise spirits. I went there this morning. The exorcist calculated on his fingers that I should go to Ajmer. He told me the name and address of someone who takes out spirits . . . if the witch has tied her threads from Ajmer, then they can be cut only from Ajmer. He said, 'If you come from the north, then go to the south.'

Ma had been startled by the mention of Ajmer. The witch had come to our house from Ajmer, and the exorcist was telling us to go back there to break the net from where it had been cast.

When we were about to set out and Ma had lifted her bundle and tied money in the corner of her dupatta, I saw the witch was standing behind the storeroom door. Ma felt that she'd come to block her way. She must have guessed where we were going and why. Generally when she appeared in front of her, my mother would give her a word of blessing. But today she was silent. She was deeply worried about my father's illness.

The witch didn't say a word either. She just stared in front of her like a stone image. Then she turned towards her own room.

We left the house. I had never driven as fast as I did that day. I did a journey of eleven hours in seven. As evening fell we were in the streets of Ajmer. Asking the way, we arrived at the place of the maulvi who exorcised spirits, whose address had been given us by the people at the Shiv temple. But here too something strange happened.

When we arrived, he was sitting outside his room. There were five or six burqa-clad women standing in the lane in front of him. Practically everyone carried a child. The maulvi was a lean, spare man with a patched cap on his head and a brazier of glowing coals at his side. He held a large knife.

One by one each woman lay her child in front of him, and the maulvi spat on the palm of his hand and rubbed it on the children's cheeks. Then he waved the hot knife in his right hand around its head. After this, each woman picked up her child and retreated.

As soon as he noticed us, the maulvi gestured us to go into his room and sit down. I knew that he had understood the desire of our hearts. We went into his room. It was smallish and dark. A grubby mat lay on the floor. To one side was a piece of jute cloth on which perhaps the maulvi himself sat. There was a niche in the wall in which burned a large diya, but the flame from the diya had blackened the whole niche.

The maulvi was very old and had a white beard and long nose. He spoke very little and nodded a lot.

Before saying anything, I placed five hundred-rupee notes in front of him—that much I have learnt, ji. Nobody minds money. When I put the notes down, the maulvi said nothing, nor did he touch them. They stayed where they were.

'Save my husband, and I will wash your feet and drink that water,' pleaded my mother.

The old maulvi sat in silence, looking at the floor and nodding. After a little while he raised his head. 'What is his trouble?'

'He has no strength, ji. He falls to one side as he sits. Before he used to walk, go to the market . . .'

The maulvi listened and with his head bowed drew lines on the earthen floor with his forefinger. At places he touched them as if he were making some calculation. Sometimes it seemed he was just running his finger over the floor out of habit. Suddenly he spoke, 'Bibi, someone's shadow has fallen on your husband.'

The moment these words fell from his lips, Ma turned to me as if to say 'Now you see I'm right, don't you?'

The maulvi continued, 'I will give you a taviz.' Then he began to explain the magical rites. 'Knead some flour and make chapattis from it. Cook the chapattis only on one side, not the other. They should be half-cooked. Smear that side with unrefined oil from an oil press. Break them into pieces and feed them to him bite by bite.'

Ma's face began to flush. She was receiving support for her suspicions. She burst out, 'Ever since the witch came into our house this misfortune started, ji.'

The moulvi's finger stopped moving. He lifted his eyes and looked at my mother. 'Witch? What did you say? Witch?'

'She comes from your own Ajmer, ji. Her home is just here behind yours. She's the daughter of Jiyaram Munshi . . .' She was totally carried away.

The maulvi frowned. Furious, he sat bolt upright. 'Wretch! Kamjat! Get out of here, get out at once . . .' And he picked up the five one-hundred rupee notes in front of him and threw them in my face.

Ma began to tremble. She didn't understand what she'd done wrong or why the maulvi was so angry. She was badly shaken. On any other occasion, she would have lost her temper and joined issue with the maulvi.

'But I said nothing, ji. Beaten and kicked by fate I have come to you.'

'Get out at once. Be gone from my sight,' shouted the maulvi.

I quietly picked up the notes and stepped outside. Ma was still shaking like a leaf. I was stepping down when, who do I see, but that shoe seller Kubara crossing the lane in front of the maulvi's house.

'Chacha!' I called out.

Kubara halted and looked back in my direction.

'What are you doing here?' I asked.

He smiled very calmly. 'I've come to buy goods. There's a shoe market at the back here. They sell wholesale.'

I glanced towards my mother, who had immediately turned her back on him and wrapped her head and face in her dupatta, as if she wanted to keep far away even from his shadow.

My car was out of Ajmer by the time my mother collected herself a little. She shook her head and said, 'I interrupted him. He was telling me how to lift the spell. I could have listened to all he had to say. He was explaining how to get out of the net, but I, muhjali, had to put my word in.'

'Mother,' I said, 'who knows if the witch didn't come to our house with the maulvi's help. Both of them ensnared us together.'

'I, muhjali, if I hadn't spoken, he was telling the way to do it. I could have heard it all.' And, as she always did, Ma shook her head and rubbed her hands together.

The moment she got home, Ma went straight into the kitchen, washed her hands and face and began to knead aata. It didn't take her long to make chapattis cooked on one side, but she didn't know what to do next. The maulvi had been talking about some mustard oil.

So she took the half-cooked chapattis, tore them piece by piece and fed them to my father.

You won't believe it, ji, but Mother just fed him those half-raw chapattis for three days, and he sat up in bed. The colour had come back to his face. He wasn't entirely well, his health didn't improve much, but he was out of the jaws of death.

But all the time Mother rubbed her hands and said, 'Maulvi was telling me the counterspell, and I, muhjali, interrupted. If I hadn't spoken, I would have heard it all.'

The car continued on its way. Now it was turning round mountain bends. Outside, the cold of Shimla was in the air. By the side of the road were hoardings for Shimla hotels. Far away, sometimes in one valley, sometimes another, the rooftops of homes seemed to beckon visitors.

Suddenly the driver slowed, and turning sharply, came to a halt at the side of the road.

'What's the matter?'

'The piston's started knocking, ji. But don't worry, I'll fix it right away.'

I'd heard no noise from the engine; it must have been very slight, but the driver's ears had picked it up.

From beneath his seat he took what must have been a toolbox, and from the glove compartment a ball of string and a scrap of cloth.

He opened the bonnet and busied himself with the engine. In just a short while the car resumed its climb to Shimla.

'Then what happened?' I asked, as if placing the thread of the story in his hand.

The witch stepped up her activities. She was on the same wavelength as the old maulvi. Exactly thirteen days after returning from Ajmer, my other sister-in-law burnt to death.

She and my younger brother lived on the floor upstairs. We heard her screams coming from there. I ask you, can anyone set fire to their clothes themselves? And why should my sister-in-law?

Bapu had not fully come out of the grip of the witch and the maulvi, but the maulvi had at least told half of the counterspell. Now the witch had taken my sister-in-law into her power. She did whatever the witch told her. The witch had bound her in her grasp. She was taking revenge on our family for going to Ajmer to that maulvi . . . that I realized when I heard my sister-in-law's screams. I ran up the stairs. When I got to the top I saw her clothes in flames, nearby the kerosene stove was alight, and the witch was standing in the middle of the room with a bucket of water in her hands.

By this time Ma too had climbed to the top of the stairs. Crying 'This is the end of me,' she picked up a blanket from the bed, wrapped it round my sister-in-law and held her tightly in her arms for a long while. The witch was still standing in the middle of the room holding the bucket.

Blisters appeared in places on my sister-in-law's body. I thought she would be saved. Ma also felt she'd foiled the witch's plans.

My sister-in-law was being treated when something odd happened. It was as if she had become the witch's disciple. The witch spent the whole time at her bedside. They kept on purring together, when the opposite should have happened, shouldn't it, ji? It was my mother who saved my sister-in-law's life. If she hadn't wrapped her in the blanket, she would have died screaming in the flames. But instead of being grateful, she went and sat in the witch's lap. My mother watched, bit her tongue and shook her head.

On the third day my younger sister-in-law died.

My mother was devastated. She had cut the witch's net, but the witch had still succeeded in dragging away my sister-in-law.

Our household was terrorized. Even Ma was now afraid of the witch. She had already taken control of my brother and left him good-for-nothing. Then she attacked my father, and he was half-dead and bedridden. Now she had devoured my sister-in-law. Even my mother began to think that nothing could be done, and worried constantly about who would be the next victim. She began to hear all kinds of noises in the night. Sometimes it seemed to her that someone was drawing lines round the house, like the maulvi drew to make his calculations.

Slowly, the witch was looking better and stronger. Sometimes at night the sound of rattling pans from the witch's room woke my mother. There's a great power in a household's pots and pans. When the witch banged pans, Ma took it as a challenge.

What was going to happen? Whenever Ma spoke, she shuddered, 'Nothing will be saved. Nothing of this house will survive. The witch's threads are getting tighter and tighter.'

Then one day I got up and saw Ma wasn't at home. Usually she returned from the temple before sunrise and started washing up. But she was nowhere to be seen— not in the kitchen, or in bed, or in the shop. Goodness knows where she'd gone. I thought the witch herself might have sent her somewhere to get her out of her way. Who was to say, ji? The witch must have known Ma was trying to cut her net.

The morning passed; Ma returned in the afternoon, a bundle under her arm. As always, her face was flushed. She climbed on to the porch, went straight to her room and locked the door from the inside. There wasn't the slightest sound out of her for an hour. The door remained locked. Then she came out, drank a glass of water and quietly went to sit in the shop.

'Ma, where have you been?' I asked her when we were alone. She put her fingers on her lips, and came up next to me. 'I went to the ojha at Himarpur. He's given me some sacred ash. Now go. I'll tell you later.'

Ma had brought sacred ash from some ojha in Himarpur.

'There is no other way. The ojha was saying that he would cast a spell, and the witch would leave the house. But I said if she leaves the house, there is no way she will leave us alone. She was in Ajmer when she took us in her clutches. Now if she goes, why should she leave us alone? Then he gave me the ash.' Ma fell silent. Then she put her mouth to my ear and whispered, 'This will turn the witch to ash. According to the method the ojha gave, at that time she should be alone in her room.' Mother bit her tongue. She does that when any inauspicious thought comes to her.

'You make some excuse and take your brother out of station on work. He should stay out all night. Then I will scatter the ash.'

The ojha had told Ma that my brother was acting as the witch's shield. Only if she got him out of the room would the ceremony work. If the witch found out, then she would leave the room in time.

'What did the ojha say, Ma?'

'He said, "Don't let your son sleep in the room at night. And before the first light of day, while it's still dark, sprinkle the ash. You will have to sprinkle the ash about her room. When the four walls have touched the ash, the ceremony will start".'

'What mantra will there be, Ma?'

'The ojha will recite the mantras. He will recite them from there, where he sits. You find some excuse to take your brother away from here. Bring him back tomorrow during the day. By then this task will be over. That's all. Just do what I've told you.'

I have never seen my mother so resolute. She was right too. If we didn't act now we would never be able to do anything. And we would be destroyed. That night I took my brother to Shimla, ji, on the excuse that we had to bring medicine for my father from an ayurvedic doctor there, and because I wanted him to take a bank loan for me. At first he tried to avoid the trip. He never did anything without asking the witch. But I persuaded him away from the house and didn't give him the chance to go home.

Before dusk we left for Shimla. In any case it's not dangerous driving in the hills at night now, ji. It's a wide road. If your lights and battery are okay, it's an easy journey. But still it was night, and it took four hours to reach Shimla.

Exhausted, we stretched out in a room built over a wayside dhaba. But neither he nor I could sleep. The witch had cast such a spell over him that without her he was like a fish out of water. I felt bad to think of the state he would be in when the witch was reduced to ash. But at the same time my mind kept turning to my mother. What if the witch found out about my mother's plan? Witches sense things miles away. What if she bound my mother? And if Ma were successful in scattering the ash, and the witch burnt to ash as she lay in her room, what then? And if she survived, what then?

I tossed and turned on my bed. Just before daybreak my heart began to pound. By now Ma must have got up, she must have started scattering the ash along the walls of the room, slowly the witch must be feeling its heat. What would Ma do with the burnt corpse? Did witches even have bodies? The ojha must have been sitting reciting his mantras. Was the witch really asleep? If she sensed something was wrong, she would pounce on Ma. When witches come to take revenge, all hell breaks loose. Ma had taken a huge risk, God alone knew what would happen. When we got back, who knew, the house might be in bedlam.

As dawn broke my tension relaxed a little. I said to myself, whatever was to have happened will have already happened. Now no one can do anything.

Somehow we passed time on the streets of Shimla, took medicine from the vaid, went to the bank, took a loan form, wandered around for a while. My brother was even more anxious to return than I was.

At about eleven in the morning we left Shimla. I have only driven that fast once before—when I took Ma to Ajmer

Sharif. But now my heart was pounding, ji, at the thought of what might be going on at home. I was driving like a lunatic.

When we came up to the house, I was astounded. Everything was as we had left it. The shop was open, and Bapu was on his seat dozing as usual. Kubara's barrow stood in front of the shop, and Kubara himself lazed on the steps of our shop.

True, Ma was not sitting in the shop behind Bapu. Where could she be, I thought. I walked through the shop and straight into the back room. I was shocked to see that the witch wasn't there. She must have fled the house, and Ma's ceremony must have failed. Now what would happen? This is what I'd feared. Now God only knew what hell the witch would create.

Just then Ma came out of the kitchen. I rushed up to her, 'What happened, Ma?'

My eyes suddenly fell on the far wall. Ash had been scattered there.

Ma said with great patience, 'I didn't sprinkle all the ash, just a little. I looked and saw she'd begun to toss and turn. I sprinkled a little more, and she began to whimper. If I'd sprinkled any more, she would have been writhing in agony. But I stayed my hand.'

'Why?'

'I was about to sprinkle more ash when I wondered why she had come to take revenge from us in the form of a witch. I must have tormented her in previous births for her to come to take revenge. Now if I reduce her to ash what would happen?'

'She won't stop, ji. She'll go on tormenting us.'

'Let her, as far as she can. Her deeds are with her, and mine with me. I will not burn her to ash. If I had sprinkled it all, goodness knows what I would have had to suffer afterwards. If I pull back my hand, who knows, perhaps she will pull back hers.'

At that point the sound of clattering pans came from the witch's room.

The witch had returned.

But now Ma was not concerned by the clattering dishes; she simply listened and kept talking to me.

'The witch is back, Ma,' I told her.

'Yes, I can hear.'

But as I said, ji, Ma had stayed her hand. The witch must definitely have realized, ji, because for some days nothing happened in the house. Bapu's health began to improve and Kubara went away too. He had found a shop to rent somewhere, ji. Ma also felt that the witch was relaxing her pressure. One day she opened the whole storeroom cupboard in front of her and gave her all the cooking pots.

Now the witch doesn't live with us, ji. Ma has taken another house for her and sent our pots and pans there. The witch has taken my brother to live there separately. It looks like the witch has stayed her hand, ji, but who knows what the future holds? When she went, Ma stroked her head and said again and again, 'May you bathe in milk, bear many sons! Sati suhaagin!'

SEMINAR

'I still say forget the seminar. It's beyond us,' he said, peering through his thick spectacles. 'Get out of it right now. It will look a bit awkward, but that doesn't matter. We can put up with it. Let's face it. We aren't in a position to organize an entire seminar.'

This irritated me.

'You just sit at home and mope. We have never backed out of anything. Now we've accepted the challenge, we'll meet it. However we may have to, we will meet it.'

At this he shook his head and said in the tone of a Shia Muslim grieving the martyrdom of Imam Husain, 'There are just five weeks to go, and you don't have a broken cowrie shell in your pocket. Without money, there is absolutely no way you can hold it.'

At once I replied, 'We'll sit on a durrie in a park. We'll put up the artists in a dharmashala. We don't need anything ostentatious.'

He smiled a smile mixed with acid. 'By all means hold the seminar on a durrie, but won't you provide a sound system? For a three-hour meeting the loudspeaker man will take two hundred rupees. Won't you announce your seminar in the press? You talk about reaching out to everyone. Won't you print any invitations? Won't you invite any well-known servants of the arts? And if they ask you for the taxi fare, will you just ask them to excuse you? What world are you living in? If you're holding a seminar, won't you feed the participants even once? Won't you offer them tea or a glass of water?'

I had just opened my mouth to answer when he launched his most devastating weapon. 'And the foreign guests you've gone and invited, what will you do with them? Will you force them to stay in dharmashalas? Will you drag all our names in the mud?'

My companion with the thick glasses always speaks harsh truths, but my attitude is different. Ever since the seminar was first mooted, I'd felt the thrill of my old enthusiasm rekindling for those days when we'd founded an artists' organization and my colleagues and I used to roam the city the whole night sticking up posters. After many years that same feeling was stirring again.

'Yes, I will make them stay in dharmashalas!' I replied excitedly. 'Let them see that we don't have money. And what meaning does putting them up in the best hotels have anyway? We are appealing for mass contact, and you don't get mass contact in hotels.'

My companions at the meeting started whispering to one another. I sensed that I had gone too far.

'If not in dharmashalas, they can stay with us in our homes.'

The immediate response of my friend with the spectacles was, 'And you'll take them to the seminar on foot. Or by cycle rickshaw. One guest will be staying in Jama Masjid, another in Model Town, another in Okhla. At least talk sense, yaar. Enthusiasm is a fine thing, but in this day and age it is not enough to organize a seminar. For that you need money and people who will work for you.'

My temperature soared.

'If you have the fire of enthusiasm in you, you have everything. What are you talking about! With fire in their hearts people scale the peaks of the Himalayas, and this is only a little seminar. Inspired by this fire, people swing from the gallows.'

At this, some of those present began to giggle.

'Someone explain to him, yaar, he's going off his head,' he said and sat down.

I should have realized then that we didn't have the means to take one step forward. Nowadays everything's gone to the dogs. Where you used to pay one rupee, you now pay ten. But ever since we'd conceived of the seminar, the good old days had whirled before my eyes. Then we used to organize things in a state of virtual intoxication. If we needed money, we would just take a collection from the audience. Somehow or other we would cover our costs. So many occasions came to mind when we laid out the durries ourselves and rolled them up. I spent many nights sleeping at the venues themselves.

We were always singing. We didn't have any money then either. So how did we organize seminars and conventions?

When I began to cite examples from a golden past, he lost his temper.

'Don't boast about old times! I know how you worked. Disorganized, disordered. You accused anyone who worked methodically of being bureaucratic. Social service to you meant having an ill-fitting cap, loose pajamas, two days' stubble on your face, never being at home, telling your family you'd be back in an hour and coming back in the middle of the night, having no regular meals, or changes of clothes, debating incessantly. Such people weren't just "servants of society" in your book, they were "images of renunciation". Running from pillar to post, lacking in sense, unreliable. This is the reason that you've lost your composure today.'

I opened my mouth to speak again, but he pointed his finger at me and asked, 'How long have you been preparing for this seminar?'

'Why are you asking me? You know as well as I do.'

'How many people came to our first meeting?' His finger was pointing like a pistol. But receiving no reply, he himself said, 'Sixteen members came to the first meeting. Then we had outlined the programme and divided the work, and this great thespian,' here his finger advanced towards me, 'kept on singing the old songs of his theatre group. But then how many people turned up for the second meeting? Only seven. And today how many have come? Only four. Someone's ill, someone has visitors, someone had to go to Chandigarh. Is this correct or not?'

'Go on, say what you have to say.' I was sorely vexed, but all his facts and figures were accurate.

'At the first meeting we decided to publish a commemorative volume. How many advertisements for it have we got? One of you promised to bring in five, another promised seven. So far we have a total of two and a half, and those are from relatives. And there are just five weeks to the seminar. Now you tell me, what do you have to say? Some of you feel embarrassed asking for ads; others say we shouldn't approach big businesses.'

Then he warned us. 'There is still time to get out of this. Send messages to the guests that for some reasons the seminar has had to be postponed, and we will be in touch with them later.'

All my colleagues were silenced. He was, after all, right.

'You don't want government funding—why should you? We should use our own resources—but where are they?'

It slipped out of my mouth again. 'That's why I say we should use a durrie in a park . . .'

He snapped, 'Learn to talk sense. Yaar, your hair is turning white with age.'

The discussion continued for a long time. In the end it was decided that we would wait and see for another two weeks, and in this time work ourselves to the bone to raise money. We would go to industrialists, traders, public institutions to find someone somewhere who would rescue our sinking boat from midstream. We would knock on the door of every wealthy connection we had.

Accordingly our chosen companions took up their shoulder bags and went forth.

But again and again we faced disappointment. I met one man who at one time used to sing with me in the same music group. Now he had trucks. He met me cordially, remembered the old days with great nostalgia, but when it came to making a contribution, he took out a ten-rupee note and offered it to me.

I met another gentleman who was an even older acquaintance. He had also become a wealthy entrepreneur. The moment he saw me he began to offer advice. 'Are you still carrying on with that? Don't take me wrong, but organizing seminars is like living on immoral earnings.'

We plodded on from one house and one office to another. We knocked on the door of another old companion. He was the same one who used to paste posters on walls with me. He too had become a prosperous figure. As well as making money he also dabbled in politics. Firstly he gave us some very useful suggestions.

'Why don't you hold the seminar in a university auditorium. Induct a university office bearer into your committee, and your work will be done for free.'

But when we spoke of a donation, he just laughed and said intimately, 'Ask me to make a speech, be chairperson. If you need to meet a minister, then I'm your man.'

Then he counselled, 'Even if you take fifty or a hundred rupees from me, what use will it be?'

We departed silently and with long faces.

As we left the building, my friend with the thick spectacles said in the middle of the street, 'Get out of this bother of a seminar now. Even if a few people do give money, what difference will it make? We have been wandering around for a whole week, and up till now all we've collected is three hundred rupees. There is still time, postpone it. Afterwards we'll organize a seminar with proper consideration and planning.'

The times really had changed, and I could not grasp the situation. I was trapped. All my enthusiasm was turning into worry and trepidation. There were just a few of us working on this project. We were all approaching old age, and now we were hurling abuse at one another.

It was the next day that I met *him*.

It was a Saturday in winter. There was mist in the air, rather like the fog that was clouding my brain and making the surrounding reality mysterious. I was standing outside my house, my bag over my shoulder, unable to decide in which direction to head, when his car passed in front of me. I didn't pay attention. I just retreated a little to keep out of its way. But the car slowed down. Someone in it had recognized me, because a short distance ahead the car stopped, and a tall man in a suit and smart shoes climbed out and walked towards me.

By now I had fallen into the habit of asking anyone I recognized for advertisements. I would discuss my seminar with them and talk about the role of the arts in the rebirth of the nation, rather like a quack doctor stands on the edge of the street and reels off the benefits of his medicines. They also have bags slung over their shoulders.

It was my old classmate Sethi who had climbed out of the car. We hadn't met each other for years. As soon as I recognized him a voice called out within me—ask him, ask him, ask him for ads. If he doesn't give an ad, he'll give money—he can't refuse.

We embraced. He examined my greying hair, and I his. Our glance fell on each other's broken and half-broken teeth, and then we inquired about each other's health and well-being and families.

I was about to mention advertisements when he said, 'You're looking a bit down, what's the matter? Have you taken a beating at home or in the street?'

In reply I laughed weakly. Then he looked me up and down and said, 'You take some sort of interest in the arts field, don't you? From time to time I read your name. What do you do? Do you paint? Write? Dance? Nowadays even circus clowns call themselves artists.'

Then he smiled, that big-hearted smile that made my eyes travel of their own accord to his tie and the handkerchief peeping from his suit pocket and land on his shining personality.

Then I mentioned the seminar and also said that I was on my way to look for ads.

'I understand perfectly. You must have already been to scores of people, but you didn't come to me.'

It struck me that this man already knew a lot about my enthusiasms.

I spoke at length of my worries. He was standing on the lofty peak of patronage, looking down, smiling, listening.

'I am in advertising myself,' he said. Then he took hold of my arm and led me towards the car. 'Come, get in.'

I liked his familiarity. Anyone who could treat you so much as his own would surely give an ad or two.

As we drove he said, 'How much have you collected already?'

'A few ads, a few donations.'

'Ads are not money. Ads are a mere assurance of giving money. Don't you even know that? How many will you be able to pull in if you go around like this?'

Then he continued in a patronizing tone, 'It's right that people like you should get treated as you do.'

When the car stopped it was in front of an office building.

'Come up to my office.'

'Will you give me an ad?'

'I will, and I'll take ads from you as well.'

What an office! All oak and cedar. The walls were covered with gleaming teak panelling, the desks shone. Everything sparkled. My eyes were dazzled.

He offered me coffee and the best cigarettes. Then when I again mentioned advertisements, he pushed a button on his desk and the next moment a rather flabby, dark-complexioned individual appeared.

'Get this man's work done, bhai. Whatever he says, do it. He's an old friend of mine. Take care of him.'

I felt a great relief. Well here at least was one ad, I told myself as I followed the man out of Sethi's office.

This flabby, dark-complexioned man proved very useful. He sat down at a small desk in the next room and, putting his ample hands on the desktop and smiling at me just as mysteriously as his boss, he said, 'Tell me, what is your command?'

He opened his desk drawer and took out a thick blue sheet of paper and put it before him.

'Please go ahead.'

I failed to understand what he was doing. Still I explained about the seminar. It was a two-day event, some foreign guests would attend. There would be an exchange of ideas, a poetry reading, a cultural programme, an art exhibition . . . he listened attentively. I imagined that he too must have had an interest in literature and the arts.

'It will be done,' he said.

I was taken aback. What would be done? I looked at him.

'We'll do it,' he said again.

'I don't understand you.'

'Now that you've come to us, you can consider your work done.'

I had thought that the blue paper he'd taken from the drawer was something to do with the advertisement that Sethi was going to give me. But I saw that he began to note down some things on it.

Despite his bulk, he turned out to be a brisk worker. He kept reorganizing the things on his desk. Sometimes he would pick up a pencil and put it in the pen stand, or move paper from one place to another, or clasp his plump, dark fingers together, put them on the desk and fire questions at me. Years of training had made him as efficient as a machine.

'How many days will the seminar last?'

'Two. But we want one day to take our guests sightseeing.'

He took a sharpened pencil from the pen stand and entered something on the blue sheet of paper.

'How many people will come from abroad?'

'Four or five scholars.'

'Four or five?'

'Take it as five.'

Again he asked for clarification, 'Four or five?'

'Ah . . . er . . . five.'

'Where do you want to hold the seminar?'

'We have spoken to someone about a hall, but we haven't been able to raise the advance booking fee yet.'

'I will find one. How many sessions will there be?'

'Two each day. In the evening a tea party and a cultural programme.'

'Those to be invited. Will you provide the list or . . . We already have many lists prepared, including Delhi-based artists and writers. If you want to give any particular names, then do.'

What did he mean? Was he going to organize the whole seminar? I felt a weight lifting from my shoulders. But I still couldn't comprehend the situation.

'Will there be one chairperson or a group?'

Again I was taken aback. I couldn't reply to that question before he said, 'What will be the topics for the exchange of ideas?'

I gave a few details, at which he said, 'I have some ready-made write-ups on these subjects. If you like, we can use them.'

Then after filling up another section of the form he lifted his eyes.

'What do you want in the cultural programme—Bharatnatyam? Odissi? Gham-e-Ghazal? Rajasthani folk songs? Folk dances.?'

I was stunned.

'Will you arrange that too?'

'It's Sethiji's orders,' he smiled. Then taking up the pencil he said, 'How will the seminar lean?'

'What do you mean?'

'Left wing? Semi-left wing? Liberal? Right wing? I have data ready for all of these.'

Then he turned to me and said politely, 'You are the organizer, aren't you? Will you prepare your own speech, or will we have to put it together?'

I was dumbfounded. Seeing my embarrassment, he assured me, 'It's necessary for me to enter everything. If you get everything clear once, then there's no confusion later.'

Then, putting the point of his pencil upon the next item on the form, he asked, 'And resolutions. There will be some resolutions, won't there? About language . . . secularism . . . multinational companies—no, no, that's for economists' meetings—unity of the nation . . . the Punjab situation . . .' He shook his head. 'But these are subjects for other meetings. You are holding a seminar of artists and men of literature.'

Then he stretched down and took a dark-grey card from his drawer. 'Beyond free verse? New standards in criticism? The short story of today? The dearth of good

Hindi dramas—the problem and its solution? The question of Hindi and Urdu? Should Urdu be the second official language of UP?'

He looked at me again and said, 'What did you say, how many sessions?'

'Four.'

'Then we will keep three topics,' he decided himself and ticked the card.

Gradually, instead of consulting me, he began to guide me, make suggestions himself and enter them on the card.

'There will be heated discussion at the seminar but . . . tension, fisticuffs, verbal abuse, rioting, breaking of heads . . . which do you prefer?'

'What?'

'It's my duty to ask in advance,' he replied, immediately entering something on the card.

'What have you put?'

'I've just put "tension". If there's not at least that, the seminar would be a washout. Beyond that, whatever you say.'

That flabby, dark-faced man had entered everything. How many bouquets, what kind of badges, folders, list of events, changes in topics, support, opposition, tea, coffee, cultural programme . . .

Just then Sethi opened the door of his cabin and walked in.

'Everything done?' he asked, thrusting his hands into his trouser pockets.

'Yaar, what is all this? Is your office really going to organize my seminar?'

'What else are we here for?'

'But listen, how much will all this cost? We have only . . .' I said hesitantly. The conversation had come to the same point: money.

'You don't have any money to give. You've only got two and a half ads.' Then turning to the flabby man he said, 'Have you made the budget?'

'Yes!' he replied, and he was holding out the paper to Sethi when Sethi said, 'Put it in the special category.'

I persisted, and Sethi put a hand on my shoulder.

'Give me a chance to be of service. Your organization is well known, and you and your colleagues are well known. It is not a small matter of pride for us to arrange your seminar. This is, after all, everyday work for us. Come with me, will you have a cold drink or tea?'

And he took me back to his office. My head was spinning, but at the same time it was feeling very much lighter. That man seemed to me a magician, who simply by the touch of his wand on my shoulders had lifted my burden and thrown it aside.

'Now tell me, what do I have to do?'

'Go home and sleep. Your seminar is easily fixed.'

For a moment he again seemed a stranger. What was his connection with art and literature? And then, these days who is anyone's friend? Will anyone do anything for anyone if there's nothing in it for them?

'Tell me, what will you get from all this?'

'First, you get something, I keep getting things all the time,' he replied at once.

I left. My feet were not on the ground. I ran to my companions who were still looking for ads and donations, their bags over their shoulders. I told them the entire story.

They raised many questions. Their spirits were dampened by uncertainty and anxiety. The one with the thick spectacles went as far as to say, 'You've sold out.'

They continued to shower me with sharp remarks, but I felt that we had passed through a time of trial. We would see what came next.

The date of the seminar approached. A week before the seminar was due, details of it appeared in the newspapers. Three days later an article about the scope of the seminar and subjects under discussion was published. A full seven days before the seminar we had received the invitations, well printed on good quality card. With them we had received a printed programme, well set out. Once or twice I phoned Sethi's office. Each time the flabby man picked up the receiver. 'It's Sethi Sahib's orders. Don't worry about a thing.'

Two days before the seminar a statement of mine together with my photograph was carried in the papers. In it were discussed the topics for consideration and the foreign participants. There were also details of the main speakers. The day before an outline of the programme was also published.

Our minds were truly at rest. We sat in cafés sipping tea. Otherwise at this point we would have been beating our heads, visiting intellectuals in their homes to insist they take part, debating with them, running around making dozens of preparations. Now there was no question of arriving on the day of the seminar and finding that no arrangements were in place. Now we would arrive in style half an hour before the start.

The morning of the seminar I went to inspect the hall. Sethi's employees were putting up the decorations. There were floral archways, festoons of flowers and green leaves and bouquets. Some people were hanging long banners on the walls. The whole hall was full of banners. Not only the hall, but the corridors and the courtyard outside as well. There were scores of them, and there was a huge pile on the floor still to be hung.

On each banner was an instructive message. On one was written in large blue letters, 'Artists and the Masses Are One Flesh and Blood'. And beneath in red letters was written, 'Take Martand Chyavanprash Tonic'.

On another was inscribed, 'Artists Are the Torchbearers of Society' and beneath, 'Tower Bulbs Give Twice the Light'. On another, 'Consumer Culture Is Choking Art', beneath which was 'The Cure for All Throat Problems—Drink Mehtaji's Joshina'.

In a similar vein another banner read, 'Make the People's Dreams a Reality', and below 'Eat Kamdhenu Digestive Powder,' 'Secularism, Democracy, Socialism'—'Courtesy International Enterprises', 'Long Live the Struggling Masses '—'Find happiness—Insure Your Life with General Insurance'.

I was flabbergasted. A couple of my companions dropped into chairs, their heads in their hands

'What is this, yaar? What sort of seminar is this going to be?' asked my thick-spectacled colleague. All I could say in reply was, 'We were after ads too. My friend succeeded in getting them.' But inside myself I was extremely agitated. At this moment the flabby man came in with two of his managers.

'What have you done?' I asked.

He looked astonished at my remark. 'What's wrong, sahib? I was most careful about the messages chosen to be written.'

'But, yaar, what about all this soap and joshina and Kamdhenu?'

He replied patiently, 'The readers' eye will first be drawn to the message; the ad they may read, they may not.'

Then he smiled and opening the palms of both plump hands, he remarked, 'You've had your say. But these are the messages you want to get across at your seminar, aren't they?'

Then Sethi arrived, his hands thrust into his pockets as ever. He was reassured by the sight of the decorations and the scores of message banners. Slapping me on the back he said, 'You see? I did your work before you could snap your fingers.'

Then he whispered, 'Before I took on your work, I'd already received three orders, all for cultural functions. In fact I was going to thank you.'

We returned. We had no alternative. The whole way we remained silent. We were all deliberating whether this was right or not.

Whatever had happened, had happened. But what happened next was unprecedented.

The seminar was due to start at five in the evening. But by a twist of fate at exactly three o'clock, just two hours before, clouds gathered. It had been overcast since the morning, but by half past three the clouds had become threatening. They were those thick black clouds that have to rain. It was, in any case, a winter evening when it begins to get dark at five. Just one and a half hours before the seminar began, the heavens opened and poured down torrents.

My heart fell. Now nothing could be done. Everything would be upset, I was agitated, I couldn't think of what to do. I was comforted only by the thought that it wasn't my hard work that was being ruined; it was the hard work of Sethi's office that was being inundated. But still, it was our seminar.

I set out from my home as the clock struck four. Whatever happened, I should get to the hall. This too was my foolishness because later I found out that Sethi had sent a car to fetch me. But going on foot and by three-wheeler I somehow managed to arrive outside the venue. By now it was already past five. My other companions also arrived, some before, some after me.

Rainwater was flowing though the streets as I paid the scooterwallah outside the hall. It was raining so hard it was becoming impossible even to cross the road. But as I approached I heard the sound of applause. What was this? Had people managed to get to the seminar in this weather?

I entered the hall through a side door. I was dazzled. The stage was bathed in light while the rest of the hall was in darkness. On the stage were the foreign guests, garlanded with marigolds, and at the lectern stood Sethi, and he was introducing the foreign guests to the audience. One after the other, young women in beautiful saris, were placing garlands of flowers around their necks. The hall was jam-packed, and towards the rear of the stage stood the flabby man.

I stood near the door in darkness. I ran my eyes over the people in the hall. Only two or three faces in the front row seemed familiar. They were the people who never miss a seminar come typhoon or dust storm. The people at the back were in darkness, and it was difficult to make them out. Then I remembered that as I was coming to the hall I had seen four large buses parked on the side of the road. Had Sethi arranged the audience as well?

After the introductions, the lighting immediately changed, and beams of coloured light fell at angles across the stage, and in between them a group of young men and women entered. The young men were in yellow kurtas and red caps while the girls were in red-bordered white saris.

The youth group sang a song worthy of great maestros, dripping with patriotism. It had revolution, a tinge of sentiment, a call to awake and arise, and at the climax, when the young men and women clenched their fists and stretched up their arms, as if taking a revolutionary vow, in place of the multicoloured beams, streams of red light criss-crossed each other on to the stage.

After introducing the guests, Sethi peered into the hall. I realized he was looking for me. My clothes were drenched, but still, knowing that at this point it was essential for me to go on stage, I was on the point of going forward when Sethi began to read from a speech in his hand. This was a welcome address. In fact I was meant to read the welcome address, but my own speech had been reduced to papier mâché in my pocket.

His speech received a good response. At exactly the right moments applause resounded through the hall. I was amazed. Why didn't such a discerning audience come to our seminars? I listened to Sethi, my head to one side. Then my eyes fell on the flabby man. He had moved from backstage and was standing by the wings in one corner. He was holding a copy of the speech in his right hand, and his left was slightly raised. According to what was written in the speech, at intervals he raised his left hand a touch higher, at which the hall resounded with applause.

One or two of the foreign guests recognized me and began to wave to me in greeting from the stage. Their faces brimmed over with satisfaction. It seemed they were very impressed by their hospitable welcome.

At the conclusion of the speech the lights went up in the hall. A ten-minute interval was announced.

When the lights went up the people seated in the packed hall began to feel self-conscious. Some felt that their work was over and were about to get up, but, when a man from Sethi's office gestured to them to sit down, they lit bidis. The photographers and journalists at the front began to flock around the foreign visitors. There was a festive atmosphere, and from backstage came the sound of Hindi film songs. I also moved forward to mingle with my guests.

THE SPARROW

There was a broad, deep courtyard outside the zenana hospital, and it was surrounded by a low wall. Nearly all the time the relatives of the patients could be seen sitting on that low wall dangling their legs. No one was allowed to enter the hospital. The nurses came out in turn and kept informing the relatives about the condition of the patients.

On this wall, next to me, sat Gurmukh Singh talking disjointedly. Sometimes he cursed his wife, who was lying in the hospital, and sometimes he began singing her praises.

'She is enjoying herself lying inside on a government bed, and I am wandering around like a lost soul. I have no peace night or day. If I have one foot in the hospital, the other is sometimes at home, sometimes in the street, sometimes in the bazaar!'

Then he suddenly said excitedly, 'But I won't let her die, ji. Even if I have to sell the house, sell the shop, I will not let her die. Just last Tuesday Yamraj came to take her away. I saved Devaki from his clutches. That is the truth, ji. If there'd been the slightest delay in giving the injection, he would have carried her off. His black shadow was really hovering on the threshold of Devaki's room. When they were giving Devaki the injection, I looked up and saw Yamraj's shadow. I said, "O Lord, if my love is true, save her." He was waiting for the time when my Devaki wouldn't open her eyes, and he would rush in and seize her.

'But that injection cost me seven thousand rupees, ji! First I was going to pawn Devaki's own bangles. I had even taken them from the steel trunk, but then my heart reproached me. "A thousand curses on you, Gurmukh Singh! Will you sell your wife's bangles to pay for her treatment?" I started thinking, ji. When Devaki was strong and healthy, I would have shiny, new bangles made and put them in the trunk. She wouldn't even know. At that point I was helpless. I had no choice. But still my heart didn't agree. I was about to put the bangles back in the trunk, when I clearly heard Devaki's voice, "Take the bangles, ji. Sell them. What is there to think about?" When I heard her voice, I stood still in amazement. How did she know that I was going to sell her bangles? But I said, "I swear by your head, Devaki, that I will find money for your treatment." That day I put the bangles back, my heart was breaking.'

'Then did you sell the bangles?' I asked suddenly. Gurmukh, who still seemed to be talking to himself, jumped and turned to me. After staring at me, he replied, 'I sold them, ji, I sold the bangles. Not just the bangles, I took a loan and mortgaged my shop . . . that happened within two months. Here every injection costs seven thousand rupees. It's as if medicines are burning, ji!'

Saying this he took a small box from his waistcoat pocket.

'It costs six thousand seven hundred. I've just bought it from the chemist's. He's a real bastard of a shopkeeper. He didn't even agree when I suggested that if the doctor says there's no need for the injection he could take it back. Son of a bastard, he said, "I don't take back sold goods." I said, "Am I running away anywhere? My wife is lying in the hospital opposite. The doctor has said bring the injection, but he also said that if there is no need, we won't use it." Now if there is no need for it, what will I do with it? Stick it up my arse?'

He continued angrily. 'But pity has died in that bastard's heart. If the doctor says there's no need for the injection, you'll get your goods back. What objection do you have to that? But no, what stone-hearted people they are! I said, "Everyone has good and bad times. Just now I'm in great trouble. Tomorrow the same thing can happen to you." So he turned his back on me and said, "Don't talk so much nonsense, sardarji! If you want the injection, then take it, but we don't take back sold goods."'

With this, Gurmukh Singh put the box back in his pocket.

The rear door of the hospital was deep in the shades of evening. Now a dimmish bulb was shining there. Just as before, from time to time some nurse or lady doctor would come out and stand and look here and there, when suddenly someone or other from among the people sitting on the wall would leap up and rush over to her. One man's wife was in labour, another's wife was about to have an operation. And after parting with essential information, she would again disappear behind that mysterious door.

Next to me the sardar kept on talking.

'I say, "Good woman, if you were going to be ill, you could have caught some small disease. Does anyone stay in hospital for two months at a time? Am I the son of an aristocrat with a full treasury? Are you to stay lying on your bed inside, and am I to keep squandering my capital? What do you say? Has it ever happened like that?" When I go inside, she asks me how Gurnam is. How her daughter is. Why don't I being them with me. Now what can I tell her, ji? Seeing the distress I'm in, my sister has taken our daughter to live with her in Meerut. When I'm not there my son used to sit in the shop. He's a seven-year-old boy, ji, what shopkeeping can he do? He can't handle the scales.

So I shut the shop. I said whatever is the will of the Guru Maharaj, we will see what happens. Now I keep doing the rounds of the hospital. Sometimes he goes to school, sometimes he doesn't. And here she keeps on asking why I don't bring him. How can I make her understand? Once I did bring him, and the moment she saw him, she began to cry. She wouldn't stop. What have you done to my son? Look at that, had I done anything, or had she? I said, "Good woman, don't cry. When you get well, then your son will get strong too." Our daughter will come home too. But she would keep crying and wouldn't stop. Now what can I tell her? After all, she's a mother. You know a mother's heart.'

Saying this, he put a hand on my knee.

'Now however much I hide it, she knows. Women have a vein of their own, ji. It begins to throb. One day I went to see her, and she said, "You haven't brought Gurnam." I said, "Gurnam is doing his homework." She was quiet. After a little while she asked, "Why hasn't Gurnam come?" Then I realized that the vein was throbbing within her, or she wouldn't have asked a second time. I repeated, "He's doing his school work. Tomorrow's his test." She kept on looking at me, looking at me. Then I couldn't bear it; I told her the truth. "Gurnam was on his way back from school when a scooter hit him. His forehead was injured, but not too badly. The doctor says he'll be fine." She still kept on looking at me. Just as before, there was fear in her eyes, ji. But when I told the truth, she went quiet and turned her face away from me. She didn't make a sound. A woman should speak, ji. She should certainly keep on chattering, keep on complaining. If a woman is quiet, it's not right. But once she had taken to silence, she remained silent and turned her face away. And tears in her eyes, she went on sobbing and weeping. Then I decided to bring Gurnam to see her so that when she saw him she'd be at peace.

'But when I saw her weeping like that, I lost my temper. "Good woman, you are lying here, and I am having to roam all over the place. The hospital people are set on flaying my hide, and still you are turning your face from me and crying, as if it's all my fault!"'

Suddenly Gurmukh began to smile. 'Yesterday I told her, ji, "Devaki, my rani, when I come to the hospital you are lying here angry, and when I go outside, there are leopards ready to attack me." One leopard is that bastard chemist. Six thousand seven hundred for one injection. I have touched his knees to beg him, "You butcher, if the doctor says there's no need, then take it back. Give me back my money. If not the whole amount, then one hundred, two hundred less." But no, ji. He just kept on repeating the same old thing, "We don't buy back sold goods", and put the box of medicine back on the shelf.

'What could I do, ji? I gave him the money, the whole six thousand seven hundred. I counted each note one by one and paid him.' As he said this, Gurmukh began to laugh, 'When I put the box with the medicine in my pocket and stepped down from the shop I heard a voice from behind saying, "Sardarji, come back. Listen to me. If the doctor says that he doesn't need it by this evening, then bring it straight back to me. I'll give you your money back, but I'll deduct two hundred rupees."

'I said to myself, "If you were going to say this, you bastard, you could have said it earlier. Why did you torment me?" I told him, "Certainly deduct two hundred rupees." He'll get two hundred for nothing, and the medicine will go back on the shelf. There's nothing bad in it for him.'

And he began to stare at the ground and comment philosophically, 'People come here to the hospital because they're in deep trouble, ji, all the unhappy souls of the city. And here they are flayed alive. If he could do it he would drink the blood of every one of them.

'Now I am just waiting, ji, for the lady doctor to come, or the nurse, to tell me whether to give the injection or not. Whether they decide to give it or not, the injection is in my pocket. Isn't that so, ji, that much consolation I have.'

And he again patted his waistcoat pocket in which lay the box of medicine. 'Even if I lose two hundred rupees, it doesn't matter. At least I won't feel the shoe-blow of six thousand seven hundred.'

The darkness was growing deeper, and when the layers of darkness began to fall on the hospital walls, they looked even more frightening than before. Misery infused the whole atmosphere.

When a nurse came out into the feebly lit doorway, it seemed that someone was bringing a mysterious message from some dark cavern. Every time a nurse came out, Gurmukh leapt to his feet and rushed forward a couple of paces as well. Every time he felt as though the nurse was coming to see him.

The darkness was complete when one nurse came out. As always Gurmukh stood up, but this time he also shouted, 'It's not the nurse, it's the lady doctor. The lady doctor's come out,' and taking the box containing the injection from his waistcoat pocket, he practically ran towards her.

Then it was like a scene being played.

Gurmukh ran to the doctor. When he reached her, I could see from his gestures that he was impatiently showing her the injection. The doctor shook her head. And Gurmukh became extremely excited and set off at the same speed holding up the box of medicine, right in the direction of the chemist's shop. But he had barely taken two or three steps before he stopped and stood stock still. The doctor was nodding and came up to him and took his hand. She was nodding constantly. Gurmukh was standing motionless and then the next moment he sat down on the ground beating his head violently. Rubbing his heels against the earth, he began to weep. It was then perhaps that he realized that his wife was no longer in any need of injections.

I don't know what happened to that box of medicine. I don't even want to know.

After that day, a few days must have passed. I myself hadn't been to the hospital. That very night my wife had given birth to a son, and two days later she'd come home.

But one day I was strolling towards the market when I saw Gurmukh sitting on a bench near the park. It was natural for me to turn towards him. I don't know if he recognized me or not. At first I was hesitant, because I thought that seeing me would cause him pain. But then, thinking that pain is felt in any case, but that it can also be shared, hearts can be consoled, I went quietly and sat down beside him.

He smiled. A very open smile was playing on his lips. But because of his smile, I was not certain that he had recognized me. A boy of around seven was sitting next to him. I realized that this must be his son, Gurnam.

We had not picked up the thread of a conversation when he chuckled, 'She's come, my rani has come! Come here!'

Gurmukh's eyes were fixed on a bush near the bench on the uppermost branch of which was perched a sparrow.

'Come, my rani, come!'

Then he smiled at me and said, 'Devaki has come, ji. She comes here every day. When I wake up, she is already sitting on the windowsill. Then she flies inside. She sits at the stove. When Gurnam goes to school, she flies behind him. After all, she's a mother, ji. When he comes back, she brings him home.

'When I went to open my shop, Devaki was already sitting by the door. The moment I saw her my heart cooled.

I said, "My rani has set her foot here. Now there's nothing to worry about. Come, my dear, come, come."'

The bird, which had left the bush to sit on the grass now, again flew up to perch on the twig.

Gurmukh said, 'We are talking, you see, and she doesn't want to place any obstacle in our conversation. That's the reason.'

Gurmukh had placed both his hands on his knees and was looking in front of him. Then my glance fell on his clothes. The drawstring of his pajamas was hanging out.

'They took me to hospital, ji, but I ran away from there. What was I going to do there? What work do I have there? When they took me there, I prayed to the Guru Maharaj, "Babaji, what will I do here alone? Even my wife Devaki isn't here." Babaji told me that if I wanted, he would show her to me. I joined my hands, "Maharaj, I see her every day. She arrives at my home early every morning. But now that I'm in hospital, how will she be able to find me?" So the Guru Maharaj smiled. He lifted his hand and tiny bells began to ring, little tiny silver bells. At the same time, fine rain began to fall. Like a waterfall, just the same sound. Then a shining Devaki was standing before me, ji. Her face just a little veiled. The jewel in her nose stud was glittering, and she was smiling gently at me from behind her veil. The sequinned orhni kept slipping from her head.

'Then as I watched, she disappeared. I said, "Devaki was just standing there, where has she gone? Where can I find her now?" I knew that she wouldn't come back. Then I ran away from the hospital. I did the right thing, didn't I? Devaki wasn't there, so what business had I there? But when I arrived home, Devaki was already sitting at the window waiting for me.'

At that moment the sparrow fluttered down from the bush and perched on the back of the bench.

Gurmukh broke into a smile. 'She's come. Now that you've come, you mustn't go. I can't rely on you at all.

Come, sit next to me. We'll talk from our hearts for a few moments. The work of the world, good woman, keeps going on. Listen to me. Sometimes listen to me. Don't be upset with me. Whenever I see you, you look angry. Come, come. Today I'll say nothing. Just look, I've shut my mouth. If you like, I shall tape it up.'

And Gurmukh looked at me and laughed.

And the sparrow hopped up and down the bench for a while and then sipped drops of water from a small pond. Then, with a whirr of wings, it flew up to the bush.

'Look,' Gurmukh said to me, 'She's gone. After all she's a woman, ji, always getting sulky. But just you see, she'll be back . . . Come, come, my rani, come . . .'

And the sparrow again flew on to the back of the bench. Gurmukh's face lit up as if within him his spirit were illuminated.

The sparrow hopped down to the pond and again sipped water before fluttering up to the bush.

'Look, ji, she's playing hide-and-seek with me. She does it like this every day.'

And Gurmukh gazed with great contentment on the sparrow perched on the bush.

BEFORE DYING

Until the day it happened, he had no inkling of his own death. True, he felt a little irritation and fatigue, but even so he was not only making plans for his plot of land but was also satisfied that he had found a solution to his problem and he could now comfortably sit and make these plans. In fact just the previous evening, he had pulled off a feat of great shrewdness: he had succeeded in pouring his heart's most eager desire into the heart of another elderly man like himself. But in view of his death, it was as if he had been enacting a drama and had run away in midperformance.

The previous day he'd had to go to the deputy commissioner's office about the land and had climbed down from the bus to complete the journey on foot. It had been nearly one o'clock, there was scorching sunshine, and there was not a single shady tree beside the long road. But he had to arrive at the office before one, because the courts work only until one o'clock. After that the officers leave, the agents light up bidis and cigarettes and don't pay attention to anybody. You can wander anxiously around the courtyards and verandas, and no one will be in the least interested. And so in that heat, with feet like lead, he endeavoured to reach the office of the deputy commissioner as soon as he could. He kept looking at his watch but, despite the knowledge that there was very little time left, he couldn't walk any faster. At one point a car horn blared behind him, and he managed with great difficulty to move to the side of the road. In the days of his youth, he could have galloped. Despite being tired, he could have taken off his jacket, flung it over his shoulder and run for it. In those days there was a sense of achievement in running; he'd at least arrive at a run, whether he was able to complete his work or not. But now he was plodding along unenthusiastically. His mouth was dry and had a bitter taste in it. His neck was covered in a film of sweat, which he no longer had the energy to wipe away with a handkerchief.

'If I arrive and find the court closed because the deputy commissioner or tehsildar hasn't come today either, then I'll sit there for a while—on a bench, on the steps of the office or on some veranda—and recover my breath before I go back,' he thought. 'If I find the commissioner in his office, I'll go straight to him—officials sit in their offices and growl like wild animals in their lairs—but even if he keeps on growling, I'll lift up the bamboo chik over the door and go straight in.'

Even at this point, he had no idea that his last day had come. As he walked through the intense heat just one thought preoccupied him: The work should be done, if not today then tomorrow, if not tomorrow the next day, but the work should be done.

The previous day, despite bribing three different agents in the tehsildar's court, his work hadn't been done. Sometimes he would pat the chin of a chaprasi, sometimes offer cigarettes to agents and clerks to plead with and persuade them. The sun was beginning to sink, the court was growing deserted, and he had stuffed money into the pockets of three agents, but still there was no sign that his work was going to be completed, and so he came to sit on the office steps. He was tired out, and his mouth was filled with a bitter taste. He lit a cigarette, knowing that on an empty stomach the smoke would go straight to his lungs. It was then that, as he drew on his cigarette, he began to consider his idiotic position. By now even his confidence in corruption had begun to wane. Before at least, you could grease a man's palm, and he would do the job; now there was no hope even of that. This sentence spun in his mind.

It was then that the meaninglessness of all of his running around came home to him: 'What am I doing? I am already seventy-three. If I do get the land, what use will it be to me? How many days of my life will I be able to enjoy it? The case began twenty years ago. Then I could have made plans, thought about the future; I could even have woven dreams of building a small home on my ancestral land, of planting fruit trees in the courtyard, of sitting on the green lawn in their shade. But now? Firstly, it's still not going to be easy to get hold of the land. It's no simple task to get an encroacher out. If I can bribe, so can he. Even though the case has been decided in my favour, he will come up with a dozen stratagems. There have been so many ups and downs over the past twenty years. Sometimes the decision went my way, and he would appeal. If the decision went his way, I would appeal. And so twenty years have passed, and now at the age of seventy-three, how am I going to build a house there?

'It's not exactly easy to build a house, and who is there to help me? Even if I do build, by the time the house is ready, I'll have crossed seventy-five. My lawyer is currently eighty years old and has begun to wander about as if he's senile. His intelligence has gone cold, and he sits with his cloudy eyes looking into nothing. He says he has his old diarrhoea problem and rheumatism in his knees. This man is in this condition at eighty. What state will I be in by the time I reach the same age? Even if I build the house, I'll only have three or four years left. For that should I rush around and break my bones? Why don't I get out of this bother? My lawyer is more sensible than I am because he has understood his situation and refused to go to the tehsil court with me. "Enough, sahib, I've done my job, you've won the case. Now you take up the task of getting possession of the land." He had flatly refused.'

Thinking this, he tossed his head. 'Should I retreat when I've gone this far? Leave the land in the hands of the encroacher? If this isn't cowardice, what is? Why should I let anyone appropriate my land for nothing? Am I so past it that while I am alive someone can come and grab my ancestral land, and I'll just stand by watching? And now the judgement has come; all that's left is to give a slight push. If I get the papers from the tehsil, if I get the Indraj copy, then the road will start to clear, the goal will be in sight.' Thinking this, he again tossed his head. Opportunities like this had come before. Then too he was wont to say, 'Once the decision goes in my favour, the road will clear.' But what happened? Twenty years had passed and he was still kicking up the dust of the courts. 'A snake with a vole in its mouth—if he eats it, he dies; if he lets it go, it blinds his eyes. Neither can I escape this trouble, nor can I leave it.'

The deputy commissioner was not in his office. It was the same as before. Someone said he'd gone to a meeting; he didn't know when he'd be back, whether he'd come back or not.

He went and sat quietly on a bench. He lit a cigarette just as he'd done the day before and began to curse his fate. 'I don't know how to get work done. I run around from pillar to post in person for the smallest things. These things are done through contacts, not by running around from place to place yourself. I roam around anxiously, sometimes at the tehsil office, sometimes throwing up dust at the district courts. If anyone else had been in my place they'd have thought up a dozen plans by now. People get scores of things done through connections, and here I am hitting my head against a brick wall.'

At that moment the deputy commissioner's chaprasi said that the sahib would not be coming back today, and he picked up the bench where petitioners sat and took it inside. The court sweeper began sweeping the veranda and courtyard. Seeing the whole day wasted like this, he began to burn inside. A shooting pain like a flame flared up inside him. 'I will not accept defeat, I am not going to give up my land. However much these people tear me apart, I will not give it up. I will bury my teeth in it, I will not rest until my work is done.'

He knew in his heart of hearts that this surge within him was actually a sign of his own helplessness and that whenever he couldn't find a way forward, he would grab the hem of obstinacy. He attempted to keep alive his sinking self-confidence through stubbornness.

That morning, before departing for the district courts, his mood had been totally different. Then he was feeling confident. He had bathed and felt fresh and full of life. When he had set out from his home, he had known that he would find the deputy commissioner in his office, that he was a good man, a just man. And, moreover, his work was very commonplace. If he had a word with him and he passed an order, it would be done in the blink of an eye. Perhaps this was the reason that when he left home the world around him had seemed as pretty as a picture. As if a haze of gloom had lifted after many years and a particular sort of light brightened all directions, a slight shimmering, in which every single thing—the expanse of the river, the white bridge spanning it, and the tall, leafy trees on its banks—had become clearer, purer. The faces of the young women travelling on the road were blooming. Every building was clean, washed in the morning sun. And in this frame of mind he had boarded the bus that was to take him far from the town to the office of the deputy commissioner.

Then, when it left the town, the bus drove along beside a stream of crystal-clear water through dense woodland. He had peered out of the window. In one place the stream had widened, and a flock of ducks was swimming on the surface forming tiny waves. Small willow trees on the banks bent over the waters, and the netted sheets of shadows danced on the surface. Now the bus was crossing a village. Small, naked children were bobbing up and down in the stream. His glance fell on a small house standing on wooden stilts on the far bank. In a window, a beautiful Kashmiri girl was combing the hair of her younger sister, whom she had seated in front of her. This scene remained before his eyes for a short while, and then the bus had coursed ahead. But seeing them, he felt a spurt of enthusiasm—he could build a little home. Once you firmly resolve on something, then somehow or other, the job gets done.

'In the shade of the willow trees, in my courtyard, I will sit out on a chair. My wife and I will take walks beneath the avenue of trees. I will step forward, stick in hand, through the fallen leaves, wearing thick-soled boots, and the cool, cool breeze will pat my cheeks. The fatigue of a whole life will fall away. How difficult is it to build a house? Don't people of my age work? They run factories, construct new factories, keep on pushing their work forward until their last breaths.'

But in the afternoon in the packed bus, being jolted around, almost numb, staring into nothing, he was returning home. His calves were aching, and the taste in his mouth was bitter.

He was irritated again with himself, with his lawyer who, right at the most difficult time, had turned his back on the case, with his relations, not one of whom was prepared to help him. He was the one running around. Most of all, he was angry with himself, at his lack of practicality, at his submissive nature, at his helplessness.

The moment he descended from the bus, he made up his mind to go to see his lawyer. He was seething.

When the time comes to collect his fees, he doesn't leave a thing undone. He'll demand a hundred instead of ten, and when it comes to work, he turns his back. Is it my job to be pushed around tehsil offices? Haven't I paid him?

Crossing the great gate of the commissionary, he turned left where, a short distance ahead, sat a line of petition writers. For some time now the old lawyer could be found here. He looked up and saw him sitting very comfortably on an iron chair in a small wooden shack. His broad face was glowing , his few hairs were scattered across his scalp. It seemed to him as if the old lawyer were wearing a new suit and his black shoes were gleaming.

Dragging his heavy feet he slowly approached the lawyer's shack. The old lawyer was bent over papers and, in his capacity as a notary public, was attesting signatures on petitions. Standing below him was his middle-aged agent, holding the notary's stamp, stamping each petition as it was signed.

'There was no work done today either,' he practically screamed, as he reached the shack. Seeing the lawyer sitting at ease like this, he erupted in rage.

'Him sitting there on his chair enjoying himself, attesting signatures and collecting money, when I am kicking up the dust of the tehsil offices.'

The lawyer raised his head and, recognizing him, smiled. He had heard what he'd said. 'I told you, didn't I?' said the lawyer, making a display of his knowledge, 'In tehsil offices, they keep you hanging around for ten days at a time. I was weary of that, and so I told you that I would no longer do this work.'

'If you won't do it, should I run around kicking up dust there?'

'This work I cannot do. This has to be done by the owner of the land.'

He felt like telling the old lawyer, 'For years you've fought this case. I paid you whatever fees you've demanded, and now when you're really needed, you are putting this work aside and telling me that it's the job of the owner of the land.'

But he held himself back and suppressed the irritation rising in his heart. 'Moreover,' he said in an extremely controlled and natural tone, 'Vakil Sahib, you know every point of this case. We've come as far as we have due to your efforts. Now we just have to give it one more small push, and that only you can do.'

But the old lawyer had turned away. Seeing this indifference, he again felt incandescent. But his eyes were on the lawyer's face. The eighty-year-old was staring into space. Despite his firmness, his eyes were dim, and as he sat his mouth fell open of itself. To expect this man to do the rounds of tehsil offices and courts seemed a great injustice. And even if he did agree, how many days would he be able to do it?

He again became aware of his own helplessness. There was no one else who could share his burden, who could give him the time to breathe freely. Of his sons, one had gone and set himself up in Bombay, and the other was in Ambala, and here was he stupidly in Srinagar. Today I'm here, tomorrow I'll be gone. But once my eyes are closed, they will find a way to solve the land problem.

'Vakil Sahib, only you can get this boat across to the other side,' he had begun, but the lawyer immediately interrupted, 'I am not able to go anywhere. Now please forgive me. This is no longer within my powers.'

Then, gesturing towards his shack, he went on, 'You've seen how this work is. If I get up from here for even an hour, some other notary will come and sit on my chair.'

Then laughing brokenly he said, 'Every one of them is sitting in wait to see when this old man dies and they can take over his seat. I cannot leave my spot. I am already of an advanced age, and here, without running around, I can earn a little. In my old age I can only work here.'

'The difficult part is over now, Vakil Sahib. There's only a little work left.'

'Only a little work?' he replied, annoyed. 'Is it a small job to take possession of land? This is the most difficult job.'

'Listen, Vakil Sahib...' he'd begun, but the lawyer joined his hands before him, 'Please forgive me, I cannot do it.'

Suddenly, looking at the lawyer's face, his mind lit up. He stopped short and stood stock still for some time. Then he said to the lawyer, 'No, Vakil Sahib, I was going to say something else.'

'Please tell me, what is it that you want to say?'

He fell into thought for a moment more, then suddenly spoke. 'If you undertake the entire responsibility of taking possession of the land, then, when possession is taken, I will give you one-third of the land.'

He lifted his eyes to look at the old lawyer who looked astonished. His mouth was hanging open.

'But on this condition: I myself will do nothing more myself. You will do all the work,' he was saying.

'I laid before you my compulsions . . .' babbled the old lawyer.

'You think about it. One-third of the land means about four lakh rupees.'

This thought had suddenly struck him. Whether due to his helplessness or whether some half-dead shoot of his downtrodden skills in managing human behaviour suddenly burst forth, his mind had opened up.

'If you can't do it, then I don't want to force you. You can suggest the name of some other good lawyer who is capable of doing the running around. You can explain the position of the case to him.' Firing one more man-management arrow at the lawyer, he said, 'You've brought the case this far, and that's a lot in itself.'

He looked at the old lawyer again. His mouth was still open, and he was staring at him.

'Now only a lawyer can complete this task.'

A slight gleam had come into the old lawyer's eyes, and he had closed his mouth.

'I am saying this because you know everything about the case. It's my duty to put my suggestion before you first. For you, nothing is difficult, and the decision in the court has already gone in our favour. When all that's left is to take possession . . .'

Seeing the effect of his words on the old lawyer's face, he began to mutter to himself, 'It looks like the arrow has hit the mark.'

'But from my side, I will do nothing more. No money, no fees, no compensation, nothing. Just one-third of the land will be yours, and the rest mine.'

As he spoke, he felt as if he'd regained his strength, and as if waves of self-confidence were flowing over him. He felt he could deliver a speech now if he wanted.

'Patwari, tehsildar, encroacher, whoever has to be bribed, you will have to do it.'

Then, very theatrically, he made to leave, and he slowly began to lift his feet in the direction of the main gate.

'Give me your decision by this evening.' Then, even more dramatically, he said, 'If you are of a mind, then I am prepared to sign an agreement forthwith.'

And without waiting for a reply, he walked towards the gate.

The next day, just a little before his death, he was sitting on a park bench, taking pleasure in the weak sunshine and ridding himself of the fatigue of recent days. In his heart of hearts he was very confident that he'd freed himself from a huge burden. Now he could sit in peace and weave dreams of the future again.

This proposal reversed the roles of both old men. At the time the owner was sitting sunning himself and watching the shining dewdrops on the green, green grass through half-closed eyes, the lawyer was standing in a packed bus heading for the tehsil offices, making plans of building his own house. Intermittently, he felt a thrill in his heart.

'My entire life I have hung in a rented flat on the third floor. I feel ashamed to tell anyone that after working all my life I haven't even been able to build myself a house. My sons are grown up and complain all the time that I've never done anything for them. Here there'll be open land, a small courtyard, two or three fruit trees. I'll make a small flower garden. At least in the last years of my life, I'll have an open place to live in. I'll not be hanging over a narrow alley on the third floor.' A wave of enthusiasm, a kind of thrill, a sort of tremor spread through his body and, tingling, made its way directly via his spine to his head. A plot of open land, worth lakhs of rupees, will be had for free, without moving a muscle. It's a good thing that the written agreement had all been signed; the client wouldn't have a chance to reconsider.

Electrified, he had boarded the bus. But after they'd covered some distance, the old lawyer's back began to hurt as he stood. It was difficult for the eighty-year-old to keep his balance with the bus's jolting. Twice he nearly fell. Once he sat down in the lap of a young woman, at which his fellow passengers burst into laughter. His feet were unsteady, but his excitement was constant.

Just a little later, his knees began to ache. First there was a shooting pain in his right knee, and he realized that it would only get worse. It was still a long way to the tehsil, and he would be in distress by the time he reached there. The pain increased, and soon he felt as if some wild animal had sunk its teeth into his body and was tearing him apart. He didn't know what state he'd be in by the time they reached the tehsil. For no reason he'd taken on this misfortune. To hell with the land and the owner of the land! And he clutched his knees and sat down on the floor of the bus exactly where he was, lamenting loudly.

At that time the bus was passing through the village where the road ran along the banks of the stream through thickets of willow trees and where the tiny waves on the water told that today too there were ducks swimming.

There, on the park bench, the owner of the land, his fatigue long gone, had gradually slipped into a doze. There were just a few minutes left until his death. He was still feeling confident. After all, he had finally escaped from the whole foolishness and wrangling. Thinking this, he had the happy feeling that he was lazing comfortably on a bench, while the lawyer, at the very same time, must be wandering around trying to get the paperwork out of the tehsil office . . . But the thought of the land gave him a jolt. Suddenly he sat up, startled. 'What have I gone and done? Given away a third of the land! The court has already decided in my favour. Now all that's left is to take possession. I would have got that in any case. I have handed over one-third of the land worth lakhs to him and that too in writing. At the very most, I'd have had to pay a lawyer five hundred to a thousand rupees over four or five months, compare that with one-third of the land! He's looted me, while I'm sitting here! Looted me!' A scream grew within him. 'What have I done? I didn't ask or consult anyone. If I was to give anything, I should have promised a one-off payment. Who on earth gives his land? Without thinking, I signed on paper, on stamp paper. What have I done!' And he saw the stamp paper stretch before his eyes. It was then that he felt a powerful shove from somewhere, and a kind of pain, first once, then a second time, then a third, and then he fell sideways from the bench face down on to the green, green grass soaked with dew.

STRAYING

The three sisters were sitting on the veranda, chatting and laughing. They were joking about the boyfriends they'd had when they were young. In our society, after marriage lovers become absurd. At first there might be pangs of separation, but after children are born, they withdraw into the mists of the past and even become objects of mirth.

The sisters' youth was waning. All three had begun to fatten, but their saris were showy, and bangles jingled on their wrists. Once they started laughing, they were tickled for a good while.

The youngest sister was saying, 'When it came for my turn, Father had started patrolling outside. He didn't let any boy anywhere near the house.'

'He did that in our times too,' retorted Didi, the eldest sister. 'But we used to go off on the sly. Do you remember when that friend of Bhaiya's wanted to paint my portrait? The poor thing brought all those paints and brushes. Father was standing downstairs. When he heard about it, he patted the boy's back and said, 'My son, why don't you paint my portrait? Do paint mine before you paint anyone else's.'

This provoked another gale of laughter.

The eldest had been the envy of her younger sisters. So many boys used to follow her around; if one was writing poetry to her, another was following her to drop her home, and another was writing her long love letters. She was vivacious and light hearted. At one time her big, big eyes used to wreak havoc, but now she was somewhat fatter than either of her sisters. She had threaded her eyebrows and was wearing a high-quality, flamboyant, tussore-silk sari and a natural shade of lipstick. She was indulging the pursuits of youth even more recklessly than before, although they had begun to seem foolish. The mischievousness in her face had long faded although she was still jovial and carefree.

Her little sisters were no longer little either. One had three children, the other two, but you could still find glimpses of the expressions and gestures of their younger days. The middle sister was still reserved and shy. After every sentence she spoke, she would bend forward and adjust the end of her sari and, with her lashes lowered, would glance first at one sister and then the other to make sure she'd not made any mistake. In a woman of her age, this seemed ridiculous, but there'd been a time when one young man would have died for this shyness and reserve. When she would glance about her in confusion, she seemed to him like a frightened deer, delicate and helpless, and he couldn't sleep for thinking of her.

The third sister was roly-poly; from the start she'd been plump. Nothing could stop her giggling. Before when she laughed, she would rock from side to side, but now, due to her increase in bulk, she would sit still, and her whole body would wobble. The wave of her laughter began at her throat, and her body would shake to its rhythm.

'Didi, do you remember the boy with dark brown ears who used to follow you on his bicycle every day and wait for hours outside the house on the pretext of meeting Bhaiya?' asked the middle sister. Then, as was her habit, she bent forward and adjusted the folds of her sari on her knees and, lowering her eyes, peeped at her sisters.

'I used to ask why he didn't stand his cycle against the wall. Didn't he get tired?'

'Didi, you were very bad,' said the youngest. 'You used to make him miserable on purpose. When he began to get tired waiting there, Didi would come on to the balcony just once and show him her face. "You want to meet my brother? He should be back any moment," she used to say this very innocently and then go and hide inside behind the window. The poor thing would just stand there and stare up at the balcony.'

'The moment he saw Didi, his ears turned red,' said the youngest, laughing. 'I used to say, "Why do his ears turn red?" The rest of his face went yellowish, but his ears went red.'

'Not red, dark brown,' amended Didi, initiating another storm of mirth.

'He began to sweat too. We used to see from upstairs. After a while his scalp began to shine,' said the middle sister hesitantly, which sent her younger sister into a collapse of giggles.

In every family, brothers and sisters have one joke of their own that only they can enjoy to the full. The three sisters were meeting after a long while. One lived in Delhi, another in Calcutta and the third in Bombay. In this chatter there was silliness, meaningless laughter, but in fact by making fun of the young men who'd loved them, they were reviving their shared memories.

'Didi, do you remember Baldevji?'

'Hae! Don't even mention him,' said Didi. 'Still when I think of him, my nose fills with the smell of lavender! One day he said—those days we lived in Kashmir—"I will come this evening. We'll go boating on Dal Lake together." I kept quiet. If I turned him down, he used to burst into tears. Such a big, tall elephant of a man, and he would stand there crying. Then I said to myself, "If he comes, he comes, I'll get a trip on the lake." So I told him, "Fine, I'll go with you." He began to babble and dance about just like a kid—an elephant dancing. When that evening I sat beside him in the boat, there was nothing but lavender, as if he'd bathed in it. And cream on his hair—uf!—I felt like my nose would burst. What had I let myself in for?'

'Stop it, Didi. He was such a nice man!'

'He was nice, but why did he sprinkle all that lavender stuff all over himself? He used to keep bringing things from his shop and presenting them to me.'

'Hae, Didi! Kanwarlal used to do that too,' remarked the middle sister, going red as she remembered. 'Once he took all his uncle's neckties and gifted them to Bhaiya and Mamaji. When they met me, they both said, "This Kanwarlal's a strange boy. He's given us old neckties. Someone's already worn them. They're grimy where the knot's tied."'

'He often used to come to see Mamaji,' said the youngest. 'He thought Mamaji would get him engaged to you.'

'Mamaji was also a character,' the middle sister began. 'He was always encouraging him. He used to show him such affection. But when he talked to me, he said, "Doesn't he look just like a rabbit?" I couldn't understand what I should say. He used to praise him, and he used to treat him like a joke. Kanwarlal was a very good boy, very well brought up, but he did look like a rabbit.'

'He was really in love with you,' said the youngest. At this Didi immediately spoke up. 'And was he not really in love with me? He was ready to jump into Dal Lake and drown himself for me. Once he actually stood up in the shikara to do it.'

The youngest sister gave a peal of laughter.

'Really, Didi?'

'Why not? The giant that he was, he'd stood up in the boat. The moon had come out, and his cheeks, wet with tears, were shining in the moonlight. He stood in the boat and began to sob loudly, "I'll die, I'll commit suicide."'

'Then?' said the youngest sister trembling with mirth.

'Such a big man was about to jump in the lake!' exclaimed the middle sister.

'He must have been doing it to frighten you, Didi. He was never going to do it.'

'Because I had thrown his ring in the lake!' said Didi.

'Hae! Didi, you could have given it to me. Why did you throw it away? Didi, you're too bad!'

'He'd given it to me as an engagement ring, so I took it and tossed it into the lake.'

'Oh, Didi!' cried the middle sister.

At this the youngest added, 'He must have wanted to jump into the lake to fish out his ring. He must have been crying because of that too.'

'Because he'd lost the ring!' And they all launched into a peal of laughter.

'He didn't even know how to swim. If he'd really jumped in, it would've been difficult to get him out.'

'You would've had to get a crane,' gurgled the youngest sister.

'A lover hanging from a crane, dripping! You could've spread him out to dry right on the bank.'

The three of them again rolled around. When they stopped, the youngest suddenly remembered Arvind. 'Do you remember that Bengali, Didi, Arvind Mukherjee, who used to paint pictures and read palms?'

'You mad thing, that was him, the one father told to paint his portrait before anyone else's.'

'Didi, you're too bad. You kept him dangling. Poor creature, he was a very good man.'

'He used to read palms very well,' said Didi. 'When he read mine, he would never let my hand go. If I would pull it away, he would say, "Now show me the left hand." Sometimes he had the left one, sometimes the right one.'

'He used to make very good statues,' said the middle sister. 'Do you remember, Didi, when we both went to his room?'

'I remember,' said Didi. 'He said that I had been the inspiration for all his sculptures.'

'He must have said that to all the girls he took up to his room,' remarked the middle sister.

'Hae! No, he really did care for Didi a lot. He used to say to me, "I made this sculpture for your Didi. If she doesn't like it I'll smash it!"' added the youngest.

'He used to tag on to me like anything,' Didi said. She was enjoying discussing her boyfriends and so was tossing her head carelessly, as if it had been a very ordinary task to win their hearts. 'But why did he used to be so subservient? Whenever he saw me, he started stuttering. I thought it was really pathetic. Either he kept on stammering, or he would sit in one corner of the room staring at me.'

'Do you remember, you called him for your birthday party, Didi? He came wrapped in a bedcover!' said the middle sister. They all hooted.

'He sat in a corner looking at me all the time, wrapped in the bedcover. I said, "Mr Mukherjee, do eat something!" But he just kept staring. He didn't even blink, just kept on looking!'

'He didn't have eyelids. His eyes were always open,' said the middle sister.

'Damp eyes. Like a fish's. Open and limpid. He was pretty off-putting.'

Both sisters laughed again. But the youngest was quiet. Then she said softly, 'That was the same man, wasn't it Didi, who presented you with a sculpture?'

'Yes, the same one! It was the day we went to his room,' she reminded her middle sister.

'That was a very nice sculpture that he gave Didi,' began the middle sister. 'When we got there, he danced over to Didi. "You've come. How are you?" he kept saying, rubbing his hands together. He was so happy that he could hardly speak. It was as if heaven had suddenly descended on earth for him. He would come and stand on her right and then on her left. He kept rubbing his hands and looking at her eyes. And that sculpture was very good. It was of a child, a lovely, smiling face, with curly hair.'

'When we brought it back, it fell from my hands on the stairs and broke!' said Didi.

'Don't lie, Didi. You mustn't tell lies. You dropped it on purpose!' retorted the middle sister. 'There was the rubbish bin on the stairs. Didi immediately threw it into it. The moment it fell, it broke. And it was such a good sculpture.'

'How could I have carried around such a heavy piece of sculpture?' asked Didi. 'It must have weighed nothing less than five kilos . . . he used to stammer a lot. Whenever you met him yain . . . yain . . . like a beggar. His clothes used to be really dirty,' Didi remarked with girlish affectation.

'He could only wear the clothes he had,' the youngest defended him.

'But why did he do all that stammering? He spoke so little, just spent the whole time gazing at me. And even when he spoke, he would rub his hands and stutter.'

'You don't know, Didi. I met him a little while ago,' the youngest said suddenly.

The other sisters stared at her.

'Really? Did you recognize him? It's been about twenty-five years. Where did you meet him?' asked Didi.

'I met him at an art exhibition in Calcutta. It was an exhibition of his paintings and sculpture,' the youngest replied. 'He's become a very well-known artist, Didi. People really respect him.'

'What were you doing there?'

'I thought it was a sari sale, but when I went in, I saw pictures all over the walls, and there was a huge crowd. Didn't you ever see him again?'

'No, I didn't! For a long time after I was married, he kept on sending me letters. Very strange letters, they used to be. In every one he used to write that he wanted to meet me, could he meet me, just for five minutes, but he never turned up.'

'Who knows, he might have come and then left without meeting you,' suggested the youngest. Then a slight smile played on her lips. 'Didi, he still remembers you. It seemed to me as if he was still in love with you. I recognized him at the exhibition and went up to him. When I told him who I was, he began to shake from head to toe. I was amazed to see a man of his age getting so emotional. So many people around wanted to meet him, but he took me and began to show me every one of his paintings. Wherever there was a picture of a woman he would say, "Her eyes are like your sister's! How beautiful they are! There are no eyes as beautiful as your sister's in the whole universe. Very beautiful, your sister, very beautiful." He was a talking as if only twenty-five days had passed, not twenty-five years.'

'Is he still as grubby as he used to be? And stammering?'

'Hae, Didi! Don't say that! Now people stand for ages in front of every one of his paintings. I saw myself. The way he took me round the exhibition and showed me every painting, with so much respect. The people standing nearby were all terribly jealous. And, Didi, he's never married. It looks like he still misses you. I asked him, and he told me that he has only ever loved once, and that his beloved was beautiful, extremely beautiful!'

By the way the sisters were discussing Arvind Mukherjee, it seemed that they had themselves leapt over the past, landing somewhere far ahead, while the mad artist was still lost in bygone days—as if their boat had left the shore long ago, while his had only just set sail and was still being tossed about in the fog of yore.

It was then that the sound of coughing came from the room behind the veranda, and Didi hurriedly rose to her feet. 'He's woken up. What were you thinking of, laughing so loudly and waking up my husband!' And with that she disappeared into the room.

'Did you see how much she's afraid of Jijaji?' the youngest sister said after her sister had left.

'If he's disturbed even once, he can't get back to sleep again,' replied the middle sister.

'Even in the daytime?' inquired the youngest, beginning to giggle.

Within the room Jijaji was truly awake and sitting on the side of the bed with both legs dangling. Slack body, bent but broad shoulders, flyaway salt-and-pepper hair, big bags under befuddled eyes.

'Who was that you were laughing so loudly with?'

'My sisters have come. Choti has come from Calcutta. She was the one chattering . . .'

'It didn't even occur to you that someone was trying to sleep in the next room!'

Didi at once took his dressing gown from its hook and laid it at the head of the bed; then she stepped forward and opened the window. With great deliberation she picked up a small table and placed it before the bed, stripped it of its cloth and replaced it with a new one with a floral pattern.

'Tea is ready, I'll just call for it.'

'If you wanted to make a noise, you could have taken them to your own room.'

'What are you saying? How can women of that age make a noise?'

From the open window came a gust of the chill October air. Jijaji put on his dressing gown, went to the window and observed the green trees outside. Tea did indeed come within a few minutes, and Didi poured it out, making small talk to amuse her husband. The effect of hot tea immediately made itself felt on his stomach. Jijaji downed two cups one after the other. He was thinking that today he might not need a fourth cup.

Didi was about to pour out the third when, collecting her sibilant sari, her youngest sister stepped chirruping into the room.

'Jijaji . . .'

This word had just left her mouth when Didi came running over and pushed her back out on to the veranda.

'Shh . . . sshhh . . . get back! Go back!'

'Why?' said Choti in astonishment, beginning to retreat. 'Why, what's happened?'

'You have spoilt everything, you silly thing!'

'How? What have I done?'

'If anyone comes in when he's having tea, Jijaji gets constipation. Then I have to start making tea all over again. You barged straight in. Now I will have to boil another kettle full.'

Choti smiled and quietly went to sit beside her middle sister on the veranda.

But Didi's preparedness saved the day. She didn't have to make another pot of tea, and Jijaji's mood wasn't even spoilt.

The piping hot tea had the required effect and, after a little while, when Jijaji came out of the bathroom, he was looking pleased. Seeing her chance, Didi insisted that he meet her sisters, and he agreed and, tying the cord of his dressing gown, stepped out on to the veranda.

If you started talking about the old days, Jijaji would happily chat away, would tell anecdotes about himself, for his past too had been full of incident.

The moment he sat down Choti started on the subject, and Didi added, 'In college everyone was scared of him. Tell the story about the time you broke the superintendent's window.'

'Do tell us, Jijaji.'

'Arré, what's so special about these stories?' said Jijaji in his gravelly voice. 'I was sitting on the lawn of the hostel eating when some man came up to me and asked where the superintendent sahib lived. I pointed to show him. But he didn't understand. I pointed again. Still he was clueless and just stood there. Then I stood up, picked up a clod of earth from the ground and threw it with all my might at the window of the superintendent's house. Three panes of glass smashed and fell to the ground. "That's the superintendent's house!" I said and sat down to finish my food.' He broke into a sawing laugh.

Didi started giggling, 'His aim was deadly.'

All three sisters laughed.

'Didn't the superintendent sahib say anything to you?' asked Choti.

Didi answered, 'What would he say? Wouldn't he have got thrashed? Everyone was afraid of your Jijaji!' Then addressing her lord and master she said, 'Now tell the story about when you upset the tuckshop man's deep-frying pan.'

'Forget all that. What's in these stories now?'

'No, no—do tell us,' said Didi. Then to her sisters she explained, 'Whenever he meets one of his old friends, they tell all of these stories. It wasn't as if he was there for only two or three years, he spent a whole thirteen years in college. They used to call him "khalifa" there, as if he was a guru!' Didi concluded with pride.

Jijaji was smiling, the corners of his mouth had turned upwards listening to his own praise. He said with half-closed eyes and a light smile, 'I was a ferryman, a boatman ferrying people from one side of the river to the other. I used to take the boys of one year up to the next class, and then come back to where I had started!' And again he gave that grating laugh.

Middle-aged Jijaji regaled them with stories of his courageous childhood and youth for some time. Evening was drawing in, and there was no sign of Jijaji's stories ending. The middle and youngest sisters rose to depart.

Didi came outside to see them off. When their car was about to set off, Didi said to Choti, 'Did you really meet that Bengali in Calcutta?'

'Yes, I did.'

'What did he say?'

'He said that I still think of your sister a lot. I could never forget her.'

Her threaded, arched eyebrows trembled a little. 'Tell him to meet me if he comes here.'

'If I ever see him again, I'll tell him. But do you think he'd come?'

Then Didi replied softly, as if to herself, 'Yes, you're right. Why should he come? What is there to see?' Then she suddenly attempted a laugh and tossed her head. 'But still, tell him to meet me. The wretch, he goes round painting such beautiful pictures inspired by me, and people don't even know who I am!'

WANG CHU

Wang Chu came into sight wandering along the Lal Mandi Road by the river bank. He was wearing a knee-length khaki cloak, and from a distance it seemed as though his head was shaven just like a Buddhist monk's. Behind stood the steep hill of the Shankaracharya and above, the pure, blue sky. The road was lined by an avenue of tall eucalyptus trees. For a moment I felt as if Wang Chu had stepped from the pages of history. In ancient times, precisely such robed monks from various different lands must have crossed mountains and valleys to come to India. Wang Chu too appeared to be strolling in the romantic twilight of the past. Ever since he had arrived in Srinagar, he had been visiting museums and the ruins of Buddhist monasteries. Now too he was coming from the museum at Lal Mandi, where there were various sculptures of the Buddhist period. He seemed from his mood to be truly cut off from the present.

'Did you meet any bodhisattvas?' I teased him as he approached.

He gave a slight, crooked smile, which my cousin used to call a one-and-a-half-tooth smile because he only lifted his upper lip a little on one side.

'Outside the museum there were many statues. I just looked at those,' he replied softly. 'One image had only its hands and feet left on its body . . .'

I thought he would say something more, but he was so overcome that he choked, and it was impossible for him to speak. We both set off for home together.

'At first, only the feet of the Great Spirit used to be depicted,' he said in an unsteady voice, his hand on my elbow. I could feel his hand trembling slightly like a fast-beating heart.

'In the beginning they didn't make statues of the Great Spirit! You know, at first, beneath the stupas they would only show his feet. They began to make images later.'

It was clear that the sight of the bodhisattva's feet had reminded him of the Buddha's and he'd been carried away. You never knew what would excite him or when he would thrill with pleasure.

'You're very late. Everyone's waiting for you. I was searching for you too under the chenar trees.'

'I was in the museum.'

'That's all very well, but we should have been at Habba Kadal at two o'clock, otherwise there's no point in going.'

He nodded his head three times with a short, jerky movement and lengthened his stride.

Wang Chu was roaming India a free spirit. He had already walked barefoot, his hands joined in supplication all the way, to the Buddha's birthplace at Lumbini. Wherever the Great Spirit had walked, there too, fascinated, had walked Wang Chu. In Sarnath, where the Buddha had given his first sermon and two fawns had emerged from the bushes to gaze at him enchanted, Wang Chu had sat for hours under a peepul tree his forehead lowered in devotion until, according to his account, indistinct sentences began to resound in his brain, and he felt as if he were listening to the Great Spirit's first sermon. He became so deeply engrossed in this devotional experience that he took up residence at Sarnath. He would see the Ganges through the haze of thousands of years as a pure current of water. Ever since he'd come to Srinagar, he would often remark to me, looking towards the snow-covered mountains, 'That's the road to Lhasa, isn't it? By that road Buddhist scriptures were sent to Tibet.' To him, the mountain chain was pure and good because Buddhist monks had used the footpaths spread across it to reach Tibet.

Wang Chu had come to India some years earlier with Professor Tan Shan. He stayed with him for some time, studying Hindi and English, and then Professor Shan returned to China and Wang Chu stayed on, obtained a grant from some Buddhist society and came to Sarnath. He was an emotional, poetic soul whose aim was to remain in the entrancing past. He didn't come here to establish facts. He had come to be thrilled at the sight of the statues of bodhisattvas. For a whole month he had been doing the rounds of the museums, but he never told us which Buddhist teaching gave him the greatest inspiration. Neither did he become enthused by the discovery of any fact, nor did any uncertainty ever bother him. He was more of a devotee than an inquiring scholar.

I don't remember that he ever opened up to me or put forward his own opinion on any subject. In those days my friends and I used to debate for hours, sometimes about national politics, sometimes about religion, but Wang Chu never used to take part. All the time he would just smile slightly and hide away in a corner. In those days, a flood of extraordinary events was taking place in the country. The freedom movement was at its height, and we would discuss it among ourselves—what policy would the Congress adopt, what form would the movement take. Actively we did nothing, but emotionally we were very much involved. Sometimes we found Wang Chu's indifference irritating and sometimes astonishing. He not only had no particular interest in the happenings in our country, he didn't have any in his own either. Even if you asked him about China, he would just smile and shake his head.

The atmosphere in Srinagar had changed recently. A few months previously there had been firing. The people of Kashmir had risen against the Raja, and for some time you could sense a new excitement in Srinagar. Nehru was coming, and to welcome him, the city was being decked out like a bride. Nehru was arriving that very afternoon. The plan was to bring him by river in a boat procession, and that was the reason I had set off searching for Wang Chu.

We were heading homewards when suddenly Wang Chu stopped in his tracks.

'Do I really have to go? As you say . . .'

I felt as though I'd been pushed. At a time when hundreds of thousands of people were gathering to welcome Nehru, Wang Chu's saying 'how would it be if he didn't come' really upset me. But then he himself reconsidered and didn't repeat his request, and we went off together.

A little later we were standing in a crowd of hundreds of thousands at Hubba Kadal—Wang Chu, two or three friends and I. All around, for as far as you could see, there were just people—on rooftops, bridges, the sloping banks of the river. I kept on watching Wang Chu from the corner of my eye to see his reaction and whether the tumult in our hearts had any effect on him. In any case it's been my habit when I'm with a foreigner to observe his face and see his reaction to our customs and way of life. Wang Chu was watching the scene in front of him through half-closed eyes. The moment Nehru's boat passed in front of us, the rooftops resounded. Nehru was standing with local leaders in a boat built in the design of a swan waving his hand in greeting. I turned and looked at Wang Chu. He was watching the scene before him motionless, just as before.

'What did you think of Pandit Nehru?' one of my friends asked him.

Wang Chu lifted his eyes and turned to him, and then, smiling his one-and-a-half-tooth smile, he replied, 'Good, very good!'

Wang Chu knew an average amount of Hindi and English, though if you spoke fast, he couldn't follow you.

Nehru's boat was far ahead, but the procession was still passing when Wang Chu suddenly said to me, 'I want to go to the museum for a little while. There's a way from here. I will go by myself.' And without saying any more, he crinkled his eyes and smiled, waved his hand gently and turned away.

We were all amazed. He really couldn't have been interested in the procession if he'd gone off so soon to the museum by himself.

'Yaar, what an idiot you've found! What is he? Where did you dig him up?' asked one of my friends.

'He comes from abroad. What interest could he have in our matters?' I defended him.

'Vah! So much is happening in the country, and he's not concerned.'

By now Wang Chu was beyond the crowd, disappearing from sight beneath the avenue of trees.

'But who is he?' another friend asked. 'He doesn't speak. You can't tell whether he's laughing or crying. He's always hiding in a corner.'

'No, no, he's a very sensible chap. He's been here for five years. He's very highly educated and knows a lot about Buddhism,' I continued to defend him.

From my perspective, the fact that he deciphered Buddhist scriptures was very important, and that he had come from such a distance to study them.

'Arré, to hell with his studies! Vah, ji, to leave the procession for the museum!'

'It's perfectly simple, yaar,' I went on. 'It's not the India of today that's drawn him here; it's the India of the past. Hsuan Tsang came here to read Buddhist scriptures too. Wang Chu is a scholar as well. Buddhist teachings are what interest him.'

We discussed Wang Chu all the way home. In Ajay's opinion, if he'd spent five years in India, he'd spend the rest of his life here.

'Now he's come here, he's not going to go back. Once an outsider comes, they never think of leaving.'

'India is a swamp. Once a man from outside puts his foot in it, he just keeps on sinking in. Even if he wants to pull himself out, he can't,' joked Dilip. 'God knows what lotus he was dreaming of picking when he got sucked into it.'

'We Indians don't like our own country, but outsiders love it!' I said.

'Why shouldn't they? You can get by with a little, the sun's out all the time, the people don't bother foreigners, they let them sit in peace. On top of this, they meet idiots like you who sing their praises and give them royal hospitality! Your Wang Chu is going to end his days here.'

In those days my youngest cousin was staying with us, the same one who called Wang Chu's smile a one-and-a-half-tooth smile. She was a vivacious girl, always joking. Once or twice I'd caught Wang Chu looking at her from the corner of his eye but didn't give much thought to it because he looked at everyone from the corner of his eye. But that evening Neelam came to me and said, 'Your friend has given me a gift. A love token.'

I was all ears. 'What did he give you.'

'A pair of earrings.'

And she opened both her hands in which glittered two bright silver, Kashmiri-style pendant earrings. Then holding them up to her ears she said, 'How do they look?'

I was at a loss for words.

'His own ears are such a funny pale brown!' Neelam laughed.

'Whose ears?'

'This lover of mine.'

'Do you like his funny brown ears?'

'Too much! When he goes shy, they go brown, dark brown!' She burst into giggles.

How girls can make fun of the love of men they don't care for! Or was Neelam having me on?

But I wasn't too upset by this news. Neelam studied in Lahore, and Wang Chu lived in Sarnath, and he was going to leave Srinagar in another week. The shoots of this romance would shrivel of their own accord.

'Neelam, you've taken these ear-pendants from him, but this kind of friendship will be hurtful in the end. Don't lead him on.'

'Well done, bhaiya. What a rustic type you are! I've also given him a present—a leather writing pad. I had it anyway, and so I gave it to him. When he gets back, it'll make it easy for him to write love letters.'

'What did he say?'

'What could he say? All the time his hands kept shaking, and his face would keep on going red and then yellow. He said, "Write to me, reply to my letters." What else could he say, poor chap with his little brown ears.'

I looked closely at Neelam, but apart from laughter, I couldn't read anything in her eyes. Girls know well how to hide what's in their hearts. It seemed to me she was encouraging him. For her this was a game, but Wang Chu would certainly take it differently.

After this I felt Wang Chu had lost his balance. That night I was standing by the window of my room looking out at the line of chenar trees in the valley when I saw Wang Chu strolling in the moonlight, beneath the trees a little way away. He generally spent a long time strolling under the chenar trees at night, but today he was not alone. Neelam was mincing along beside him. I was angry with her. How cruel girls are! Knowing that this game would upset him, she was encouraging him.

The next day at the dining table Neelam began making fun of him again. She brought a broad aluminium container from the kitchen. His face was as red as hot copper.

'I've brought some rotis and potato curry for you. There's a piece of mango pickle too. You know what mango pickle is, don't you? Say it, just once, "pickle". Say it, Wang Chuji, "pickle".'

He looked at Neelam with lost eyes and said, 'Bickle!' We all burst out laughing.

'Not bickle, "pickle".'

'Bickle.' There was another torrent of mirth.

Neelam opened the container. Taking out a piece of pickle she showed it to him and said, 'Pickle, this is what you call pickle!' Holding it in front of Wang Chu's nose, she added, 'The smell of it makes your mouth water. Is your mouth watering? Now say "pickle".'

'Neelam, what nonsense are you up to! Sit down quietly!' I scolded her.

Neelam sat down, but she didn't stop her tricks. She implored, 'Don't you forget me when you go to Benares! Be sure to write to me. And if you need anything, never hesitate to get in touch.'

Wang Chu could understand the words, but he couldn't catch the irony behind them. He was feeling more and more emotional.

'If you need a sheepskin or some kind of rug or walnut . . .'

'Neelam!'

'Why, bhaiya, won't he read scriptures sitting on a sheepskin?'

Wang Chu's ears had begun to change colour. Perhaps for the first time he sensed that Neelam was mocking him.

His ears really were turning dark brown, just as Neelam used to joke.

'Neelamji, you all have shown me the greatest hospitality. I am deeply indebted.'

We all went quiet. Even Neelam was embarrassed. Wang Chu had certainly understood her joke. He must have been hurt. But it also occurred to me that in a way it was good if his feelings for Neelam changed, or he would have been the one to suffer.

Perhaps, despite understanding the situation, Wang Chu had fallen prey to a natural attraction. An emotional individual has no control over himself. He only realizes his mistake when he faints and falls.

Towards the end of the week, he began to bring a gift a day. Once he even brought a cloak for me and insisted, like a child, that we both put our cloaks on and go out. He still used to go to the museum. Once or twice he had taken Neelam with him, and when she got back, she spent the whole evening making fun of bodhisattvas. In my heart of hearts I welcomed Neelam's behaviour as I didn't want any of Wang Chu's inclinations taking root in our home. The week passed and Wang Chu returned to Sarnath.

After he left, my contact with him remained of the kind that is usual with an acquaintance. At times he wrote to me; sometimes I got news of him from people passing through. He was one of those people who restricts himself to the sphere of formal acquaintance for years and never crosses its boundaries to come closer nor distances himself and disappeares from sight. I received information that even his daily routine was unchanged. For some time I retained an interest as to whether the relationship between him and Neelam had progressed, but it seemed that love too had failed to dominate Wang Chu's life.

Years passed. In our country in those days, a great deal was happening. Every day there were satyagrahas, a famine broke out in Bengal, there was the Quit India movement, firing in the streets, the navy in Bombay mutinied, there was bloodshed, then Partition, and all the time Wang Chu stayed put in Sarnath. He seemed content with himself. Sometimes he wrote that he was studying tantra; sometimes I heard that he was planning to write a book.

After this I met Wang Chu in Delhi. That was in the days when the Chinese Premier Chou En-lai was about to arrive on a state visit. I suddenly came across Wang Chu in the street and took him home. I was happy that he'd made it from Sarnath to the capital for the visit of the Chinese Premier. But when he told me that he'd come in connection with his grant, and he only learned about Chou En-lai's visit after he'd arrived, I was amazed at his attitude. His nature hadn't changed one bit. Just as before, he smiled his one-and-a-half-tooth smile. He was just as inert, out of touch. All this while he hadn't written a single book or dissertation. He didn't even seem keen to, nor was he very enthusiastic about tantra. He kept on talking about one or two scriptures on which he was making a commentary. He also spoke of a piece of writing that he was currently working on. Neelam and he had continued to write to one another, he told me, though she had married long ago and was now the mother of two children. With the passing of time, even if our basic views don't change, our level of enthusiasm does. He discussed his studies, but a kind of steadiness had entered his zeal. He was not so emotional as before. He didn't go around sacrificing himself at the feet of bodhisattvas. He was content with his life. As before he ate a little, studied a little, wandered a little and slept a little, and he was enjoying following the path that he had chosen on an impulse in his dim and distant childhood, at a tortoise pace.

After our meal we began a discussion. 'Without understanding social forces, how can you understand Buddhism? Every area of knowledge is linked with every other, is linked to life. Nothing is separate from life. How can you cut yourself off from life and hope to understand dharma?'

Sometimes he smiled, sometimes shook his head, and all the time looked at me with a philosopher's gaze. It seemed that my words were having no effect on him, as if I was pouring water on a greasy pot.

'If not in our country, at least take an interest in your own! At least find out what is going on!'

He smiled and nodded. I knew that, apart from one brother, he had no one in China. Some political upheaval had taken place in 1929 in which his village had been burnt to the ground and all his relations had died or fled. Altogether he had one brother who had lived in a village near Beijing. Years ago they had lost contact with one another. Wang Chu studied in his village school and then in a college in Beijing. From there he had come to India with Professor Shan.

'Listen, Wang Chu, the closed doors between India and China are opening. Contact is being established between both countries, and this is of the greatest importance. The same study you have been doing all alone up till now, you can now undertake as the respected representative of your country. Your country will arrange a grant for you. Now you don't have to be all alone. You have been more than fifteen years in India, you know Hindi and English, you have been studying Buddhist scripture, you can become an invaluable link of cultural contact.'

His eyes began to gleam slightly. He really could get some resources. Why shouldn't he take advantage of them? He had also been impressed by the goodwill between the two countries. He told me that when he had recently gone to Benares to collect his grant, ordinary people on the street embraced him. I advised him that he must return to his own country for some time, witness and understand the great changes taking place there, that there was no point in his sitting all on his own in Sarnath.

He listened, nodded and smiled, but I couldn't work out if I'd had any effect on him.

About six months later I received a letter from him saying he was going to China. I was very happy. If he went back to his own land, then he wouldn't be like a dhobi's dog any more, belonging nowhere. He would belong somewhere. A new vigour would enter his life. He wrote that he was leaving his trunk, containing some books and research papers, in Sarnath, that after living in India for years he considered himself an Indian, and that he would return soon and again take up his studies. I chuckled to myself. Once he returned to his homeland, he would never come back here.

He stayed in China for about two years. He sent me a postcard of Beijing's ancient royal palace and one or two letters, but I received no details of his state of mind.

In those days China was in tumult, there was enormous enthusiasm, and practically everyone was caught up in it. Life was taking a new turn. People went to work in groups, singing, with red flags in their hands. Wang Chu stood by the roadside watching them, at a loss. Because of his shy nature, he couldn't go singing with the groups of workers, but he stood watching them rather astonished, as if he had landed in a different world.

He couldn't find his brother, but he did find an old teacher, a distant aunt and one or two acquaintances. He went back to his own village. A lot had changed. As he went from the station to his village, a fellow traveller told him, 'There, beneath that tree, all the landlord's papers, all his documents were burned, and the landlord stood there with his hands tied.'

Wang Chu had seen the landlord's mansion in his childhood. He still remembered the stained glass windows. He had also seen the landlord's buggy a couple of times on the town's streets. Now that mansion was the village administration centre. A lot of other things had changed too. But here too he was in precisely the same position as he had been in India. He felt no enthusiasm. Others' enthusiasm just slipped off him. Here too he roamed around a spectator. In the beginning he was given a warm reception. On the initiative of his former teacher, he was invited to the school. He was honoured as an important link in China–India cultural relations, and he spoke at length about India. People asked all kinds of questions about customs, pilgrimage places, fairs and festivals. Wang Chu could give satisfactory answers only to those for which his knowledge was based on his own experience. But there was much that, even though he lived in India, he knew nothing about.

A short time later, the campaign for the Great Leap Forward began to gain strength. In his village too people were collecting iron. One morning he too was sent out with a group of people to collect scrap. He stayed with them the whole day. There was a pervasive new zeal. People were bringing every single piece of iron proudly, showing it off, and throwing it on to the pile. At night, amid the leaping flames of the fire, they began to melt it down. The people sitting around the fire were singing revolutionary songs. All of them were joining in the community singing with one voice. Only Wang Chu was sitting quietly, his face turned away.

As he stayed in China, gradually a kind of tension grew in the atmosphere and a darkness began to surround him. One day a man in a blue coat and blue trousers came to him and took him to the village administration centre. On the way the man remained silent. At the centre he found a panel of five individuals waiting for him sitting behind a table in a rather large room.

When Wang Chu sat down in front of them. One by one they began to ask him about his stay in India. 'How long were you in India?' 'What did you do there?' 'Where did you go?' and so on. Then, having learnt about his fascination for the Buddhist religion, one of them asked, 'What do you think, what is the material basis for Buddhism? How do you evaluate Buddhism from the point of dialectic materialism?'

Wang Chu still didn't understand the question, but he babbled an answer. 'In man's spiritual development for his happiness and peace the guidance of Buddhism is of great importance. The teachings of the Great Spirit . . .'

And Wang Chu began to give an exposition of the eightfold path of Buddhism. He had not managed to get to the end of his story when the person with sharp eyes sitting on the headman's chair interrupted him and said, 'What do you think of India's foreign policy?'

Wang Chu smiled, his one-and-a-half-tooth smile and said, 'You honourable people know more about that than I do. I am a simple student of Buddhism. But India is a very ancient country. Her culture is the culture of peace and goodwill to all men.'

'What do you think of Nehru?'

'I've seen him three times. Once I also talked to him. He is somewhat more influenced by Western science, but he highly praises India's ancient culture.'

At this answer some members began to shake their heads, others to fume. Then they began to ask various kinds of pointed questions. They found that as far as facts and present conditions were concerned, Wang Chu's information was incomplete and laughable.

'Politically you are zero. You cannot assess Buddhism from the view of social science. I cannot understand what you were doing sitting there all this time! But we will help you.'

The interrogation went on for hours. The party officials gave him the job of teaching Hindi, and at the same time they gave him permission to work in the museum in Beijing two days a week.

When Wang Chu returned from the party office, he was exhausted. His head was humming. He did not feel at home in his own country, and today he felt even more uprooted. He lay beneath the thatched roof, and suddenly the memory of India began to torment him. He remembered his own room in Sarnath in which he would sit the whole day reading manuscripts. He remembered the leafy neem tree beneath which he used to sometimes rest. The chain of memories grew longer. He recalled the cook at the canteen in Sarnath who always greeted him with affection, always joined his hands and welcomed him with 'Tell me, bhagwan, what can I do for you?'

Once Wang Chu had fallen sick, and the second day the canteen cook came to his room himself. 'I was saying the Chinese babu hasn't come to drink tea for two days! Before he used to come, and I was blessed by the sight of him. If you had told me, Bhagwan, then I could have called the doctor babu. Can I ask, what is the matter?' Then before Wang Chu's eyes came the banks of the Ganges where he would roam for hours. Then suddenly the scene changed and the lakes of Kashmir appeared before him and, behind, the snow-covered mountains. Then Neelam came to him, her wide open eyes, sparkling pearl-like rows of teeth . . . his heart became troubled.

As the days passed, the memory of India began to disturb him more and more. He writhed like a fish out of water. In the monastery at Sarnath there was no interrogation. Wherever you lay, you lay. Food and accommodation was provided by the monastery. He had neither the patience nor the curiosity to study and understand the scriptures from a new point of view. After years of proceeding in a particular way, he was nervous of change. After that interview, he began to shrink from others. Here and there he had also heard comments against the Indian government. Suddenly Wang Chu began to feel endlessly alone, and he felt in order to remain alive, he had to return to the daydream of his boyhood when he used to imagine wandering in India as a Buddhist monk.

He suddenly resolved to return to India. It was not easy. It was not difficult to get a visa from the Indian embassy but the Chinese government raised many objections. It was a question of his citizenship and several other matters. But relations between India and China had still not deteriorated much, and so, in the end, Wang Chu received permission to return. He decided in his heart that he would now spend the rest of his life in India. It was his intention to become a Buddhist monk.

The day he arrived in Calcutta, there was a skirmish between Chinese and Indian troops on the border, and ten Indian soldiers were killed. He found that people were staring at him. He had just left the railway station when two police constables came and took him to a police station. There for a whole hour an officer examined his passport and papers.

'You went to China two years ago. What was the purpose of going there?'

'I had been living here for many years, I wanted to return to my country for some time.' The police officer looked him up and down. Wang Chu was self-assured and smiling the same one-and-a-half-tooth smile.

'What did you do there?'

'I worked with a team farming in a commune.'

'But you say you study Buddhist scripture?'

'Yes, I had begun to teach Hindi in an institute in Beijing, and I had permission to work in Beijing museum.'

'If you had permission, why have you run away from your country?' asked the police officer angrily.

What answer should he give? What should he say?

'I had just gone there for a limited time. Now I have come back.'

The police officer stared at him again, taking him in from head to foot. Suspicion welled in his eyes. Wang Chu began to feel agitated and confused. It was his first experience of standing before an Indian police officer. When he was asked for references, he first mentioned Professor Tan Shan and then Tagore, but they were both dead. He mentioned the name of the secretary of the institution in Sarnath, and one or two old companions he remembered in Shanti Niketan. The superintendent noted all the names and addresses. His clothes were searched three times. His diary, in which he had written several quotations and comments, was taken, and the superintendent wrote next to his name that he must be kept under surveillance.

When he took his seat in the railway carriage, the passengers were talking about the shooting. When they saw him, they all fell silent and began to stare at him.

After a while, when the passengers saw that he knew a little Bengali and could speak Hindi, a Bengali gentleman sprang to his feet and, gesturing with his hand said, 'Either you admit that your fellow countrymen have betrayed us, or get out of our country. Get out! Get out!'

His one-and-a-half-tooth smile had disappeared. In its place on his face was alarm and distress. Fearful, Wang Chu sat in silence. What should he say? He had also felt a deep shock when he heard about the shooting. He had no clear knowledge of the cause of the dispute, and he didn't even want to know about it.

Yes, when he arrived in Sarnath, he was truly overwhelmed. As he drew close to the ashram, his bag beside him in the rickshaw, the canteen cook rushed out,

'Have you come back, bhagwan! You've come back, my Chinese babu! You've blessed me with your presence after such a long time! I was saying, such a long time and the Chinese babu hasn't come back. And tell me, is everything happy and well? You weren't here, and I was saying, when will you return? When you were here, we would chat a little every day. I would be blessed with the company of a good man. There is much merit in that.' And he stretched out his hand to take Wang Chu's bag. 'Can I pay for the rickshaw, babu?'

Wang Chu felt as if he had returned home.

'Your trunk, Chinese babu, is with me. I took it from the secretary. Another gentleman came to stay in your room so I said, 'Don't worry, leave this trunk with me.' And, Chinese babu, you left your lota outside by mistake. I told the secretary, "This lota belongs to the Chinese babu. I know him. Leave it with me".'

Wang Chu's heart overflowed. He felt as if his unsettled existence had regained its equanimity. The tossing ship of his life had again begun to steer through calm waters.

The secretary also met him affectionately. He was an old acquaintance. He even opened up a room and gave it to him, although he said Wang Chu would have to apply again for the grant. Wang Chu again spread out his mat in the centre of his room, and the same scene rose before his eyes outside its window. His lost life had returned to its rightful place.

It was then that I received his letter saying that he had returned to India and had begun to work hard studying Buddhist scriptures. He also wrote that he was a little worried about his monthly grant, and in this connection, if I wrote to a certain gentleman in Benares, it would be helpful in securing it.

The letter made me feel uneasy. What mirage had drawn him back? Why had he returned? If he had stayed there longer, he would have begun to feel at home among his own people. But there is no cure for an obsession. Now that he was back, I had no option. I wrote to a 'certain gentleman' and a small arrangement for Wang Chu's grant was made.

But ten days or so after he returned, he was reading sitting on his mat in the early morning and thrilling at the experience, when a shadow fell across his book. He looked up to see the thanedar standing there with a piece of paper in his hand. Wang Chu's heart sank. What new worry was about to descend? Wang Chu was summoned to the main police station in Benares. His heart filled with trepidation.

Three days later he was sitting on the veranda of the police station in Benares. With him was another Chinese man of advanced age who worked as a shoemaker. Finally he was called and Wang Chu lifted the bamboo blind and went and stood in front of the senior officer's desk.

'When did you return from China?'

Wang Chu told him.

'In your statement in Calcutta you said that you were going to Shanti Niketan, so why did you come here? The police has had a great deal of trouble locating you.'

'I had talked of both places. I only wanted to go to Shanti Niketan for two days.'

'Why did you come back from China?'

'I want to live in India!' he repeated the answer he had given before.

'If you wanted to come back, then why did you leave in the first place?'

This question he had heard many times before. In reply he could think of no other answer but to refer to his interest in Buddhist texts.

It was not a very long interview. Wang Chu was instructed to report to the Benares police station on the first Monday of every month and register his name.

Wang Chu came out beginning to feel depressed. It was no great thing to come to the police station once a month, but it was an obstacle, an obstruction to his even life.

Wang Chu began to feel so distressed that, after returning from Benares, instead of going to his room, he first went to that quiet place of merit where centuries earlier the Great Spirit had given his first sermon, and he sat there for a long time in reflection. After a very long while his mind began to regain its composure, and waves of pleasant emotion began to rise in his heart again.

But Wang Chu was not destined to have peace. A few days later war suddenly broke out between China and India. A great storm raged through the country. That evening policemen arrived in a jeep and took Wang Chu in custody to Benares. What else could the government have done? Those in power did not have the leisure at a time of crisis to travel around examining the circumstances of each and every enemy citizen with sensitivity and fellow feeling.

For two days both Chinese were kept in the same cell at the police station. They had nothing in common. The shoemaker chain-smoked, muttered with his elbows propped on his knees, and Wang Chu, confused and weak, sat leaning against the wall, staring into nothingness.

While Wang Chu was attempting to comprehend his situation, two or three rooms away his small bundle of possessions was on the desk of the superintendent of police being searched. In Wang Chu's absence, a police constable had brought his trunk from his room. In front of the superintendent lay a package of papers, on which were quotations, some in Pali and some in Sanskrit. A large part of the writing was in Chinese. The officer flipped through the papers for a while, put them under a lamp to search for secret messages and finally ordered that the package should be tied up and dispatched to the officials in Delhi, as no one in Benares knew Chinese.

The war ended after five days, but Wang Chu received permission to return to Sarnath after one month. When, as he was leaving, he was handed his trunk and he opened it, he was stunned. The papers on which he had recorded his comments and writings over the years and which in a way were the sum of his possessions, were missing. When the police officer told him that they had been sent to Delhi, he began to tremble from head to foot.

'Please give me my papers. I have written so much on them. They are essential.'

At this the officer said bluntly, 'What do I want with your papers? They are yours. You will get them.' And he sent Wang Chu off. Wang Chu returned to his room. Without his papers he felt half dead. He didn't feel like reading or copying out fresh quotations. And then he was under close surveillance. Just beyond his window every day a man could be seen sitting under the neem tree. A stick in his hand, sometimes he sat on one side, sometimes the other. Sometimes he stood up and strolled around; sometimes he sat on the edge of the well; sometimes on the canteen bench; sometimes he stood at the gate. In addition now, instead of every month, Wang Chu had to report to the Benares police station every week.

It was then that I received a letter from him. After giving all the details, he wrote that the secretary of the Buddhist monastery had changed and the new secretary hated China, and Wang Chu was afraid that his grant would be discontinued. Secondly, whatever way I could, I must save his papers. As soon as possible they should be taken from the custody of the police and sent to him in Sarnath. And if instead of every week, he could be allowed to report to the police station every month, it would be convenient for him because at the moment he was spending around ten rupees a month in fares, and then he didn't feel like working because it was like having a sword hanging over his head.

Wang Chu had written the letter, but he had not considered that a man like me was not capable of doing this. Here nothing can be done without connections and contacts. And the most influential contact I had was my college principal. But still I went to one or two MPs. One of them sent me to another, the second sent me off to a third. I wandered all over the place. I received a lot of assurances, but they all asked, 'When he went to China, why did he come back?' Or they asked, 'He's just been studying for the last twenty years?'

But when I mentioned his manuscripts, they all said, 'Yes, that shouldn't be difficult,' and noted something on the paper in front of them. I received a lot of assurances like this; they all noted the request on the paper in front of them. But the ways of government are like the ways of a chakravyuh, and at every turn someone or other is always putting you in your place. I replied to Wang Chu listing the details of my efforts. I also assured him that I would be meeting the same people again, but at the same time I suggested that, when the situation improved, he return to his homeland, that this would be better for him.

I don't know what effect my letter had on him. What must he have thought? But in those tense days when I myself was enraged by China's action, I couldn't regard Wang Chu's predicament with much sympathy.

Another letter arrived. In it there was no mention of returning to China, just of his grant. His grant was still forty rupees, but he had earlier been informed that after a year they would reconsider whether he should continue to receive it or it should be terminated.

About a year later Wang Chu received a note telling him that his papers were being given back to him, and he should come to the police station to collect them. Those days he was ill, but sick and unsteady as he was, he reached Benares. He was handed only one-third of his papers. The bundle was half open. At first Wang Chu couldn't believe his eyes, then his face turned pale, and his limbs began to tremble. At this the thanedar said roughly, 'I don't know anything. Take them and get out or enter here that you refuse to take possession of them.'

On shaking legs, and with his bundle of papers under his arm, Wang Chu returned. Only one complete essay and some commentaries were left.

From that day, dust began to blow before his eyes.

I received news of Wang Chu's death a full month later, that too from the secretary of the monastery who let me know that, before he died, Wang Chu had insisted that his small trunk and few selected books should be sent to me.

By the time you reach my stage of life, you are accustomed to bad news, and it doesn't wound the heart deeply.

I couldn't go to Sarnath immediately, neither was there any sense in going, because Wang Chu had no loved one there whom one could console. There was just a trunk. But after a while, when I got the opportunity, I went. The secretary said words of sympathy about Wang Chu—he was a very good-hearted man, a Buddhist monk in the true meaning, and so on and so forth. I signed for the trunk and it was handed over to me. Inside were Wang Chu's clothes, including the tattered old cloak which at one time he had bought in Srinagar. There was a small tooled-leather writing pad, which Neelam had presented him as a gift. There were three or four books of Pali and Sanskrit. There were letters, some of which were mine, some Neelam's and some from other people.

I had picked up the trunk and was on my way out when I heard footsteps behind me. I turned and saw the canteen cook running towards me. In his letters Wang Chu generally used to mention him.

'The babu used to miss you a lot. He used to talk about you to me many times. He was a very good man.' His eyes became moist. In the whole world perhaps this was the only living being who had shed a few tears on Wang Chu's death.

'He was a very innocent-natured man. The police harassed him badly. To start with, they used to keep a watch on him twenty-four hours a day. I used to tell the havildar, "Bhaiya, why are you troubling this poor man?" He would say he was just doing his duty.'

I have brought the trunk and the bundle of papers back with me. What can I do with these papers? Sometimes I think I should have them published, but no one will publish an incomplete manuscript. My wife loses her temper with me every day because I am filling the house with rubbish. Two or three times she had already threatened to throw the things out, but I keep on moving them. Sometimes I put them on a takht; sometimes I hide them under a bed. But I know that one day they will be thrown out into the street.

RADHA-ANURADHA

Reverberating through the air came the cry, 'Ra . . . dha!'

This meant that the dhobi was at work and was sitting in the alleyway heating his iron and his daughter Radha had arrived to clean pots and pans and sweep houses. Every half or three quarters of an hour the dhobi would shout to her as he sat by his iron, and thirteen- or fourteen-year-old Radha would finish off the work in one house and move on to the next. For the past few days the dhobi had not been shouting, and Radha had not been coming to work. The dhobi had been alone pressing clothes. The dhobi's shouting was not so much to call Radha as for the people who lived in the houses where she worked. All sorts of people lived in the locality. When they heard his voice, they remembered that the girl's father was outside.

'Come in straight by the front door, Radha. Don't you dare jump over the back wall!' came Shyama bibi's voice.

But Radha would not have been Radha if she did anything straight. No one had ever seen her opening the door and walking in. She always climbed over the courtyard wall or walked along the top of the neighbour's wall and jumped into the courtyard.

'One day you will have such a fall that you will be forced to come to your senses.'

'I won't fall. Can't you see, bibiji, how I'm walking? Nothing will happen, see . . . '

And balancing on the courtyard wall, she stepped forward singing a film song, 'Mujhe buddha mil gaya'—'I got an old man.'

'Come down!' screamed Shyama. 'One day you'll fall and break your skull.'

'I also want, bibiji, to break my skull.'

'If you want to, go and fall from someone else's wall. Come down immediately!'

'I'm coming, I'm coming . . .' and Radha leapt down. 'What film's on the television today, bibiji?'

'To hell with the film! First do your work. It's still a long time till evening.'

'Will they show hell on the film this evening?' Radha laughed. 'And if they don't then?'

'Go indoors and get to work. Don't talk when you should be working.'

'I'm not talking, bibiji, I'm laughing,' and Radha began to rock with mirth.

As she scrubbed dishes in the kitchen she began to sing, 'Mujhe buddha mil gaya . . . '

'Keep quiet when you work.'

'Bibiji, tell me anything else you like, but don't tell me to keep my mouth shut. That I can't do.'

'Why didn't you come for the last three days?'

'How could I come, bibiji? I was ill.'

'You were ill, you liar. You can't get away with that, Radha. I've told you. The next time you don't turn up, I'll make other arrangements.'

'All right, please do, and when I come back, take me back again.' She chuckled.

'Get on with it. I don't like the way you talk.'

Compared with other houses where she worked, Radha liked working for Shyama bibi. Even though she would lose her temper and scold her, she was good at heart.

Shyama bibi liked Radha too. She worked smartly, had a sunny temperament, used to relate the news of the locality and never stole anything. But she was talkative, she gossiped the whole time, and she laughed at everything like an idiot.

'Would you like tea?'

'Yes please, bibiji.'

'Shall I give you a roti with it?'

'Yes please, bibiji,' replied Radha with a laugh.

'So did your father beat you again?'

'He beats me every day. He beat me yesterday and the day before. He'll beat me today and tomorrow and the next day.' And Radha laughed at her own predicament.

She had eaten the roti, but Shyama could still see hunger in her eyes.

'Shall I give you another roti?'

'One more.'

'Did you have anything to eat this morning?'

'No, nothing. Or last night. But so what? I go to sleep on an empty stomach. Nothing happens to me.'

'All you people bring you own food.'

'But, bibiji, there were no rotis left, so how could I have?'

'What do you mean?'

'I had made them. I made two, and my brother took them to school with him. Then I made three more, and my father brought them to work with him. Then I made two more, and my mother packed them away. Then the dough was finished!'

'You could have kneaded some more.'

'How could I? When they don't give me any, how can I ask? They send me to your home, bibiji, because they know that you give me something to eat. They don't have to feed me.'

'What are you talking about? You don't speak about your mother and father like that. A father is a father.'

'And a mother is a mother, and a brother is a brother, and Radha is Radha.' And she burst into a fit of giggles. 'All right, I won't laugh any more,' she said, stuffing the end of her dupatta into her mouth, and then removing it the next moment, she continued, 'Fathers are butchers, and mothers are witches, and brothers are donkeys.' And she giggled again.

'Get along with you, you don't talk like that,' repeated Shyama bibi. And Radha stuffed the cloth into her mouth again.

'Now get up and work.'

'What film is coming today, bibiji?'

'No film-vilm at all. Go straight home.'

'Why don't you tell me? Today's Sunday. There must be a film.'

'You go straight home.'

'Look, bibiji, whatever film it is, I'll watch it, and then I'll go home. When I go home, I have to cook for everybody. Here I work in seven houses, and there I go and cook food. If I see the film and then go, I'll just get a beating. I won't have to cook anything.'

'And you won't get anything to eat either?' asked Shyama Bibi in Radha's own tone.

'So what? I will sleep on an empty stomach. Nothing does me any harm.'

Shyama was silent. She knew that Radha wouldn't go home without seeing the film first, even if they flayed the hide off her. Radha knew the songs and plots of dozens of films. She would sing the songs constantly. She new the dialogues of several films by heart.

'Now quickly do the dishes. Your father is going to shout in a minute.'

'Hae, bibiji!' Radha lamented, rising slowly to her feet. 'Why do I feel sleepy when I come to your house? I don't get sleepy at anyone else's. When I come here, I feel like lying on the floor and going to sleep. The day's not started yet, and I'm dozing off.'

Radha turned round at the door to the kitchen.

'Do you know, bibiji, why I didn't come for the last three days?'

'No.'

'Because I'd taken poison.'

Shyama was shocked, but she didn't believe her. Radha was a gossip and kept on making things up in her mind.

'I took poison, but I didn't die,' she continued, opening the palms of her hands and laughing.

'What nonsense!'

'It's true! Those pills you put down for killing rats, I ate those. But I didn't die.'

Shyama bibi just stared at her.

'I said to myself, when these people wake up in the morning, they'll find me dead. Then mother will cry, "Hae! My darling has left me!" Then my father will cry, "Hae! Now who is going to earn seventy rupees?"' Radha imitated her parents and gave a laugh. Then, holding up her hands, she said, 'But I just didn't die,' as if her not dying was nothing less than a great miracle.

Shyama was still looking at her. Radha was showing slight shoots of womanhood. Her little eyes were carefully drawn. Her pale, ordinary face was always covered with a fine film of sweat, her eyes were constantly tired, weighed down, but even her dull face betrayed a kind of savoury charm.

'I ate five pills, bibiji. That Madrasi babu whose house I work in, I took them from there. I tossed them into my mouth, shut my eyes and lay down. I thought I'll die in my sleep, but, bibiji, after a little while such a pain came in my stomach, how can I explain? I began to writhe around. I immediately stuffed a cloth in my mouth. Everyone was asleep. Then I began to feel a burning inside me as if there was a fire in my stomach. Then I couldn't lie down any

more. I got up and ran out of the room. I felt as if someone
was cutting up my stomach, as if it was burning. I went at
once and drank from the water pot, a lot of water. But
still my stomach was burning just the same. How can I tell
you? I felt like going to a cold place and lying there. I
couldn't even sit. Then, I felt really sick and I vomited.
All five pills, whole, totally whole, came out.' And she
laughed, 'Such big, fat pills.'

'You mad girl! Well, at least you've learnt a lesson. Now
you'll never take poison again.

'You put down poison to kill rats too, don't you, bibiji?'

'Yes, I do.'

'Hae! Don't put that poison, bibiji. It's very bad.'

'Does your father know that you took poison?'

'How could I tell him, bibiji? If I told him he'd only
beat me more.'

'You really are mad. Does anyone eat poison? And what
reason did you have? Even if your mother and father are
bad, you're not going to live with them forever. In a year
or two you'll get married and go to your own home.
You're not going to live with them.'

'Hae, bibiji. They were going to get me married. That's
why I took poison.'

'You never told me that you were getting married.
What's the matter? Didn't you like the boy? Is that why
you took poison?'

'He's no boy; he's an old man. And, bibiji, he's deaf
and dumb, and lives in a far-off village.' Shyama was quiet.
This was an everyday tale for these people; there was
nothing new in it. But still she was angry with the dhobi
for handing a young, innocent girl to an old man.

'It's all been fixed, and so I thought nothing could be
done. These people are going to marry me off any day.
That's why I ate poison. Otherwise why should I? But I
didn't even die.'

Radha was still talking as if it were a joke.

'What possible need is there for them to marry you off to an old, deaf-mute man?'

'Why not, bibiji? If they marry me off to a young man, they will have to spend money from their own pockets, and if they marry me to an old man, it's the opposite, and they will get money. It's just that simple fact. Nobody has told me, but I've heard. When I go to bed at night, these people whisper among themselves. I squeeze my eyes shut and lie there. I hear everything they say. The old man lives somewhere near Meerut and will give my father a full seventeen hundred rupees. And my father has already taken two hundred from him.'

'Doesn't your father earn well?'

'Not at all! He earns two or two and a half rupees a day.'

'That's all?'

'That's all,' Radha nodded. 'Ever since the committee people took his handcart away, the work's not been good.'

Shyama bibi too remembered this incident because when his handcart had been taken away the dhobi had come to ask for money from her too. They had taken the handcart and his iron and told him to deposit a sum of sixty rupees. And he couldn't even raise that.

'Look, bibiji, the money that he'll get, he can get by on it for a year or two. And by then my brother will have grown up and started working.'

'And what else have you heard?'

'What else! My father was telling my mother, "What is there to be embarrassed about in this? If she has good karma, she'll find happiness even there. If she hasn't a store of good karma then she'll have to wander from door to door like us."'

'That's true, Radha. If he's a prosperous farmer, at least he'll keep you in comfort. You won't have to scour pots and pans in seven households.'

'Hae! Who can live in a village, bibiji? I couldn't stay there for one day. If I'm going to live anywhere, I will live in the city. I'll die out there in the village. I will live in the city and come to watch your television.'

'He lives off your earnings, so why does he beat you?'

'How do I know, bibiji, why he beats me. He gives my brother milk to drink every day and doesn't even give me food.'

At that point the dhobi shouted from outside, 'Ra . . . dha!'

'Today I'm late, bibiji. Today he'll really lose his temper with me.'

This made Shyama bibi angry. 'Let me catch him losing his temper with you! What nonsense is this? You've just got here, and already your father's shouting from outside. You didn't come to work for three whole days.'

But a little while after Radha went quietly into the kitchen and started washing the pots, Shyama bibi called out from the sitting room, 'Finish the washing up and go. Do the rest of the work in the afternoon.'

'I don't feel like working anywhere else but here, bibiji. Keep me here to work the whole day. Really. But you won't pay me seventy rupees, will you? That is also true. And my father won't agree to anything less than seventy, that's true, that's also true.' And then she giggled again and, wiping her hands on her dupatta, descended the steps of the house.

At the age of thirteen Radha had already learnt a valuable lesson of life: It makes no difference, nothing makes any difference. If you eat or not, sleep or not, arrive late, arrive early—nothing makes any difference.

The sunshine had become hot, and she'd only finished one house. At the end of the alley in the shade of a tree sat a group of Madrasi servants. They had made that spot their regular meeting place. When any of them finished their work, they would come and sit here. Passing them

Radha said in a loud voice, parodying their mother tongue, 'Gut-gutaiya gudduppoo!' Chelamma, who was sitting on the edge of the group, shook her head and smiled, 'She's mad, quite mad.'

Radha turned and said again, 'Gut-gutaiya gudduppoo!' and, laughing, walked round the bend in the alley.

She paused before climbing the steps to the Bengali babu's house. She'd got very late today. His wife would already have left for work, she thought. The Bengali babu himself left later. He would be alone in the house at the moment. This was another calamity. When the mistress of the house was there, she could scour the pots, and all the work went satisfactorily.

She found the Bengali babu standing on the steps of his house scratching his paunch, chewing paan and smiling at her.

'You're late today, Radha. I thought you wouldn't even come.'

'I got late at Shyama Bibi's,' she said as she dodged past him and went straight to the kitchen. The Bengali babu was imagining that she'd come late on purpose.

He did everything gently and simply. He thought that love for him was maturing in Radha's heart due to his gentleness and simplicity. He was different from the sort of men who pounce on maidservants, who go into the kitchen, leap on them, show them a ten-rupee note and take them in their arms.

For a long time Radha sang to herself and went about her work, and the babu kept his ears on her.

'Radha!'

'Yes!'

'Come here and clean the table.' Radha understood, tossed her head, picked up the duster and entered the babu's room.

'Did you sweep this room?'

'Yes, I did.'

'See how much dust there is! Look at the table.' And the Bengali babu ran his finger over the table and showed it to Radha. There really was dust on the table.

'There's a lot of dust blowing around these days,' replied Radha, starting to wipe the table.

The babu was enjoying the girl's proximity. Her body had acquired a kind of smell born of perspiration, and its sharpness carried the scent of adolescence.

'Look, you didn't clean the telephone either. Lift up the receiver and see how much dust there is underneath it. Wait, I'll show you.'

The next moment he was standing behind her. Then, placing both hands on her shoulders, he said, 'Lift the receiver, not like that, like this,' and moving forward and stretching one arm over her, which left one of his cheeks touching one of hers, and with his shoulder against her back, he lifted the receiver.

Radha felt weary, disturbed. Her forehead was burning. She waited. The babu thought she was encouraging him.

'I'll just clean it. Give it to me.' And she began to wipe the receiver and the phone with the duster. The Bengali babu again put both his hands on her shoulders. His breath sounded like a pair of bellows, and he was thinking that even at his age he could win a young girl's heart. When the telephone was clean, he bent down again to replace the receiver and again his cheek rested against Radha's. Radha drew away without a word.

She thought of threatening to tell his wife. That would make him back off, but she might also lose her job. She'd said the same to a Sikh once, and the very next day his wife had sacked her. She'd lost a job worth fifteen rupees.

Radha had already slipped into the kitchen when she heard her father's voice from below, 'Ra . . . dha! ! !', and she rushed towards the steps.

'You're going already? You haven't finished the pots yet.'

'There are just two left, I'll come and do them in the afternoon, when bibiji comes back.' And she reached the foot of the steps. On such occasions she appreciated her father's shouting, and the fact was that the dhobi watched over every house, shouted, just so the master of the house would realize that Radha's father was standing outside.

This was another reason for getting Radha married. Some neighbour or relative or the other would warn him every day, 'Stop her working.'

'If I stop her working, how will I eat? She brings in a whole seventy rupees.'

'And if one day she gets pregnant, then what? What will you do?'

'So what should I do?'

'Put henna on her hands and send her off to her in-laws. However you do it, send her away. Don't you see where the times are leading?'

'Where will I get the money?'

'Some way will be found.'

And a way really had been found.

After leaving the Bengali babu's house, Radha walked towards a house of Sindhi traders. There was no risk in going there at this time. It wasn't really difficult to escape the hands of the Bengali babu, but there Dayaram the cook used to grab hold of her, and it was very difficult to escape his clutches. After their lunch, the Sindhi trader, his wife and children used to go to sleep in their air-conditioned room and lie there the whole afternoon. They didn't come out once, and they couldn't hear any sound from outside either. That was why it was essential to get to the Sindhi trader's house before lunch. For the same reason she had to get to the Bengali babu's house before breakfast.

After finishing the Sindhi trader's house, she had to go to Maji's house, where an old widow lived with her daughter, then from there to a doctor sahib's house and then after lunch she had to go to all these people's houses again to do the washing up from lunch. She kept up her circuit until the late afternoon.

That evening Radha did not go to watch television at Shyama bibi's. Shyama bibi paid no particular attention to the fact. The next day Radha didn't come to work either. Shyama bibi was irritated, and she asked the dhobi, who replied as if to stall her, 'She'll be coming just now, she's just around here.' When she hadn't arrived by the afternoon, the dhobi said, 'How do I know, bibiji? She left the house. I don't know where she's sitting. I'll go and look for her. If I find her, I'll send her to you.' But the afternoon drew to a close, and there was no sign of Radha. The dhobi was certainly hiding something; otherwise, if Radha had come, he would have been calling her name. He wasn't, and so this meant that she'd not come to work. Shyama bibi muttered, but still she managed to get her work done.

Radha didn't come the next day either, and the following day the dhobi didn't either. Shyama bibi sensed something was wrong. There was obviously some mystery somewhere. It must be that he was getting Radha married. Perhaps Radha was telling the truth that her marriage had been arranged with some old, deaf-mute. But who knew if it wasn't something else! When the dhobi didn't turn up the third day or the fourth and there was no sign of him or Radha even on the fifth, Shyama bibi employed a Madrasi woman to clean her house and pans. Once or twice she wondered whether something hadn't gone amiss, but gradually her attention shifted from Radha.

Then one day the dhobi came back to work. He was sitting in the alley, setting light to the charcoal for his iron when Shyama bibi saw him. She went straight out to him.

'Tell me, have you had Radha married?'

'What, bibiji? Whose marriage?'

Shyama bibi hesitated. She felt a little embarrassed that she had spoken without any knowledge.

'Where's Radha? She hasn't come to work for such a long time.'

To this the dhobi responded, 'She'll come back in a few days, bibiji.' He turned his attention to the charcoal.

'Tell me precisely, dhobi. Will she come or not? If she's not going to come I'll make some other arrangement.'

'She'll come, she'll come.'

'When will she?'

At this the dhobi burst out, 'Now, bibiji, what do I know what's in her heart? The bitch, she told us nothing, said nothing and went off somewhere. I don't know if she's gone to her sister in Mathura or to Lakshmibainagar, where her other sister lives. She didn't tell anyone before she left. When she comes back, I'll send her to you.'

Shyama bibi returned to her house. There was certainly something wrong somewhere. Girls nowadays seem very simple when they talk, but they drink water from all kinds of different sources. God only knew what she'd been up to.

Then one day, in the evening, Shyama bibi was knitting in front of the television when whom did she see standing in the doorway but Radha.

'Arré, where have you come from?' she asked in amazement. Then she took in Radha from head to toe and began to laugh. 'Well, look at you, all done up!'

'I'm married, you see, bibiji.'

'You're married? To whom? The dumb man?'

'No,' replied Radha with a smile.

'Does your father know?'

'How would he know? He doesn't know a thing.'

This reply alarmed Shyama bibi, and she immediately stood up and closed the door opening into the alley. 'You've come in secret? You silly thing, one day you will die, and you will also get me into trouble. Your father is sitting outside in the alley. What would happen if he saw you?'

'How will he? I've just walked straight past him.'

'Didn't anyone see you?'

'No one, really, bibiji,' Radha giggled.

Shyama bibi's eyes rested on her cheap earrings and her loud sari.

'Where did you get that sari?'

'*He* gave it to me,' Radha giggled.

'Look at you trying to behave like a married woman! "*He* gave it to me." When did you get married?'

Radha really was being bashful like a new bride. Her eyes were half-shut and rather heavy as before. Her forehead was flushed as always.

'You're looking very beautiful, Radha, truly you are.'

'I am not beautiful, so how can I look it?'

'No, you're looking very nice.'

'Then say nice, not beautiful.'

Shyama Bibi went and brought a little sugar on a saucer.

'Here, sweeten your mouth. You have come to my house after marriage.'

Radha laughed and dropped a pinch of sugar into her mouth. But from her gesture, goodness knows how, Shyama bibi guessed that she was hungry.

'Would you like something to eat?'

'No, bibiji, nothing. I'm not hungry.'

This convinced Shyama bibi even more. She went and brought a few slices of bread and a little pickle. Radha took them and downed them in a moment.

'Whom have you married?'

'Just near here, not far away at the back. He works in a boys' hostel.' She was anxious to talk about her wedding. 'Do you know, bibiji, how I ran away?'

'You ran away from home?'

'No, I ran away from your house,' she giggled again. 'He was standing waiting outside with his bicycle, I simply quietly went and sat behind him, and he took me straight to the hostel.'

'Where was your father?'

'He was in the alley behind. I went out into the alley in front. How would he have known?'

'Where do you live there? Has your husband got quarters?'

'I am in hiding,' she chattered, as if relating the plot of a film. 'When we got close to the hostel I jumped off the bicycle and stood pressed against a tree. He took the cycle straight inside. Then he came out again and told me the way to get in from the rear. He'd left the back door open. That's all.' And Radha let forth a peal of laughter. 'No one caught on there either. How could they when I hide all day. Do you know, bibiji, the old watchman comes there on his rounds at night. At ten o'clock, before lights out, he makes his first round and peers into every room. But he doesn't see anything. I stay crouching in a corner.'

'Some day you'll get caught, you mad girl.'

'If I get caught, I get caught,' said Radha waving her hands carelessly as always.

'What do you do all day? He must go to work.'

'That's all, I hide in the room. I don't say anything.'

'When did you get married?'

'Five or six days ago.'

'Did you know him before?'

'Yes, he worked around here. He used to come to have clothes pressed by my father.'

Shyama bibi smiled. 'Where was the wedding held?'

'In the temple.' Then she volunteered, 'There's a temple behind the hostel, there.' Then, seeing Shyama bibi regarding her doubtfully, she said, 'Behind our room on the veranda, bibiji, there's an image of god in a niche. We both went and stood in front of it and got married.'

'There was no pandit?'

'What for, bibiji? We held hands in front of the image and got married. It happened just like that in the film *Anuradha* too. Don't you remember? I saw it on your television. So we got married in the same way.'

'You will always be mad. Is that any marriage?' replied Shyama bibi and stared at her at a loss. 'You hide there the whole day every day?'

'The first two days nothing happened, but yesterday I was very tired. I forgot what day it was. This morning when he told me it was Sunday I said I will definitely go to bibiji's home today. I will see a film. What film is it today, bibiji?'

Shyama couldn't bring herself to say what film was being shown. 'If anyone had seen you, what would have happened?'

'How would anyone, bibiji? I veil my face. I've just walked right past my father. I pulled the end of my sari over my face and kept close to the wall. He's never seen me in clothes like this.'

'If he finds out, then what will happen?'

'So far he knows nothing at all,' she chirped. 'Do you know, bibiji, my husband, he comes every day to have clothes pressed by my father and at the same time asks everything.' She laughed.

'What does he ask?'

'Whether my father has been to the police or not, whether he's looking for me or not. He hasn't gone to the police yet. That's good, isn't it, bibiji?'

'Where will you live? This marriage is no marriage!'

'His mother and father live near Nainital. He'll go there.'

'Will he take you with him?'

'Yes.'

'And if his parents don't accept you?'

'So what, bibiji? I'll come back.'

'Is he from your region?'

'No, he's not. He's a Garhwali.'

'You idiot. What need was there to get into a marriage like this? If he leaves you, what will happen?'

'He's not like that. He's very good.'

Shyama bibi gave a laugh. 'He may be, but many aren't.'

At this Radha tossed her head and said, 'If he leaves me, he leaves me. So what? I will start scouring dishes again.'

'Where is he now?'

'He'll come to pick me up at ten o'clock.'

'Where will *he* pick you up?' asked Shyama bibi.

'I'll find him sitting on the steps of your house. He'll come by cycle, and I'll at once go and sit behind him.'

But Shyama was not happy with this idea. This was an alarming matter and risky. If anyone found out, a dozen people would turn up at her house. Nowadays you couldn't rely on anyone. A runaway girl. Her father outside in the alley. How did she know who was who? As Shyama thought about it, she became more and more concerned and afraid that this might lead to trouble for her. And Radha was growing further and further from her, until she seemed to be a stranger.

Controlling her voice, Shyama said, 'This is not right, Radha. You go away from here. When your wedding is formally conducted, then please do come back here. It's your home. But now if someone comes up the steps and sees you and goes and tells the dhobi downstairs, there'll be a dreadful problem. That's true, isn't it? Now go. And don't come back to my house until your marriage is properly formalized and your father knows about it.'

'But I've come to see the film.'

'No, Radha, go.'

'But how can I go without seeing the film? I have come from there just to see the film,' Radha insisted like a small child.

Shyama's voice became sharp. 'No, no film. Get out of here.'

'But, bibiji, he's coming at ten o'clock. What will I do until ten o'clock?'

'No, no, you go. That's the only right thing to do,' said Shyama bibi, even more greatly disturbed. She wanted to get Radha out of the house at any cost.

Radha paused. She looked at Shyama with wide, wide eyes for some time. Then she stood up, 'All right, bibiji, I'm going.'

'But how will you go? You should wait until night falls, then go.'

'Oh, no, bibiji, nothing will happen to me.' Radha stood still for a few moments and then left just as she had come.

Shyama ran to the window and looked out. Radha had veiled her face, and slowly she walked right in front of the dhobi and past him before turning left and disappearing from sight.

Shyama bibi came and sat down on a chair and, as was her nature, hung in a dilemma. Why hadn't she let her sit here? Who would've come to see her? It wasn't even dark outside yet. But then she shook her head and said, 'No, it's good that she's gone. If there'd been trouble, what would have happened? These things can't remain hidden.'

THE WONDROUS BONE

By the time Maharaja Udaygiri of the Golden Land had reached the age of fifty, he had become a king of kings. His emblem of victory had fluttered across many countries; there was no limit to his exploits. Various captive rajas were passing the last days of their lives staring at the dark walls of his dungeons, and beautiful young women from their own lands were adding to the splendour of the inner apartments of his palace. Whenever the Maharaja's army returned from crushing a state, his vast sums of gold increased, and new gems sparkled in his golden crown. But the eyes of the Maharaja were still fixed upon the horizon.

It was the last day of the rainy season. The Maharaja was with his ministers, hunting in the northern mountains of his kingdom. The afternoon was drawing to a close when he lost his way in the pursuit of a young adult deer. In the excitement of the chase, he set his steed galloping for miles, though there was no sign of the deer. He reached the edge of the forest and stood, tired out, beneath a tree. But the next moment he raised his eyes and was enraptured. Before him, in the rich light of the setting sun, stood a massive mountain, its proud forehead raised high; at its feet spread a wide, blue lake. The lake was as pure and fresh, as if it were a mirror to reflect the unplumbed beauty of nature. The shores of the lake were laden with deodar cedars. On its bank to the right was a small town, where the roofs of the houses, in the dim light of evening, could be seen extending into the distance.

The Maharaja was gazing at this peerless scene when his companions found him.

'I never knew that there was such a beautiful province in my kingdom,' he said.

At this his chief minister joined his hands respectfully and replied softly, 'Maharaj, this state is beyond the borders of your kingdom. Your rule ends here, where you are standing.'

'So this is not a part of my kingdom?'

'No, Maharaj, this is a small, independent state, whose people make their living catching fish.'

The Maharaja felt a searing pain in his heart, and his eyes became unsteady with envy. 'This is not a part of my kingdom.' Then, curling the fingers of both hands together to make one fist, he said with unshakeable resolve, 'Return today and prepare the army, Chief Minister. I myself will attack this state. The border of my kingdom will now be that mountain peak.' With this, he set out on his return journey.

Not even ten days had passed since that captivating encounter when that quiet forest began to resound with the battle cries of warriors. Even the wild animals of the forest were disturbed and fled from the valourous deeds of the Maharaja. The peaceful expanse of the lake, on which formerly fishermen had sung as they fished, now ran red with their blood. The rain of arrows from the heroic troops of the Maharaja destroyed even trees and rocks.

Three days passed. The Maharaja's army had crossed the lake and reached the walls of the town. But still the fishermen did not surrender. At night, while the Maharaja's troops loudly rejoiced in their victories, the silence of the cremation ground descended on the town. There was not even a single flickering oil lamp to be seen. The fishermen would fight all day, at night they would take account of their dead companions, and when they saw no hope in this dreadful darkness, they would touch their mother earth and vow to sacrifice their lives.

It was morning. The Maharaja was sitting with his ministers in his camp initiating new assaults when the guard at the door came and saluted him. 'Maharaj, a man standing at the door wants to meet you.'

'Who is he?'

'Some old man, Maharaj.'

'He must be some ambassador,' said one minister.

'Or some soldier in disguise,' ventured another.

'He has no weapon, Maharaj. He is very old, and he finds it very difficult to stand even leaning on a stick.'

The Maharaja gave him permission to enter and in a short while an old man in a long, grubby loose shirt, weighed down with age, walking bent over a stick, came and stood before him.

'What is it, old man? Who are you? I have very little time.'

The old man folded his hands respectfully and said, 'Maharaj, I too have very little time. The four directions are resounding with your glory and praise. Before I die I have come here with the desire to behold you.'

The Maharaja was silent for a little while and then said slowly, 'Have you come from the enemy country, old man?'

'No, Maharaj, I am a servant of your kingdom. My hut is a little way away on the shore of the lake.'

The Maharaja asked again, slowly, 'What is it you want, old man?'

'I have come here to plead for alms, Maharaj! Because of the war I cannot work.' With this he put his hand into the pocket of his long shirt and, taking out a tiny piece of white bone, said, 'Only give me the weight of this bone in gold, Maharaj. I want nothing else.'

The Maharaj looked at the bone—it was not bigger than a fingernail—and burst out laughing. 'Men go mad in old age. The equivalent of this bone will not even be a single grain of gold, old man.'

'To me even that will be a treasure hoard, Maharaj,' replied the old man.

Laughing, the Maharaja ordered a pair of scales to be brought, and taking two gold coins from a silver tray lying near him, he threw them towards the old man. 'Weigh them against the bone,' he said, and he returned to his counsels.

The scales arrived. In one scale was placed the piece of bone and in the other the two gold coins. But when the minister weighed them against the piece of bone, the bone turned out to be heavier. The Maharaja was embarrassed and immediately took two more coins and put them on the scale. Even if the request of a petitioner is small, the gift of the giver should be generous.

But the bone again proved heavier.

The Maharaja was astonished and picked up the bone from the scale to look at it. Then he excitedly picked up a whole fistful of coins from the silver tray and put them on the scales and, holding the scales himself, he weighed them.

But just as before the bone was heavier.

All the courtiers drew close in amazement. The old man joined his hands and said, 'Maharaj, I will take my bone back. Perhaps you don't have its weight in gold to give away.'

The Maharaja could not endure this insult. He ordered a larger pair of scales to be brought and, picking up the bone, began examining it, rubbing it over and over again. The larger scales arrived, and on one side was put the insignificant-looking bone, and on the other was poured the whole trayful of shining gold coins.

But the bone, just as before, was heavier.

'This is a magic bone, old man. You have come here to insult me.' The Maharaja's eyes became red with arrogance and anger. Neither could he throw out the bone, nor could he muster its equivalent in gold.

An even bigger pair of scales was called for. Instead of gold coins, gold bricks were put on it.

But the little white bone was still heavier.

Like an insane gambler, the Maharaja began to squander his hoard of gold on the scales. The courtiers stood motionless watching this strange transaction. Beads of sweat broke out on the Maharaja's brow.

The old man stood beside him and said softly, 'Maharaja Udaygiri, your kingdom is very great. But, leave alone the wealth of your kingdom, in all the kingdoms of the world there is not gold to equal this bone.'

The Maharaja was panting. He looked at the old man. 'What did you say?'

The old man bowed his head and said, 'Yes, Maharaj, even if the seven seas of this world were to turn to gold and come here, the thirst of this bone would not be quenched.'

The Maharaja was silent and started to stare at the old man's face. Then he said softly, 'What is it , old man, what is the secret of this bone?'

'This is the bone of desire, Maharaj. It's thirst always increases, is never quenched.'

The Maharaja was dismayed. In his expression frenzy was replaced by defeat and anguish. His gaze shifted from the old man to the wondrous bone. 'So, old man, will the wealth of the whole world be lighter than this bone?'

'Yes, Maharaj,' replied the old man, and he continued, 'The wealth of this town of fishermen could not even touch the scale.'

'So, old man, can nothing in this world equal this bone?'

The old man smiled, then slowly took a dagger from the hand of a soldier standing near him and the next moment cut his own hand.

'What have you done? You have cut your own hand?' asked the Maharaja in astonishment.

The old man let a drop of his blood fall from his hand on to the scales. At once, the scale with the bone in it began to rise, for the drop of blood weighed heavier.

'Maharaj, there is no throbbing, no life in my old blood, but the slightest touch of blood from a young man, or the body of a simple child, can shake this bone.'

The Maharaja was disturbed and silently left the camp and came to stand before the lake. The rain of arrows was still falling with the same velocity, and from the direction of the town, the uproar of war was even louder than before. Standing in silence for a long time, the Maharaja looked sometimes at the bone and sometimes at the bloodstained water of the lake.

They say that the next day at dawn when the time came for the drums of war to sound, the fishermen saw that the armies of Maharaja Udaygiri were going back, and the birds and animals that had fled the forests were returning.

VEERO

Today they had come again, playing their jingling chaine-kartal. Day had not broken when their song became audible in the distance.

Salima was dozing when their melody and rhythm dissolved in her sleep, and a gentle shower of sweet voices began to fall upon her inner being. As she heard them, her whole body thrilled. The words of the song were indistinct, but the tune was familiar. She had absorbed it in the far-off days of her childhood.

Suddenly she rose and ran those same few steps on to the balcony and stood peering out from behind the bamboo blinds. A woman of advancing years—so eager, so distracted.

The cool morning breeze was stroking her forehead. Outside the moonlight had begun to mix with the half-light of dawn. The enchanting voices of the singers drew closer and closer.

The group of pilgrims had again reached the small town.

This was not the first time. They had been coming for years, every year on this day of the month of Baisakh. Now they were on their way from the railway station and, in the evening, again to the accompaniment of chaine-kartal and stirring Salima's heart, they would return to the railway station. The waves of their song would gradually be lost, sink into the air. Again a kind of quiet would descend, and slowly, as time passed, their visit would begin to seem a dream.

Salima's gaze, as she peered from behind the blinds, was fixed on the approaching group. She was already trembling, and, her heart now surged, sending hot tears flowing from her eyes. This too happened every year. On this day of Baisakh she first felt unmatched happiness, then unfathomable disquiet. Even as she slept, tears would burst from the corners of her eyes. Then she would get up suddenly, as if wounded, and rush to the balcony.

The pilgrims were close by. They were passing her house. By now another layer of darkness had dropped away, and shapes were clearly distinguishable.

In front walked five Sikhs in yellow turbans and long blue cloaks that covered their whole bodies. They were all elderly. Some had greying beards, some silky white ones. Behind them were the musicians. One had a drum slung round his neck, another a harmonium, one carried a jangling pair of chaine in his hands while another played on the kartals. They were all engrossed in their singing. Behind them came a party of twenty or so pilgrims whose feet threw up a slight dust from the street of the small town. Some had hands joined in prayer, others walked with them clasped behind their backs. Most of them were elderly too. The younger ones laughed, talked among themselves, and looked about them, sizing up the place.

Salima's whole being was swinging between eagerness and hope. Every moment, every fraction of a moment, the group would advance. The faces on whom her eyes had fallen would pass in a few seconds, and she would feel a stabbing pain in her heart, and she would be left in misery.

She wanted to run down the stairs, stand in front of them and demand, 'Tell me, sardarji, are you my brother? Or a relative? Do you know him? Has he ever come with you to look for me? Every year, year after year, I search for him.'

But how could she? Women from good families who kept purdah did not run barefooted and bareheaded into the street and that too behind a group of strange foreigners on a pilgrimage.

By now the pilgrims were far ahead. Now they would cross the Dhakki. Her locality would be left behind. Then the gleaming dome of the gurdwara would appear before them. Bright in the light of sunrise and singing hymns, the group of Sikhs would enter the gurdwara.

Salima again began to feel as if she'd been dreaming. If it was just today, she wouldn't complain, but this happened to her every year. And it would continue in future and, weeping and lamenting, she would leave this world, giving false comfort to her unquiet heart. She was losing her sanity in pursuit of an unattainable desire.

Suddenly she heard a noise. She turned. On the threshold of the room behind her stood Salim, her youngest son.

'What is it, Mother? Why are you standing there?'

'For no reason. The Sikhs have come from Hindustan, the ones who come every year. I came to see them.'

'You're crying, Mother. Why are you crying?'

'What have I to cry about? May my enemies cry. I was standing in the breeze, that's why.' And Salima wiped her eyes with the end of her dupatta and, to hide her embarrassment, took her son into her arms.

'My dearest boy, may you live for ever. Why should I cry? Now, let's go inside.' And they both stepped indoors.

Then Salima had managed to hide her tears, but in the afternoon she wept again.

Salim was sitting on the courtyard wall, his legs dangling, learning a poem by heart, and Salima was sitting in the middle of the courtyard with a piece of embroidery spread in her lap sewing with gold thread. She was listening intently to her son's poem. She had heard it several times before, and every time it touched her.

The poem told a story. Once upon a time a flock of saras cranes was returning home, flying and sporting in the sky, when a huntsman fired. The other cranes escaped, but one female saras was wounded and fell to the ground. Close to where she fell was the hut of a holy man. He was moved by the sight of the crane and brought her to his hut and began to nurse and heal her.

When Salim reached the point where again the flock of saras returned, and the distraught and wounded saras calls out to them, Salima again gave way to tears.

> One day she saw the line of birds
> flying aloft.
> She gave a cry
> fit to shake the earth.
> Saras! Tell me, pray,
> Is my beloved among you,
> Or have you news of him?
> I have been waiting long.

Her heart filled.

'What is it, Mother? Why do you cry when you hear this poem?'

The down on his upper lip was turning into a moustache. He looked so lovable! Her tearful eyes caressed him.

'I shall tell you today what I have always hidden from you. I shall tell everyone in this house.' Then she said softly. 'By birth I am a Sikh.'

For a moment Salim's eyes widened, but quickly a smile spread over his lips.

'So how does that matter, Mother? What is there to hide?'

His mother was quite shocked. She had imagined that her son would be somewhat stunned, but he hadn't been at all.

'When Pakistan was made, I got lost. My mother and father and relations all boarded buses and went away. I got lost somewhere in the crowd. I was very small then.'

A smile was still playing on Salim's lips. His mother, strands of whose hair were now turning white, had once been a little girl, losing her way!

'Where did you get lost, Mother?' Salim asked with a laugh.

'Here, right in Hasan Abdal.'

Salim's interest began to grow.

'Where did you use to live? What lane?'

'How do I know, beta, which lane we used to live in? If I ever see it, perhaps I'll recognize it.'

'Then what was your name, Mother?'

'They used to call me Veero-Veero.'

Salim erupted with mirth.

'Is that a name? So who gave you the name Salima Begum?'

'I don't know, beta. Whoever gave me refuge, took me into his house, he must have.'

At this they both laughed together.

'Then you must have been like a little doll. Tiny, lively, running in and out of the alleyways. You must have tied ribbons in your hair,' said her son.

He couldn't find the lineaments of childhood however he searched the face of his middle-aged mother. For Salim the truth was what was before his eyes.

Salima began to feel something like despair. Her inner turmoil held no meaning for her son.

So was it meaningless for her too? What would happen if she did find one of her relatives? Her life wouldn't change. So why did she keep crying and tormenting herself like this?

Salim had no idea of small-town life before Pakistan. It was difficult for him to imagine a time when Hindus lived there and Sikhs too. Hindu and Sikh women would have walked in the streets without their faces and heads covered, and there would have been one shop belonging to a Hindu, another to a Sikh and another to a Muslim. All this seemed very odd to him.

'But, Mother, what is there to cry about? Why are you crying?'

His mother was still astonished that he couldn't understand.

'Every year when the Sikhs come to bow their foreheads in the gurdwara, I look for my brother among the pilgrims.'

Salim watched her face intently.

'Does your brother come with the pilgrims?'

Salima shook her head. 'How do I know if he comes or he doesn't? But my heart tells me that perhaps he does. After all, he lost his sister here, didn't he?'

As she spoke, her emotions again overtook her.

'As I remember and miss him, who knows, perhaps he remembers me, and my family remembers me.'

'And every year, every time the pilgrims come, you stand behind the blinds and look for him.'

'Yes, I do.'

'Mother, what strange things you're saying. The Sikhs left decades ago. If your brother did come back here, couldn't he have asked where his sister was?'

'If he'd asked, who would have told him? No one.' Then pausing, she said, 'Who knows if he came, if he asked. How would he know where I am now?'

Salim had understood a little, but still he couldn't fathom the depth of his mother's distress.

'Do you really believe that you'll be able to recognize him by looking down from behind the blinds? After so many years?'

Salima felt like saying, 'Yes, I will recognize him, every pore of my body will recognize him.' But she said nothing.

She stared at her son, thinking, 'My son is more sensible than I am. He sees how untenable my position is, but still I cling to my self-deception.'

Salim spoke suddenly. 'If today he were to recognize you, would you go away with him?'

She was stunned. What was he suggesting?

'Hae! How could I go? My home is here. My children, my heart, my life are here.'

'But you keep on crying.'

'I cry just for one glimpse of him.' Salima was alarmed. What a thing for her son to say! But he could doubt her, anyone could.

It was as if she had woken from a dream.

Now a different concern began to fill her mind. This could cause trouble. Her family would think that she didn't want to stay here any more. Hae! What had she done? Why had she told Salim what was in her heart?

'If anyone had come to search for you, it would have been in the beginning. Who will come now? Don't cry for no purpose, Mother.'

For some time Salima was silent. Then she said, 'You don't know how I feel when I hear the sound of the chaine-kartal. I was very small when I used to listen to them. That's the reason I cry.'

But Salim, perplexed, was still watching her. It was very difficult for him to understand the fine, invisible threads that bind us to our past. Years afterwards, and despite realizing her circumstances, Salima was still bound by them.

Her brother could have been alive or dead. Her youth was drawing to its close. He must be an old man by now. Would she be able to recognize her young brother in his lined face?

Salima loved his mother very much. All the family loved her. She was everyone's favourite. Today she'd told him a secret that he could really show off about to his brothers and sister. No one else could know that she was a Sikh. Even his brothers wouldn't know, but Father must. His father's sisters must also know—but until today no one had told him.

The shades of evening had begun to fall by the time the sound of the chaine-kartal came once again. The pilgrims were returning, heading towards the railway station. But this time Salima did not get up. Something else was worrying her. What she had been doing was total foolishness. It could cause a lot of trouble. The thread of emotion that had bound her and moved her for years had been insanity and had no substance.

The pilgrims had stirred up dust as they arrived, and now they stirred it as they returned.

Innumerable fragments of memories from her past lay scattered in her mind. Sometimes one rose up before her, sometimes another, seeming, for a few moments, enchanting. But then they faded. These scattered fragments only existed in her mind. And there too they were only shadows. It was strange that things that did not exist, that had no meaning, could still distress her so much and had done so for so long.

The pilgrims left. Gradually Salima extracted herself from the whirlpool of her emotions. Gradually her far off childhood family became lost in the twilight of the past, and it was as if Salim, Mahmud, Rafiq and her daughter, Maksuda, came running to her and surrounded her. Maksuda climbed straight into her mother's lap. In that full and whole family she was content in every way. The days passed. Salima's heart was back in its rightful place; she again began to talk and laugh.

Her sons were immersed in their work. The youngest son, Salim, was busy revising for his exams. The eldest son traded in dried fruit from Kabul. The middle son looked after the farm. After his exams sometimes Salim went to Kabul with his brother; sometimes he landed up in Lahore. Everyone was occupied. Salima was busy preparing for her daughter's wedding. The days and months passed without them noticing.

The next year when the band of pilgrims came, none of her sons was at home. Salima's husband was in the railways and was always at one station or the other. He came home only occasionally.

This time too when the pilgrims arrived, playing their chaine-kartal just as before, Salima's sleep was filled with delight. This time too as she dozed, she felt her body thrill, but she turned over. Somewhere she had reached the firm conclusion that relationships from the past were just apparitions; they had lost their substance years before. There was no point in clinging on to them, and it could cause doubt and suspicion in the family.

But when the sound of the chaine-kartal came close, she again rose, went to the balcony, and stood behind the bamboo blinds looking at the familiar scene she had watched for years.

Moonlight was again dissolving in the half-light of dawn by the time the pilgrims approached the balcony. A band of nihangs decked out in blue robes, the same yellow turbans on their heads, was heading the procession. Behind them the same group of musicians equipped with a drum, harmonium and chaine-kartal. But what was this? On the edge of the street, walking with the Sikhs, was her son Salim. He was walking slowly, talking to some tall, elderly sardar.

What was he doing there? Salima's heart began to pound. Her whole body tingled. Whom was Salim talking to? Who was this tall sardar?

Later, beneath the balcony, the family was in the sitting room that opened on to the street. Goodness knows how all the brothers had arrived—the eldest one's wife and little Maksuda, too, and other members of the family. On one side, quietly sitting on a chair, his eyes lowered, was an elderly, wise-looking sardar with a slightly lopsided turban.

When Salima entered, he raised his eyes. He stood up. He was looking at her while the family looked at him to see the moment the light of recognition appeared in his eyes. But he couldn't make out the face and features of little Veero in this middle-aged woman. Not even a distant glimpse of her.

Salima was in the same position.

When she sat down, the sardar joined his hands and said, 'I also come from here, ji. At Partition I certainly did lose my little sister. I searched for her a lot too. I even came here from Hindustan to look for her, but I never found her. My name is Kulbir Singh, ji. My little sister, who was lost, her name was Kulwant.'

At this Salim at once said, 'But, Mother, you said your name was Veero.'

'Yes it was,' Salima replied.

'In many homes people used to call little girls Veero, ji,' the sardar said. 'I also used to call my sister Veero. We lived a little way away in a locality behind here.' Then, joining his hands again, he asked, 'Tell me where you used to live. Your father's name.'

'Darji!' Salima immediately replied.

'That's not a name, ji. In Sikh houses you call the father Darji. Brother's name?'

'Virji.'

The sardar smiled again. 'Among Sikhs that's what we call our elder brothers, ji. Tell me something about where your home was.'

But Salima didn't know the name of the locality or her lane.

'There was a stone pillar at the end of the lane, and the house next door had green doors and windows. One window was broken. There was a buffalo tethered outside our house, and somewhere just near was an open space with a tree.'

Even after discussing all she remembered of her home for a long time, they couldn't establish anything for sure. The afternoon was drawing to a close, and in a short while the band of pilgrims would return with the chaine-kartal. The elderly sardar was doubtful and had begun to feel uncomfortable. It would be better if he left with his own party. Why had he come? He'd been taken in by the words of that young boy.

There was a remoteness between Salima and the sardar. Salima had thought that the moment she laid eyes on her brother every atom of her body would respond and she would immediately recognize him. But she felt no stirring within her at all. They were sitting opposite one another like strangers.

Just then the sound of chaine-kartal came from the direction of the gurdwara. The sardar heaved a sigh of relief and stood up.

'I don't recognize her. If she remembers anything of me, please could she say?'

He stood there. Slightly stooping shoulders, his brow crossed with lines. Salima was thinking how her brother's face used to glow. He would either be climbing trees or jumping. He didn't walk; he bounded along.

The sardar was also thinking. What a difference between his vivacious little sister and this ageing woman, whose face muscles had grown slack.

The sardar addressed Salim. 'Young one, you have made a mistake. My sister certainly was lost in these lanes, but who knows where she is now.' He started to leave.

Salima felt sharply that by trying to hold on to the hem of the past she had been left with just a handful of dust. It was as if a hideous truth had begun to open before her eyes.

The party of pilgrims, with their chaine-kartal, had come closer.

The sardar turned towards the door that opened on to the street. The moment he turned his back on Salima she said, 'Wait a moment, sardarji.'

The sardar paused.

'May I ask you something?'

'Yes, behen.'

'When you were a child, did you ever fall from a tree? Behind our house there was an open piece of land with a tree in it. My virji used to climb it a lot.'

'In the village, behenji, all boys climb trees. I also used to climb them.'

Salima was hesitant. But a scene from her childhood was spinning before her eyes.

'Once my virji fell out of the tree, and he hit his leg against something on the ground and cut himself. He bled a lot. My family tore up my chunni to make a bandage to tie on the wound. There was a lot of blood.'

The sardar went suddenly still. His eyes widened.

He returned to the sitting room, sat down and lifted the bottom of one leg of his salwar. Above his ankle there really was the scar of an old wound, like a raised line.

'That is true. My family did tear up Veero's chunni to make a bandage.'

A sparkle had come to the sardar's eyes. He smiled and looked at Salima.

'We had a tonga too,' she was saying, 'and we used to go on outings in it to the waterway.'

Salima was agitated, the image of that pale line of flesh on his calf was raking her, but her mind was still not prepared to accept that this ageing sardar was her brother. She kept glancing up at the tall Sikh and then lowering her eyes.

The band of pilgrims had drawn close to the house. The sardar rose to leave. He was still uncertain. Although the moment when he had fallen from the tree had come alive for him, the constraints of doubt had still to loosen.

He joined his hands in farewell.

'I must go now, behenji, but if I have met my sister, then I am truly fortunate! Someone I had lost for so many years . . .' His eyes filled with tears.

Salima too was moved, but she restrained herself. She had still felt no quiver of recognition. She was thinking, 'Who knows, perhaps this will all turn out to be untrue or just a dream.'

About six months later Salima and her family were sitting in a train laughing and chatting. Kulbir Virji had insisted that everyone come to Amritsar. Beneath the seats were baskets of fruit and sweets. Two cases were full of gifts. Salima had brought a piece of phulkari that she had embroidered with her own hands. It felt like they were going to a fair. The girls were excited about seeing Hindustan.

It was Kulbir Virji's youngest daughter's wedding.

'After the wedding, I'm going straight to Ajmer Sharif to offer prayers,' the middle son was saying, 'and straight from there to Agra.'

They were all making their own plans.

On one side of Salima sat Salim, who was telling his mother how he had managed to find his 'Mamaji', all the places he had looked.

'Mother, I know you don't believe this, but I did find him by accident. I was sitting in a bus. There was an old sardarji sitting next to me, and I just asked him if he'd ever been on a pilgrimage to Hasan Abdal, Punja Sahib. He hadn't been to Punja Sahib, but he had come from a town nearby. I was so exhausted I was about to come home the next day. But that old sardarji told me where to find

Kulbir Mamaji. He was the one who told me Kulbir Mamaji had lost his sister. "Kulbir's father and I used to study in the same school," he told me. "Go and meet him. Who knows whether your mother isn't his sister."'

Salima listened to her son, caressing his face with her eyes.